HOT SHOT

A NORTH RIDGE NOVEL

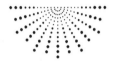

KARINA HALLE

METAL BLONDE BOOKS

Cover by: Hang Le Designs

Photo by: Wander Aguiar

Edited by: Roxane Leblanc

Proofed by: Laura Helseth

❀ Created with Vellum

For all the heroes with broken souls

PROLOGUE

PAST

WAFFLES.

The smell of waffles was by far and large the best part of weekend mornings for Fox Nelson, especially now that weekdays had changed for him.

This year, Fox started attending Kindergarten, which was actually something he enjoyed and looked forward to. What he didn't like was how early he had to get up. Maybe it had to do with the fact that his family lived on a ranch far outside of town and he had to catch a bus at a certain time. North Ridge was a small place, but it was rural and mountainous. A lot of kids lived on the ranches, farms and cabins on the outskirts and they all took the school bus, even in Kindergarten.

Mornings at home were cold, especially by October when the sun started spending less time in the sky. His father was always complaining about bills and electricity, so they heated most of their house with the wood stove and even though his mother was always up way before him to stoke the coals from the night before to get the fire roaring again, Fox's bedroom was freezing.

Those mornings he'd slip on his biggest sweater and his

fluffy slippers and shiver his way downstairs where he'd eat cold, mushy cereal (the boring kind, his mother never let him have the ones with tons of sugar) and drink orange juice while his younger brothers John and Shane were still sleeping. Sometimes John would be up too, just wanting to tag around his mother and Fox, but Shane, being a baby, would be definitely sleeping.

His mother seemed to prefer it that way. She often talked about Shane sleeping like it was best thing in the world. Sometimes Fox wondered if she even liked Shane since every time the baby was awake, he was crying or wanting their mother and it always seemed like a huge weight on her shoulders.

On cold dark mornings, that weight seemed heavier than normal. Fox had a feeling that after she walked him to the bus stop down the road on the other side of the river, that she'd go back to bed. Maybe even cry. Sometimes Fox would glance at her as the bus pulled away and she'd still be standing on the bridge, staring down at the water below.

Sad. She seemed impossibly sad, which made Fox want to be a better son, to do what he could to cheer her up. His father and grandfather were like that too, always being extra kind and understanding to her, but they operated the ranch and were almost always busy.

But weekends, on weekends that sadness seemed to lift just a bit. Fox liked to think it was because he was at home with her and not at school and so she now had a helping hand with Shane and around the house. Fox liked feeling needed, feeling special. He liked the responsibilities of being the oldest.

On this particular morning though, on a sunny, cold Saturday in late October, his mother could barely get out of bed. In fact, she didn't even wake him up like she usually did.

He went down the hall to her bedroom and found her

sitting in the rocking chair by the window, staring at nothing.

"You didn't wake me up," he said.

But she said nothing. She didn't even look at him.

"It's Saturday," Fox went on and for some reason this morning, the fact that she didn't wake him up, the fact that he should be smelling waffles right now, it bothered him. "Where are the waffles?"

"You make your own waffles, Fox, I'm sick and tired of it," she said in a dull voice. She wouldn't look at him.

"I don't know how, I can't even reach the cupboards," he whined, feeling this was completely unfair. She knows he can't do it.

"I can't do everything!" she snapped at him. "You make your own waffles, you take care of Shane, you take care of everyone. You're the oldest, it's your responsibility now."

And even though she broke down and started crying, Fox was upset too. She took something he was looking forward to and she ruined it.

"I hate you," he said to her and then stormed out of the room and down the stairs.

The fire wasn't even on this morning and it was cold as hell. He flicked on the TV for a few minutes and tried to watch his favorite cartoons until the guilt started to get the best of him.

Maybe his mother was sick. Maybe he really was old enough to do everything now.

So Fox got up and went into the kitchen and tried to figure out how to make waffles on his own. He brought out the buttermilk she used for it, the eggs, the butter. The waffle mix itself was high up in a box so he brought a chair from the kitchen table over to the counter and climbed up on it.

Normally he would never be able to do this but since his mother told him to make the waffles, then this was what he was doing. While he was up there grabbing the waffle mix, he also found a box of chocolates and snuck a few of them into his pockets to eat later, maybe share with John, if John didn't end up annoying him.

Then he climbed down off the counter, brought out the mixing bowls and attempted to make the waffles. Fox was smart and could already read quite a bit, so he tried to make sense of the directions on the boxes but with the tiny print and the words he didn't know, he ended up giving up and winging it.

He made a mess. The entire kitchen covered in spoons and broken eggs and flour and he wasn't even sure if what he had put in the bowl was the right thing or not. What he did know for sure though was that even if he ended up making them correctly, he wasn't allowed to cook them.

Then he heard footsteps coming down the stairs.

His mother.

He expected her to smile at him, say she was sorry, or just yell at him for making a mess. But she didn't say either. She didn't say anything.

She just walked past him like he didn't exist at all, like he was a ghost in one of grandpa's stories. She took his bowl and dumped the contents in the garbage and then started to make the waffle mix herself.

Fox backed away slowly. It was starting to scare him that she didn't even notice the mess he had made, that she was standing in bare feet amongst sticky eggshells and flour and she didn't care.

Maybe she was the ghost.

With that troubling thought, Fox went into the living room and started watching cartoons, trying to forget all about it. Luckily his favorite, The X-Men, was on.

Soon John was up and joined him on the couch.

Then the smell of waffles filled the air and when he and

John went to go sit at the kitchen table, it was almost like everything was normal again. The kitchen was cleaner. A pile of fluffy waffles with maple syrup was on the table.

But things weren't quite right. Shane started crying from upstairs in his crib.

Both John and Fox looked at their mother, expecting her to go upstairs but she didn't. She just stared out the window, not moving, like she didn't hear him.

Finally, John said, "I'll go tell him to be quiet." Though John was only four, he liked the baby a lot and was often wanting to talk to him and be around him.

"Good," their mother said, her voice so absent of life that it sent chills down Fox's spine. "I'm going to go pick some flowers."

She walked out of the kitchen and over to the front door, still in her nightgown, still in bare feet.

Fox watched all of this happen as if in slow motion. He knew he should yell after her to tell her to put on some clothes, tell her it was cold out. He knew that there were no flowers growing at this time of year. He knew that Shane needed her to go upstairs and take care of him, not leave it to John.

But he didn't say anything. He was still mad. And now, a little scared.

So she walked out the door and he ran to the window and watched her go down the hill toward the river, the breeze rippling through her nightgown, the sun low in the sky and lighting her up.

She went down but she never came back.

* * *

FOX DIDN'T REMEMBER much of the actual funeral. It was something that his mind blocked for him. He remembers the

5

casket going into the ground, the fact that it had snowed earlier that morning and there were still a few traces of it on the graves. He remembers everyone in black, crying. Even people from the town, like his Kindergarten teacher, Mrs. Matthews, and the old lady at the library, and the guy from the toy store. They were all there, everyone, crying and crying.

He doesn't know if he cried or not. Perhaps he was still numb. Perhaps it had just been a dream.

But he remembers when he left the funeral, he was lagging behind, not realizing that his mother would forever be buried here and that he could come see her anytime he wanted. He thought that this would be his last chance to say goodbye.

So while his family walked off, baby Shane in his father's arms, his grandfather holding John's hand, Fox took a moment to say goodbye.

But he didn't know what to say.

There was really nothing for him to say except, "I'm sorry," because Fox knew, he knew that he was the reason she died. She was so upset that he said he hated her, that she died from it. From a broken heart.

Now Fox had that broken heart.

It weighed him down like lead.

It would weigh him down for the rest of his life.

He turned away from the freshly-churned dirt on the grave and started walking back through the crowd to catch up to his family.

On the way he was stuck behind two old women who walked so slow they were like going through molasses, arm in arm.

"It was the baby that did it," the one woman said. "Baby Shane. They should have seen the signs."

"They should have. Even I knew she wasn't well. She

should have never had that child, they were struggling with that ranch enough as it was," said the other.

Fox was shocked. How on earth could Shane have killed his mother?

"He didn't kill her," Fox said to the women, both of whom had the faces of wrinkled cabbage. "I was with Shane, he didn't kill her. He's only a baby."

The ladies stopped and looked at each other. Finally, one of them gave him a sad smile and patted him on the head, to which he flinched. "Some things you'll understand when you're older, young man. Why don't you run along to your family, they need you right now more than ever."

Fox didn't have to be told twice. He started pushing through the crowd, trying to run, until finally he found his family at the long black car that they were using for the day.

"Fox, there you are," his grandpa said with a sigh of relief. "Get inside the car before you run off again."

Fox was going to protest, going to tell them that he hadn't run off, that he was trying to say goodbye and he didn't know how.

Then he was going to tell them what the women said.

But he didn't say any of that.

He just looked at baby Shane in his father's arm, his poor father who never looked more tired or sadder in his whole life than right at that moment, and Fox started wondering if maybe, somehow, this was the baby's fault and not his.

But try as he might, the blame he would put on Shane was only a deflection for the blame he put on himself.

It was his own fault she was dead, that he knew deep inside with unwavering certainty.

His fault.

His fault.

That night the tears came for Fox, in waves, in torrents, in relentless gusts. He held onto a stuffed cow that his mother

7

had gotten him years ago, a cow that reminded him of her back when she was alive, when she was happy, back when he had a mother, back when he was happy.

He cried and cried as the shame inside him deepened and darkened, carving out an ugly place inside him that would never go away.

He cried calling out her name.

Saying he was sorry.

He cried for the little boy he was before she died.

The person he would never be again.

SUMMER

1

DELILAH

PRESENT DAY

Love is wildfire.

I don't care what the Hallmark cards say, I don't care how many romance novels you read or the stories you hear about true love. I don't care if you watch your friends fall headfirst into love only to be lifted up by the same undertow that dragged them under. I don't care if love is all we need, love is what will save us, love will keep us alive.

In my book, love is a devastating force of nature, a raw, primal element that threatens all who dare to indulge in its flames. It's a wildfire that spreads and consumes until all that's left is a charred heart surrounded by ash and bone. There's no taming it, no fighting it back. No matter what you do, love will burn you to the ground.

Some days I'm okay. Some days even his smile will fill my heart with an immeasurable joy, like I'm being flooded with a warmth I don't know how to turn off. Some days I stand before him and I think "Do you see me now? Do you see me at all?"

And some days there isn't any wondering.

Some days I know the answer.

Today is one of those days.

The answer is no.

My name is Delilah Gordon, and all my life I have been head over heels in love with the boy next door, Fox Nelson.

And all my life I have been acutely aware that he is not in love with me.

"So," I say, trying to sound nonchalant as I wipe my hands on my jeans. "Have you seen Fox's new girlfriend?"

A strained hush falls over Riley and Rachel, my two best friends, and I steal a glance at them over my shoulder. They're exchanging a look, not sure what they're supposed to say. The only reason I'm even bringing it up is that for the last hour of our horseback ride through Ravenswood Ranch, I can tell it's been on the tip of their tongues in terms of town gossip and they've been trying hard to not bring it up.

Better to bite the bullet. Or at least try to.

"What?" I ask them when they haven't said anything. "I know you've seen her."

The horse I've been riding, Sugar, raises her head from the patch of dried grass she's munching on and gives me a dirty look. We've ended up by the shores of Willow Lake, the morning sun beating down on us, the first chance the three of us have had to hang out since the start of July. With Rachel's wedding coming up in a few weeks and Riley working for North Ridge Search and Rescue, they've been busy.

Me, I've just be running the The Bear Trap Pub. Same old, same old.

Riley gives me a bright, albeit cautious smile as she gets to her feet where she's been sitting on a log with Rachel, their horses tethered around the end. "She seems nice enough," Riley says casually, tucking her blonde hair behind her ear. "I've only met her yesterday. Mav and I dropped by Fox's and she was over…" she trails off and looks away.

I ignore the pang in my heart and my mind refuses to go there. I've trained it so well.

"I haven't seen her," Rachel says quietly, staring up at us with her haunting blue eyes. "I thought maybe Fox would have brought her by The Bear Trap by now."

"Well they've only been going out a few weeks," Riley points out. "And during two of those weeks, he was off fighting the fires. I'm sure it's nothing serious."

They're both looking at me again, with the pity in their eyes I've grown to expect.

I've never told them—or anyone—that I love Fox, that I've always been in love with my friend. But I think they know. I think everyone knows except for Fox, and thank god for that. The last thing I need is for twenty-seven years of friendship to go down the drain. Fox thinks of me as his little sister, always has. That's never going to change.

In fact, I remember being twelve years old and at a friend's party. While their parents were upstairs watching TV, we were all downstairs in the basement and playing spin the bottle. There were about ten of us and Fox got to spin the bottle before I did.

That entire time I watched the Coke bottle make the rounds, past my friends and classmates, all I could pray for was *please, please, please let it land on me*. Let it be me. Let Fox be my first kiss.

And…it did.

The bottle stopped right in front of me, pointing directly at me like a big flashing arrow.

I couldn't even play it cool. I was already grinning like a dumb idiot.

Fox, on the other hand, looked immensely bothered by this. So much so that without even a glance at me, he reached over and spun it around again before getting to his feet and saying, "This is stupid."

Everyone rolled their eyes but didn't say anything because it was a miracle that Fox agreed to play spin the bottle anyway. He was even more quiet, moody and irritable back then than he is now.

So Fox walked away, and I was left sitting there with my legs tucked under me, feeling the weight of the world crush my chest. I laughed it off, of course, telling everyone it would have been so gross because he was like a brother.

But even though I'd known Fox since I was six years old, he was never that to me. His brothers Shane and Maverick (real name John) were but Fox had carved a fathomless place in my heart from the very beginning.

Loving Fox is all I've ever known.

"As long as he's happy," I eventually say to them. I force another smile and then look up at the sun. "It's getting hot, maybe we should head back."

Rachel gives me a small nod while I can tell Riley is fighting hard not to roll her eyes. Riley only moved to our small town of North Ridge earlier this year, and while she quickly became part of our girl gang (especially since moving in with her boyfriend Maverick), she has a hard time keeping her mouth shut about some things. Mainly, Fox's and my relationship, which she says is rife with unresolved sexual tension or UST as she often says ("There was so much UST at the bar last night, you should just bang him and get it over with").

Rachel, on the other hand, is quieter and has been through so much in her life and with Shane, that she understands. She was there with me and Fox, growing up right alongside us.

Because of that, you'd think I would have admitted to her at some point how I feel about him, but I can't bring myself to do it. I guess I'm hoping that the feelings will go away. They have to, right? Either that or I'll continue to live with it and deal with it. And by dealing with it, I mean pretending it doesn't exist. Feelings with a capital F.

It's not like I've pined away for him locked in my room either. I've dated. I've tried to fall in love. I was even engaged to a lovely man for a while, Robert, another former friend from high school. But as much as I loved Robert, I knew that marrying him would be a huge mistake and completely unfair to him. For as good, calm, kind, and patient as he was, he wasn't enough for me. The world is too big, this life too short, to want anything less than magic with someone.

Even though it was my idea to head back to the ranch, I lag behind, with Riley and Rachel ahead of me. When Sugar tries to eat the dry grass, I don't rip her head up and let her have a few mouthfuls instead. If Shane could see me now, or his father Hank, they'd give me a talking-to about spoiling the horse.

It's a gorgeous day and I take a moment to tilt my head back to the wide blue sky. Summer is in full swing, which in North Ridge is both a beautiful and dangerous time. Each year the summers get drier and hotter, increasing the risk of forest fires. Even though the town is located in the mid-south of British Columbia, near the Washington and Idaho border, the weather can be shockingly hot compared to the rest of Canada.

As such, the fire season gets increasingly longer and more intense, which means Fox's life is more and more in danger. He works from May to October as a wildland firefighter or "hot shot," one of those crazy and beautifully brave people who head out to be smack in the middle of raging forest fires. He's getting busier and busier, the job getting riskier and riskier. I try not to worry—he's been doing this for so long, I should be used to it—but I can't help it.

I've barely seen him lately either. Usually he's gone for at least two weeks at a time with a week off here and there and during those days and weeks off, we'll be hanging out, maybe at the ranch, often at the bar. But not since he last got back. He hasn't even texted me, which is odd.

I have a feeling it has something to do with his girlfriend.

God, I can barely stomach the word.

When we get back to the ranch, my ponytail sticking to the back of my neck, the horses coated with a sheen of sweat, we get their tack off their backs and take turns hosing them down outside the barn before we turn them loose.

Though I grew up on the ranch and have been riding since I was seven years old, and Rachel is now a bonafide cowgirl after getting engaged to Shane, Riley is still getting used to the whole horseback riding thing. The horse she rode, Apple Jack, is about as sweet and docile as can be and yet she's throwing her ears back and giving Riley side-eye (though "side-eye" is pretty much the only eye horses can give) until somehow Riley ends up being more soaked from the hose than the horse is.

"Of course Riley manages to turn this into a wet T-shirt competition," Shane's voice comes from behind us.

We look to the barn to see him sauntering over, a faint flush of red on his tanned cheeks. The thing about Riley is that, yes, she does happen to be wearing a very wet white T-shirt right now, but she's also a megababe with her long limbs, big boobs, long blonde hair and blue bedroom eyes. Every guy that gets within twenty feet of her immediately starts drooling.

Shane being Shane though, tries his hardest to hide it, especially around Rachel. Rachel is equally as beautiful, the Veronica to Riley's Betty, and rarely has any insecurities with Shane. I mean, the man is so hopelessly in love and devoted to her, like he's been his whole life. If I didn't adore the two of them like family, I'm pretty sure I'd be lime green with jealousy.

Riley rolls her eyes. "Good thing Mav isn't here."

"Mav?" Shane asks with a grin, tugging on the brim of his cowboy cap. "He's nothing but a pussy cat. He working today?"

She sighs and wrings out the end of her shirt while giving Apple Jack a dirty look. "If I'm here, he's working. If he's here, I'm working. I'm telling you, having the same job sometimes fucking sucks."

"Yeah but you get to see each other all the time otherwise," I remind her. "You should try my job. I just see the same damn drunks day in and day out."

"You mean us," Shane says, walking over to Rachel and pulling her into a hug, placing a quick kiss on the top of her head.

"Do I?" I say wryly. "Because lately it's just been me, Old Timer Joe and his denture-less gal pal, my high school gym teacher who nurses his beer and sits alone in the corner crying, and a bunch of college freshmen from the city who have claimed North Ridge as some sort of craft beer haven and mountain biking nirvana. Never mind the fact that I don't serve craft beer."

"They're just trying to get in your pants," Riley says. "Delilah Does the Mountain Biking Team does have a nice ring to it."

"My point is, I barely see any of you guys anymore. The Bear Trap feels so empty without you there."

Shane and Rachel exchange a glance. "I guess we have just been so caught up with the wedding," Rachel says.

"We'll come by tonight for a drink," Shane decides. "Promise."

"I'll see if Maverick can put someone else on call," Riley offers. "Other than me." She pauses, a faux-innocent look coming across her big eyes. "Maybe he can convince Fox to come too."

With his girlfriend? I finish in my head just as Shane and Rachel look at me with those pitying eyes again.

I plaster on a smile that feels shaky at the corners. "Great."

* * *

THE HALF HOUR or so before I open the bar is definitely my favorite time of the day. It's just me and the bar, no drunk customers, no eyeing the tip jar and wishing for more, no getting trapped for hours talking to the same annoying person who won't get the hint.

It's a quiet time too. I don't play any music—lord knows I get enough of that with the jukebox later—I just enjoy the stillness and the silence, save for the small hum from the refrigerator. I've worked as a bartender here since I was twenty-years old, managed to save up and buy it from the old owner, Dwight, a few years ago and it's been mine ever since. Even though it's not the nicest bar in town or the hippest, it's the most authentic. It feels like a second-home to me and I take a great amount of pride in it.

As part of my pre-opening ritual, I polish all the wood on the booths and wipe down the chairs, bar stools, and tables. I disinfect the seats, vacuum any extra crumbs or dust. I run a dusting brush over the walls, over the paintings of bears done by local artists, the dartboard, and the neon signs I've scooped up from eBay and Craigslist.

Then I artfully scatter peanut shells on the floor. I know that seems especially redundant after all the cleaning I just did, but this is what the pub is famous for—a warm environment for the locals to drink and a place to eat peanuts served out of small copper bowls with the tradition of tossing the shells onto the floor. Of course, over time the shells get stepped on and gross so I'm always putting a fresh layer on.

I sigh when I lean against the bar and take it all in, the

bright sun streaming in through the windows, illuminating the stray dust motes in the air. As much as I love running the bar, being my own boss, and having my own business, I've started wondering if it's what I'm going to be doing for the rest of my life. I'm thirty-two years old and I know I have a good thing going on here, but some days my mind wanders. There's a restlessness in me that keeps growing, carving out a hollow space and I have no idea how to fill it.

I think about a life beyond North Ridge. Growing up I was never one of those girls who wanted to shuck the small town life behind and leave for the big cities like Vancouver or Calgary. That's what Rachel did. That's what a lot of girls I knew did. They left for university with their big dreams of a career and husbands and kids and ended up living interesting lives elsewhere, only coming back to the town around Christmas time, usually with their new families in tow.

For me, I guess I was just happy living in this town. I was born here and though my dad left when I was just a baby and I was raised by my mother alone, who would later become the nanny to all the Nelson boys, I had a relatively happy childhood. Maybe it's because I grew up on the ranch and even though Hank Nelson isn't exactly the fatherly type, he was still a father figure in my life and Shane, Maverick, and Fox became my family.

Or maybe it's because Fox is here. Maybe it's him that's always held me to this town like an elastic band. No matter what I think or do, I'm always snapping back to him.

But as much as I don't want to think about it, what happens when he finally finds someone else? I've seen girlfriends come and go out of his life and it's never really affected me. Maybe because I knew they wouldn't last long— it's hard to be in a relationship with someone when he's gone for most of the year fighting fires. Either way, it was easy to just pretend they didn't exist and I continued on in my friendship with Fox like they just didn't matter. Because they didn't. Not to him.

Now though, I feel a change. Maybe it's because I haven't seen him since he's been back. Maybe it's because he's with someone new and while I haven't met her yet and have no reason to think anything more of it, I feel like things could be getting serious. Fox is the same age as me and the older the both of us get, the more likely that he's going to eventually settle down with someone.

Someone that isn't me.

A knock at the door snaps me out of my depressing daydream with a jolt. I quickly glance at the clock on the wall. Six p.m. Right on the dot.

I give the bar a once over and then head to the door, flicking on the neon OPEN sign in the window before unlocking the door.

"I thought maybe you forgot about me," Old Joe says, holding his cowboy hat between his fingers and giving me a toothless grin.

"You? Never," I tell him, opening the door wider.

Old Joe has been here since the dawn of time and if he's ever not here at six p.m., I start to worry. The bar is closed on Sundays so I can have a day off, and I have no idea where he goes or what he does then.

He's also a pain in the ass, sometimes smoking inside or forgetting to pay for drinks, but at least the old dude keeps me on my toes.

"You're looking sad today, what's wrong?" he asks as he shuffles inside, throwing a glance over his shoulder at me before taking his place at his usual booth. I swear there's an indent from his ass in the cushion.

"I'm fine," I tell him with a big smile that's purely for show as I go behind the bar and get him his glass of whisky on the rocks. He likes to start his day off with that before moving on to beer.

"You always say you're fine, muffin," he says. "Sometimes I wonder how that can be true."

I roll my eyes and scoff as I bring the drink over to his table and plunk it down. "Hey, it's a gorgeous summer night. I'm here, you're here. It can't get much better than this."

He narrows his eyes at me suspiciously as he takes a sip of his drink. Then he visibly relaxes and shrugs. "You're right. Can't get much better than this." He pauses and looks at me with puppy dog eyes. "Maybe if I had a cigarette."

"If you go outside to smoke, you can have one," I tell him before heading back to the bar.

"Doctor says I need to cut back on cigarettes. It was either that or drinking."

"He gave you a choice?" I ask just as the door opens and Finn, Ted, and another regular come in.

Joe shrugs again. "Hell, I can't quit both."

The bar is mostly empty with a handful of the regulars until about eight o'clock when most people decide to show up for the evening, including the damn mountain biking squad that won't stop hitting on me. I go along with it, of course, because the more I do, the better they tip, and I could use a new refrigerator.

The entire time though, I'm waiting for either Shane and Rachel or Riley and Maverick to show up. I'm also wondering if Fox will, and if he does, if Julie will come.

It's about nine when the door opens and before I even glance over at it, my heart is in my throat.

It's Fox.

Alone.

My breath hitches in my chest as he shoots me a smile that seems to paralyze me from the inside out.

I haven't seen him for over two weeks and though that

doesn't seem like a long time, every time he returns I feel like I'm seeing him with new eyes. It's like I fall for him all over again.

And how can I not? Fox is tall, about six-one which is good since I'm five-ten, has a lean, muscled body and is in super-human shape thanks to the strenuous physical demands of his job, and has the most gorgeous face I've ever laid eyes on. Square masculine chin and jaw, usually accented by a dark beard or large amount of scruff, brooding green eyes that are beautiful whether they are full of rage or sincerity, and full lips I've hopelessly dreamed about kissing.

Tonight he heads straight over to me, his magnetic eyes locked on mine and I give him a wide grin in return. I can never play it cool around him, even if I try.

"Hey," he says to me, as he places his large hands along the edge of the bar and leans in slightly, his eyes searching my face. "How are you?"

Am I nervous? Damn it. I'm actually nervous around him. This is new.

"Good," I tell him, trying to keep my eyes on his face and not on his arms and chest which are straining against a tight black T-shirt, showing off his tan. "I was wondering when you might show up. I heard you've been in town for a few days."

I keep smiling as I say that, not wanting him to think I'm bothered by it. I'm not even sure why I brought it up at all but my mouth just wants to babble on about something to fill the space between us.

He scratches at his beard and gives me an adorably sheepish look. "Yeah, sorry. I've just been busy. Took a few days to recover, that was a pretty wild one."

"I was watching on the news," I tell him. "They had to evacuate the whole town."

He nods. "It made things a lot of more difficult given that

we didn't have as many men as we should have and we had buildings and houses to protect but somehow we did it." He pauses, giving me a soft smile that makes my knees feel weak. "I didn't think you still followed the fires, I told you to not watch that stuff. They always make it seem worse than it is."

I shrug. "I just happened to see it."

"Right. Well you know I don't want you worrying about me."

"Someone ought to," I tell him, though it suddenly occurs to me that maybe that's not my job anymore. Maybe it's Julie's.

Ask him about Julie. Ask him how she is. Ask him when they started dating. Get it over with.

But I clamp my mouth shut before I have a chance to and bring out a beer from the fridge, sliding it over to him. "Here. It's your welcome back beer. On the house."

He reaches over and takes the beer from me, his finger pressing against mine as he does so, holding on for just a little longer than he normally does. "Thank you," he says earnestly. "I have to say, I missed this place."

I laugh and pull my hand away and start polishing high-ball glasses with a soft cloth. It's a thing I do when I'm bored or nervous. There's certainly nothing in this bar that *needs* polishing. "You say that like you've been gone forever."

"It feels like forever sometimes," he says this with some weight to his rough voice and I glance at him. He's staring down at his beer bottle, like he's working through something. This is nothing new—Fox, for all his bravery, is always working through *something*. Sometimes I think I have an idea. Other times I can only guess. Even though I feel closest to him, there's still a lot of himself that he keeps in, choosing to wrestle with his inner demons by himself.

He clears his throat. "Sometimes I close my eyes and all I see are flames. We lost one house up there, a farmhouse, no different than the one we grew up in. We thought we had it under control but then the wind changed and someone fucked up and then the flames were on the roof, spreading down and I swear I saw faces in the window. Faces screaming for me to save them. I almost started running in until a buddy pulled me back. When I looked again, there was nothing there. The house had been evacuated days earlier."

I'm watching him, listening, a bit stunned. Fox rarely opens up about his job and he certainly doesn't do it here at the bar. Though the place is busy, no one is in earshot of us but even so, it's unlike him.

That said, I want him to continue. I want him to open up to me like this, it doesn't matter where we are.

"I can't imagine what you must go through," I tell him softly, afraid I might break the spell.

He shrugs and raises his head, his eyes meeting mine. They look pained and for the first time I'm noticing they aren't clear. They're glazed, rimmed with red. The poor guy must be exhausted, even though he's been home for a few days now. "You'd think it would get easier with time. It never does."

Why don't you quit? I want to ask. But every time I've broached the subject with him before, he ignores it. And I don't blame him. Sometimes we do a job despite the hardships, because what we get out of it is worth the risks in the end.

He slugs back the rest of his beer in one go and then taps the bottle with his fingers, his eyes fixed on mine. "Del, darling, I think I need another."

I turn around to get another beer out of the fridge.

"Listen," he goes on while my back is turned to him, "I have something I need your help with."

"Yeah what's that?" I ask, rummaging past a few bottles of Corona before I find a pale ale.

When I turn back to him about to give him his beer though, he's on his feet and waving at the door.

Maverick and Riley just walked in.

And a short woman with high cheekbones and a pixie-blonde haircut who is beaming over at us. Or should I say, beaming right at Fox.

My heart sinks.

Julie.

This must be fucking Julie.

And when Riley's eyes meet mine across the bar and she winces apologetically, then I know it's *definitely* her.

"Del," Fox says, clearing his throat as he looks back at me. "I want you to meet someone."

Oh fuck.

I'm frozen, wide-eyed, even as I see someone else at the end of the bar trying to signal for my attention. I can't tear my eyes away from Julie as she comes forward with Mav and Riley.

Traitors.

Not only is Julie especially petite but she's built like a bird, all delicate and dainty, wearing a white sundress, lacy sandals and bright pink lipstick. With my height and muscles thanks to my competitive swimming background, the P90X programs I work out to in the living room, and my early morning runs, she makes me look like positively Amazonian.

"This is Julie," Fox says to me and I'm noticing that now he's not meeting my eyes, though he doesn't sound like he's ashamed either.

"Hi," Julie says to me, giving me a small wave that makes the silver bracelets on her wrist rattle. "I'm Fox's girlfriend."

Girlfriend.

There. She said it.

To quote *Friends*, well isn't this kick-you-in-the-crotch, spit-on-your-neck fantastic?

"You must be Delilah," she goes on. "I've heard so much about you."

"Oh really, that's great," I say slowly, trying hard to blink. I don't think I'm blinking. I'm certainly not *breathing*.

"I just moved to North Ridge a few weeks ago," Julie goes on and she smiles sweetly at Riley over her shoulder. "Thank god for meeting Riley though, it's nice to not be the only newbie in town."

Riley's avoiding my eyes now too, which means only Maverick is staring at me with a strained expression on his face.

Julie goes on about where she moved from and what she's doing here but honestly I'm not listening at all. I'm just trying to pretend that none of this is affecting me, none of it hurts like a knife to the heart. I've been in this position before. I've done fine.

You and Fox are just friends.

You've always been just friends.

This is normal.

But then Fox puts his arm around Julie.

Leans in close.

And I quickly turn around, fixing my attention on the customer at the end of the bar, avoiding what I'm sure is Fox kissing her, something I don't think I'm ready to handle today.

I don't see how I can handle it any day.

This is my reality now.

Forget love being wildfire.

Love is a fucking bitch.

2

FOX

FIRE HAS ITS OWN LANGUAGE.

It's only heard by those that have witnessed its beauty, only understood by those who have seen its destruction.

I speak it fluently.

I listen.

It listens.

It invades my dreams.

Like now.

I know I'm asleep. I'm a lucid dreamer more often than not, always aware that I'm sleeping, that this isn't real, always trying to be in control of the situation.

I rarely am.

Right now I'm standing at the edge of a forest, right along a freshly dug fireline. An axe and hoe lie beside me, the tips of my worn boots pressed against the earth of the line. This line is the lifesaver, the land saver, the fire stopper. The fire will race and rage, consuming all brush and life in its path until it reaches this dirt. Then it will stop.

But here, now, in this dream, I'm staring deep into the forest and I'm waiting. The trees are close together and thick, a hybrid of pine and fir, and they're already dead. Each tree is charred, spindly-limbed, and interlocked with each other like blackened figures forming a chain.

I'm waiting and I'm listening.

The fire is speaking.

I can't see it but I can feel the heat, the glow, as it gets closer and closer, coming from somewhere behind the black curtain of trees. The hiss and whine and crackle and roar of the flames all sing the same song in a different pitch. They all say the same thing.

I am coming for you.

I hear malevolence in the tone even though I know that fire doesn't take sides. It isn't evil, just as the air or any other element isn't evil. It's apathetic in its destruction, it's humble in the way it renews. It may roar like a tornado and rumble the ground like a 747, but its intentions are always neutral.

But here, now, in this dark shadowy place, it tells me it is coming for me.

It will not bring about my rebirth.

It will only destroy.

The fire roars louder, like I'm surrounded by a busy interstate highway.

I start to see light through the trees, a warm orange glow that spreads and spreads until suddenly the fire has legs, galloping toward me like a herd of wild horses made of flames.

It rushes at me and I'm hit with a wall of heat that makes my eyelashes burn off, my nostrils singe.

The line holds it back, the fire licking the dirt but unable to go forward. There's nothing left to burn.

I stare into the flames like I've done so many times before, often hypnotized. I see faces. Mouths open, screaming. I see animals fleeing, lit on fire. Deer, bears, rabbits. I see a woman, the same woman I always see. She never runs. She just stands still and watches me with unseen eyes until she is burned alive.

I have a feeling she's dead to begin with.

I have a feeling she's my mother.

A flame reaches forward like a hand, fingers outstretched toward the dirt line.

It jumps across in an arc of flames.

Wraps right around my throat, squeezes me with a pain I've never known.

And in that moment, the moment of my death, I realize there's nothing to fear.

It's just relief.

That it's all over.

That I don't have to worry anymore.

That I don't have to live in pain anymore.

That I don't have to hate anymore.

The world burns away and somewhere in the dark skeleton forest, I know there is peace.

Just out of reach.

I wake up with a gasp, my throat and lungs feeling like they've been burned from the inside. This isn't because of any dream though. After being on the job, it's only natural. Even though we often wear masks when we fight the fires, the damage still takes place.

I roll over, trying to breathe, my eyes lazily focusing on the glass of water and the pills beside me on the nightstand, then on the light streaming in through the blinds behind it.

I clear my throat as I sit up, coughing, then take three pills from the vial and slam them back in my mouth, swallowing them down with the water.

A rustle sounds from the corner of the room and despite myself, I'm smiling. I get to my feet and walk over to the wire cage I had got from the pet store the other day and crouch down until I'm at eye level with the shoebox I had placed inside it.

I wait and watch, seeing the box twitch until finally a bunch of wood shavings spill out of the hole I had cut in the side, followed by a tiny head with big eyes.

I still don't have a name for him. I still think I'm a bit insane for doing this in the first place.

The day our team was sent home, after the biggest blazes had been contained and the replacement crew had been trucked in, I was walking just outside the perimeter of the fireline where the fire didn't touch the forest and saw a small creature wriggling beside some leaves. It was a baby squirrel, just past the stage of opening its eyes, skinny, small, with a thin coat of fur.

I don't know why I did what I did. I've seen so many horrible things in this line of work, usually I'm numb to it. Or maybe I did it because of all the death. Sometimes, after the fire has burned through an area and you're in there, looking for any flare-ups, you'll find wild animals frozen in spot, encased in ash. So many of them never escape the fires and are torched along with the landscape, sometimes a shade of nuclear white.

But this time, I felt hope. Like this was something I needed to do. I was tired of seeing so many things burn and die. So I searched the squirrel's nest and found it abandoned. The mother may have already fled from the fires, leaving the baby behind.

That settled it. I picked up the baby squirrel and brought it back to camp inside the pocket of my jacket. I went into the mess hall and took a Tupperware container that I lined with fabric, then went to the medics and asked them for anything that could help. They armed me with Pedialyte and a medicinal syringe.

Now that I'm back home, I'm wondering if I've made

some mistake. I'm not the type of person to have a pet of any kind and I know the right thing to do would be to get the squirrel to a wildlife rehabber because who knows when I'll be called out again.

And because of that, I need help.

I watch as the squirrel ducks its head back in the box and know I have to feed it soon since I gave it applesauce and water just before I went to sleep last night. But I don't want to do it alone.

I pick up my cell and text Delilah, even though it's early.

You up?

I wait for her response and when I don't see one right away, I go into the kitchen and make myself a pot of coffee. Like I've been noticing ever since Maverick moved out a few months ago, the house feels too big, too empty. There's a loneliness in these walls that was never there before, something ominous and dark that presses around me.

I try to shake it off and take a moment to turn my face into the sun coming in through the kitchen window, trying to remember what feeling safe feels like. Then I take a bottle of whisky out from the cupboard and pour a large splash in my cup.

I've gone through two cups of coffee by the time Del responds.

I am up now, what's up?

I text: **I meant to ask you at the bar last night but I need your help with something. Come over?**

The three dots appear and disappear.

Finally: **When?**

Now, I text back.

Why?

For some reason I feel a sharpness in my chest. Normally Del wouldn't hesitate or question. Maybe she's just in an off mood, although that's rare with her. Even on my darkest days, she's always been the sun.

I need your help. Come over.

I'll be bossy if I need to.

A few moments pass before I see that she's typing.

K, give me a few

I smile in relief and then get out the honey from the cupboard, knowing exactly how Del likes her coffee and that she'll want one as soon as she steps inside.

She lives on the other side of town, but it's a small town, so twenty minutes later Del is knocking on my front door.

Which, again, is odd because normally she walks right in like she owns the place.

I open the door and give her a puzzled look.

"Why did you knock? Did you forget I live here?"

She gives me a quick smile, not as broad as it usually is, and still doesn't come in. "I thought maybe you had company over."

Oh. Right. That.

Julie.

I had wondered if it was going to be weird between us when I started seeing her. I don't know why it had even crossed my mind, I guess because the last time I was seriously dating someone was a long time ago. About the same time Del was engaged to that douchebag, Bobby Barrett.

And Del and I are just friends. Hell, she's practically my sister, the girl who grew up next door to me on the ranch, her mother my nanny. This sort of shit shouldn't matter at all. I'm just going to blame Maverick for this, he's always hinting at something going on between the two of us, even though there isn't.

Not that I haven't thought about it. I mean, that's only natural, isn't it? Del is a beautiful girl, always has been. Even now as she stands in the morning sunshine, wearing just a grey tank top and black leggings, her face free of makeup, hair pulled back into the usual ponytail, she looks like she could be a runway model. Her face is both angular and round, with the brightest smile I've ever seen. She has a sweet, unassuming beauty that stirs something in your soul.

It doesn't help that she's not wearing a bra. I have to avert my eyes, lest I start leering at her. That's something that definitely does my head in and I have to remind myself that she's family and it's just so fucking wrong to even think of her that way.

"No, it's just me," I tell her. Kinda. I open the door even wider. "You coming in or what?"

She gingerly comes inside and looks around. "So how long are you going to keep me in suspense for?"

"Huh?"

"Why am I here?"

Do you have somewhere else to be? I frown. "Are you okay? PMSing?"

She rolls her eyes and punches me in the shoulder. Now that's more like it. "Shut up. And no. I'm just tired…it was a late night last night." She seems to think what she says over, rubbing her lips together. "Anyway."

Without thinking, I reach out and grab her hand for a moment, leading her toward the stairs that lead up to the rest of the house. It's a ski-lodge style chalet which means that the first floor is basically a basement and garage, with the second-floor housing the bedrooms, bathrooms, kitchen and living room. I bought it about five years ago and Mav was my roommate until he fell in love with Riley and they found a place together.

I don't know if it's my imagination that Del seems to snatch her hand away pretty fast when we reach the main level and I start to let go. I ignore it and usher her into my bedroom.

She stops in her tracks, noticing the cage before anything else and points at it. "What is that?"

"That's what I need your help with," I tell her.

She steps back as I open the cage and take out the box, placing it on the dresser before lifting the lid.

"Oh my god," she says breathlessly, hand at her chest. "Is that a…a baby *squirrel?*"

I can't help but grin. The squirrel is sitting up, or attempting to, and looking at us with wide-eyes, nestled deep in its bedding. "That's exactly what it is."

"And why do you have a squirrel?" she asks, her voice still high and breathy and I watch as she wiggles her fingers at it, a wide awestruck smile on her face. She looks positively radiant, causing my chest to feel hot. It's amazing the affect she has on people and she doesn't even know it.

"It was orphaned. I found it beside a nest, right near the fireline. On the side that wasn't burned. The mother must have fled from the fire but ended up leaving this one behind."

"Oh poor thing," she coos at it and I swear it cocks its head and looks at her. Then Del glances at me with a soft look in her eyes. "I can't believe you did that."

I shrug. "I can't either. I guess I was just tired of everything dying all the time. I couldn't let this little guy go."

She stares at me for a moment and I hold her eyes and wonder what she's thinking. Sometimes she looks at me with an admiration that I don't deserve. I often think it's because of my job—it's amazing the amount of respect you get when people find out you're a wildland firefighter. But when I think about it, Del was looking at me that way even when we were growing up. God knows why. I never did a thing to deserve it.

I clear my throat. "Anyway, I need your help. I don't know what the hell I'm doing."

She shakes her head, looking back to the squirrel. "And you think I do?"

"I don't know, you're a woman. You seem maternal," I tell her.

Her eyes roll. "And apparently so do you since you've kept this little thing alive so far. You mean to tell me you've had a baby squirrel since you got back?"

I nod. "I know I should give it to a wildlife rehabber, which is where I thought you'd come in."

She straightens up and gives me a wry grin. "Fox, I am many things but I am not a wildlife rehabber nor a baby squirrel mama."

"I'll be called back out again soon, there are already fires cropping up in the Okanagan. Who is going to take care of him then?"

"How do you know it's a he?" she asks, smiling at the squirrel again. "Did you check?"

"Well I have been feeding it. Here, let me show you how to do it."

I reach in and bring the squirrel out, holding it gently in my hand while I bring out the syringe I preloaded with baby sauce. The squirrel immediately reaches out with its tiny hands, grabbing onto my fingers and the end of the syringe as I very slowly push the applesauce out. I can feel its heart beating rapidly against my skin but I know it's not scared. This little guy doesn't know fear yet.

"Oh my god," Del whispers, coming in close to watch. "Fox, this is the cutest most precious thing I have ever seen. I might die."

"It's pretty easy so far," I tell her as the squirrel eagerly slurps down the sauce. "I alternate between this and baby formula. Don't worry, I looked it all up. It's what the online help things recommend."

"Can I try?" Del asks hopefully.

"Be my guest." I delicately take the squirrel and place it in Del's hands, then hand her the syringe. The squirrel seems only a bit hesitant to feed—I guess he's used to me already—but then as Del coos and beams at it, the squirrel finally begins eating again, nose twitching.

"He is so adorable," she says softly, looking up at me with big eyes. "Does he have a name?"

"All I got so far is Squirrel Nutkin. Remember him? Your mother got you all those Beatrix Potter books for your birthday one year."

She looks momentarily flattered then shakes her head. "No way. Do you even remember that story? He taunts the owl, provoking him to do something until the owl finally bit off his tail. I don't blame him. Squirrel Nutkin was an asshole."

I laugh. "Well I'm an asshole too, so I guess he takes after me."

"Yeah you're right."

I give her a wry grin. "Hey."

"You're my kind of asshole," she says. Then I swear to god she blushes at that. She quickly clears her throat. "So back to the name."

"You name him."

"Why me?"

"Because you'll be taking care of him."

"Fox," she says, her gaze sharp. "You can't just give me this responsibility."

I shrug. "I need your help. You're welcome to find a wildlife rehabber in town. I just know that when I go, he needs someone to look after him and that someone should be you."

"What about Julie?" she asks in a light tone, her eyes focused on the squirrel.

I frown. "What about Julie?"

"She's your girlfriend isn't she? Maybe she should be taking care of him."

It's almost as if I hear a challenge in her voice. "Del. You're my closest friend. Maverick is never around and I'm pretty sure his dog would try to eat him. My dad would probably shoot the thing. My grandpa would forget to feed it. Shane…"

"Yeah, why not ask Shane?"

"Nah," I say quickly, not wanting to involve him. "He's got too much on his plate right now with the ranch and the wedding. Same goes for Rachel. Riley is just as busy as Maverick is, especially now that they're living together and probably fucking like idiots every chance they get. Then there's the guys from my team and that doesn't help much better. You're my only hope, Del," I tell her in my best Princess Leia voice, which isn't very good.

"But what about Julie?"

Jesus, what is with her harping on about Julie?

I cock a brow. "Julie is great, but you know we've only been dating for a few weeks and most of that I was away."

"Where did you meet her?" Her voice has dropped, grown quieter. I guess these are totally normal questions, especially since I'd only introduced the two of them last night and with Del getting so busy at the bar, they never really had a chance to talk.

"She moved to town a few months ago from Vancouver, has a teaching gig at the high school in the fall. Math."

"Oh," she says. "Then she's smart."

I give her a funny look. "Of course she's smart. You think I'd go out with someone who wasn't?"

"I don't know," she says carefully. "I never really see you with anyone."

She's right about that but still. "Anyway, we met at the grocery store."

"How cute."

"I thought you of all people would approve," I tell her, getting annoyed.

"And why would you think that?"

We stare at each other for a few long seconds until I realize the food is all gone and the squirrel is trying to wriggle out of her grasp.

"Here, give him to me," I tell her, opening her hands and removing him. Sometimes I've been letting him hang out in the pocket of my bathrobe as I walk around the house but now I just put him back in his box, then back in his cage.

Something has changed in the air around us, there's tension where there was never tension before. At least nothing I've picked up on. I don't see why me dating Julie could be making things worse, unless Del is jealous.

The thought creeps into my brain slowly.

Could Del actually be jealous of Julie?

Why?

"Hey," I say to her gruffly, taking a step closer. "You have nothing to worry about with Julie."

"Nothing to worry about?" she squeaks, looking up at me.

I put my hand on her shoulder, the heat of her soft bare skin feels like electricity to my palm. I give it a gentle squeeze. "You'll always be one of my best friends, Del. Aside from Maverick, you know me best. You always have. That doesn't change when I start dating someone else. You should know that."

She slowly stiffens under my grasp until I take my hand away and she swallows hard. "I know. I'm sure Julie is great. I'm sorry I didn't get a chance to properly meet her."

"Well you will tomorrow night, dinner at the ranch. I know you and your mom are coming, right? Unless it's just wishful thinking on my grandfather's behalf."

"No," she says quietly. "We're coming."

"Great," I say but for some fucking reason it sounds forced. "So about the squirrel…"

She sighs and runs her hands down her face. "Fine. I'll take him."

"You don't have to now, just come by here when I'm gone and feed him, spend time with him."

"I thought you wanted me to take him completely," she says folding her arms. "Then find him a proper home or return him to the wild."

"I do…but maybe the change of environment would be too jarring for him." The truth is though, I think I just want Del in my house when I'm gone. I hate leaving, I hate the pressure and the strain and the danger of the job, feeling precarious from one second to the next, then coming home to this empty place. The silence, the hollowness, it starts to choke me sometimes. A panic attack or something that sneaks up from behind. My mind starts wandering, then racing, toward something thick and dark.

If Del were here, she would give warmth and life to the place, like she always does. Even The Bear Trap, forever our watering hole, took on a whole new life and vibrancy once she took ownership. She has this talent of turning everything to gold.

"You sure?" she finally says, seeming to consider it.

"I'm sure."

"Okay," she says. A small smile tugs at the corners of her lips. "On one condition."

"What?"

"You give him a name. Now. And no, not Squirrel Nutkin."

I gnaw on my lip for a moment as I peer down at the squirrel's tiny face. For a moment I think of calling him Avocado since he seemed to go crazy for the little mushed

39

bits of avocado I'd given him yesterday. Then the hint of red fur along his sides, and his tiny size, gives me an idea.

"Conan," I say and the moment I say it, it already feels right.

But Del doesn't look too impressed. "Like Conan O'Brien or Conan the Barbarian?"

"Both. He may be small but he is mighty."

She laughs. "All right. I guess we'll have to do with Conan." She looks at the time on her phone. "Oh, I should probably get going."

"Why?" I ask. "I was hoping we could get lunch together at Smitty's."

She cocks her head at me, as if what I've said has completely puzzled her. The wheels are turning behind her eyes but for the life of me I can't figure out what she's thinking. We usually get lunch there.

"My mom has a doctor's appointment, I'm taking her," she finally explains, heading out of my bedroom and toward the stairs. "I'll see you tomorrow night."

She gives me a slight wave and with that, she's gone, leaving me and Conan alone with that strange tension again.

"That, my tiny squirrel friend," I say to Conan, "is a woman. They're just as confusing as they are beautiful."

I swear he squeaks back at me in agreement.

3

DELILAH

MY MOTHER IS MY ROCK. EVEN THOUGH I WAS RAISED without a real father, she's woman enough, bold enough, to make me feel like I was never missing anything. She loved me enough to fill any possible void. She loved the Nelson boys with the same sort of ferocity too, hoping that she could make up for what they lost.

But with the Nelsons, their loss was much greater than mine. My father never died. He just left. Of course I've dealt with abandonment issues growing up, but there was a time in my teens where he reached out to talk to me, tried to be a part of my life again and I said no. I didn't need him. At least I didn't at the time, fueled by teenage pride.

For Shane, Maverick and Fox though, my mother could never replace the mother they lost, the mother who drowned herself down in the river one morning. I'd say Shane might have had the easiest time of it—he was just a baby when she died. He has no memories of her. But he has to contend with the guilt, that it was the post-partum depression that happened after his birth that caused her to commit suicide.

Of course it wasn't Shane's fault but Fox was quick to

throw the blame around when he was younger. Because of that, the two of them aren't close and it's something I wish they could address before it's too late. Not that I think they're both in any danger—save for Fox's job—but life is terribly short and the longer something burns you up inside, the harder it is to move past it. In fact, sometimes I see that darkness and anger flickering inside of Fox and I know so much of it has to do with that. Every time I've tried to bring it up though, he just shuts down. His demons are never up for discussion.

And so while it was Maverick who had the horror of discovering her in the river, it is Fox who has taken it the most to heart. He is the oldest, the one closest to his mother. The day she died I imagine a light inside Fox's heart was forever snuffed out. From what his grandfather, Dick, has told me on more than one occasion, is that the boy Fox was before his mother's death was someone very different from the Fox we have now.

Maybe in some ways, that's why I'm so drawn to him— there are layers to him that I don't get to see, that even *he* doesn't see, a beautiful light somewhere under that brave and hardened façade. I also think I have a bit of a savior complex going on, though that isn't all that uncommon. I know I'm not the first woman who has wanted to save a man from himself and uncover his hidden heart.

The only problem is, the longer I feel this way, the longer I hurt myself. I've done so well over the years and it's finally coming to a head. The pain is finally starting to settle in the cracks in my heart, something I can no longer ignore.

My mother is the first to spot it.

"Delilah," she says softly to me as I stand over the stove, slowly stirring the bone broth in the pot and watching the fat rise to the surface.

I glance at her and wonder if she's feeling alright. It's the same tone of voice she takes on when she's having a flare-up. My mother has extremely bad arthritis, which has since morphed into chronic fatigue and other auto-immune disorders. It's why after I broke up with Robert and moved out, I moved back into my mother's house. She's okay some days and seems to steadily be improving on a special paleo diet I have her on (when she sticks to it, that is), but she often needs my help and when I can, I cook most of our meals and clean the house, doing whatever I can for her.

"What?" I ask her, hoping it's nothing serious. Sometimes the medication she takes can make her tired or anxious.

But her eyes are alert and they have a softness to them. A look I've been seeing too often lately.

"Are you okay?" she asks as she watches me closely.

I give her a placating smile. "Of course I am. Why wouldn't I be?"

She continues to study me before sighing and sitting down at the table. "We don't have to go tonight, you know. I can tell Hank I'm not feeling well. They're used to it by now."

I frown, though I can't help but feel relief at the thought. "Why wouldn't we go? Are you actually not feeling well?"

"I feel fine. It's you I'm worried about."

I stiffen at that and pour the broth into two large mugs. "I'm doing good mom, really."

I place the mug beside her and hope to god she drops this because I really don't want to get into it. After going over to Fox's place yesterday morning, I feel like I'm barely being held together by the most fragile string.

"Sweetheart, you know you can talk to me," she says imploringly as I sit down beside her. "You just seem so...sad lately. I know you're trying to hide it and you're putting on a brave face and a big smile but...I can feel it off of you. Don't think a mother can't."

I try to swallow but my throat feels thick. My eyes avert

to the cup of broth and I try to focus on it, to keep my emotions buried, to keep the thoughts, those painful thoughts, out of my head. "I'm fine," I say, but my voice snags.

She puts her hand over my hand and I watch as she tries to uncurl her fingers, to hold on, shaking slightly. Her wrinkles and sunspots and veins are so familiar to me and yet I'm suddenly hit with the realization that time is going too fast.

"Delilah," she says, grasping onto my fingers.

And that's all it takes.

I burst into tears, sobbing so loudly the broth almost spills over in the mug.

My mother gets up and leans over me, enveloping me into her arms, holding on as tight as she's able to. "It's okay," she says soothingly, a shaking hand running down the back of my head, making me feel like a little kid again. "Let it all out."

And I do. I cry and cry and cry, letting the overwhelming fear and rejection and sorrow run out of me, giving life to my tested heart.

It feels like ages go past before I finally calm down, my head pounding, my eyes burning, my nose stuffy.

My mother takes my hand and leads me over to the couch in the living room and sits me down, then brings out a box of tissues and the bone broth which has probably gone lukewarm.

"Is this about Fox?" she finally asks.

I stare at her with puffy eyes. How the hell can she tell?

"Sweetheart, I know he has a girlfriend," she says gently. "When I called Vernalee to ask what I should bring to dinner, she let it slip that he's seeing someone, Julie I think, and that she'll be there."

I take in a deep breath, but even so, I feel like I'm drowning. I nod, afraid to speak.

"Del...you're in love with him, aren't you?"

Don't cry again, keep it together, deny, deny, deny.

But I can't deny it, not to her.

"Yes," I whisper, my voice shaking. "I love him. Not as a friend. I love him as more than that. So much more."

"I hate to say it, but I have been waiting for this day you know," she says.

I glance at her curiously. "What do you mean?"

"Oh, sweetheart. It's always been obvious to me. I know you. I've raised you. I've raised him, too. Both of you together. And you've always looked at Fox in a way I've never seen you look at anyone else. None of your boyfriends, not even Bobby. I just wasn't sure if you were aware of it or not."

"I've been aware," I tell her, feeling overwhelmingly tired all of a sudden. "I just thought it would eventually go away. I thought...I thought maybe it was normal, that it was just a crush. That he was my friend, practically a brother, and I was attracted to him as anyone would be. I mean, look at him."

She gives me a wane smile. "He is a very handsome man. Very troubled, too."

"I know. But can you blame him? After all he's been through, his job..."

"That accounts for some, but not for everything," she says thoughtfully. "You know Fox has always been hard to figure out but what I do know is that there's something inside him that stops him from feeling happy. I saw it in him growing up, plain as day. He did alright, and despite his temper, he was a good kid. Still, I'd watch him sometimes. Often, actually. I worried about him the way I worry about you now. Knowing that there was something underneath that caused him pain. What I noticed was that even when he was laughing, even when he was happy, he was holding himself back like he didn't deserve to have that happiness."

I'd noticed that too, of course. But when you've known someone for so long, even their afflictions become a part of them. You learn to deal with the bad as well as the good. Fox is so many things, good and bad, and I've accepted every part of him.

"And," she goes on, "I think it's something he's going to have to contend with for the rest of his life, unless its brought to his attention." She pauses and has a sip of her bone broth. "Oh, this broth is good," she says brightly.

"Good. I tried a new kind I found in the frozen section of the health food store." Then reality comes slamming into me again and my heart squeezes. "Did you know that's where Fox met Julie? Can you imagine? It's like some cheesy romance where they're both reaching for the last banana or something."

My mom doesn't laugh. "Delilah. You have to tell him."

Now I laugh. "Tell him what?"

"How you feel about him."

I shake my head. "No. No way. That's not happening."

"It's what's best for everyone."

"No it isn't," I cry out. "It so isn't. Mom, please, believe me. This is how I've always dealt with it. It's unrequited and it will stay that way."

"It's preventing you from finding someone else and being happy."

"No it isn't," I say, trying not to raise my voice, but god, I'm lying. "It isn't. Once I find the right guy, whatever I feel for Fox will go away."

"Love," she says. "You feel love for Fox. And love doesn't go away. You can ignore it, you can bury it, you can pretend it doesn't exist. But it will continue to grow and it won't grow from a happy place. Love gets twisted, tangled. It can eventually choke you if you don't face it."

"That's easy for you to say," I tell her. "Fox is my best friend. I am not about to ruin that. I can't lose him."

"But aren't you anyway?" she asks. "This is the first time

I've seen you visibly upset over him. The first time I've seen you want to skip out on the dinner. Don't pretend that it didn't cross your mind. You need to tell Fox and get this horrible weight off your chest."

I get to my feet. I can't sit still anymore. Everything inside me is coming to a rolling boil, the pressure rising.

"And give that weight to him? That's not fair. He has a girlfriend. What kind of person would that make me?"

"He has a girlfriend right now but if you said something to him..." she trails off and looks down at her mug.

"What? You think it wouldn't be a colossal mistake? I love him mom. He does not love me."

"You don't know that," she says softly.

God. Oh god, don't say things like that, don't give me hope.

I manage to swallow. "He doesn't."

"How would you know if you don't ask?"

"Because. I've never picked up on anything like that before. Back in high school, he had the chance to kiss me and he didn't. We played spin the bottle and he wouldn't do it."

She laughs richly. "Oh, sweetheart. You're basing it off of that? Listen, I won't pretend to know how Fox feels or what he's thinking. But I've watched you both grow up together. You have chemistry. The basis for attraction is there. You're both beautiful people who get along like nothing else. Your connection is stronger than steel and I know that no matter what, you can't damage that bond. If you sit him down and tell him how you feel, not only will you finally feel free from that cage you've put around your heart, but you'll give him something to think about. Maybe you'll give him that same sense of freedom."

I don't agree. None of this makes any sense. Fox won't "think" about it. I'll scare him off. I'll sever the connection between us. For all I know, things with Julie will continue to get more serious. I might have been the one he invited over to take care of the squirrel, and then later for lunch, but that's just old habits. I've always been the one who's at his beck and call. It doesn't even shame me anymore. Back when we were younger, I'd sometimes do his homework just because he asked.

"It wouldn't work," I tell her. "You don't know it until you're in it and I'm in it. I've been here a long time, I can handle more. Besides, maybe he will get serious with Julie and maybe she's meant to be with him and maybe I'm not supposed to get in the middle and fuck it all up."

"Language," my mother warns.

I roll my eyes. "Anyway, I'm glad I finally told you. Lord knows I've had to tell someone. But that's all I'm willing to do. I'll get over it one day, I swear I will. I know this makes me all sorts of crazy but…it's just the way things are. This is my life."

She stares at me, a hard look in her eyes, the wheels turning in her head. "I can't tell you what to do, Del. All I can do is be there for you and stand behind your decisions. You're a grown woman with a great head on her shoulders and I'm very, very proud of you. But, you have to know that there are consequences for keeping secrets as big as this."

It's not a secret, I want to say. *It's not big.*

But that would be a lie.

She goes on, "Unrequited love is a poison for the heart. Something that works slowly over time, like adding arsenic to milk, little by little, day by day. Undetectable on the surface but destroying you underneath. Love will give and give and give but unless you let it loose, it will only take from you until there's nothing left."

Fuck. Though my mother is usually fond of lectures, I've never seen her be so serious before, especially over something as personal as love. I have to wonder if it has something to do with my father. Even though she's dated a few men off and on over the years, no one has really stuck it out.

Despite my long overdue confession, the tears and the ominous love lessons, my mother and I still agree to go to dinner. In a way I do feel better about the whole thing, probably because I know my mother knows the truth. It feels good to have someone on your side, who has your back.

That said, I do take a little bit of extra time to make myself look good for the evening. Normally I put my hair back in a ponytail and wear jeans or shorts and a loose tank top and be done with it. This time I decide to wear my hair down. It's shockingly long, past my breasts, shiny thanks to some serum I slicked over it, light brown with gold streaks through it that I get when I'm out in the sun. I usually can't stand the feeling of my hair around my shoulders or face so that's why it's often pulled back, but I'll deal with it for tonight.

I also do some light makeup—tinted moisturizer, smudgy rust-colored eye shadow and a few coats of mascara to bring out my hazel eyes, a bit of peachy lip balm and a swipe of subtle gold highlighter. For clothes, I put on black skinny jeans with rips at the knees that I know for sure Dick will make fun of and a simple white V-neck T-shirt.

Then I add the pièce de résistance, a necklace with a fox pendant. Fox had gotten it for me one year when we went to a flea market together at the next town over. He said it was to remember to "don't give a fox." Which of course was a lame pun but I swear I fell in love with him twenty times over that day. I don't wear the necklace often since I'm not actually a fan of jewelry, but it's always hanging in my mirror where I can see it and no "fox" are given.

I smile at my reflection but the smile doesn't meet my eyes. I know I look good but I also know that it doesn't really matter to someone like Fox, who has seen me both at my best and my worst. Oh well, can't hurt to try something new.

My mother and I get in the car and soon we're leaving the boundaries of town and crossing over the Queen's River Bridge toward Ravenswood Ranch, the sun low in the west. The Nelson's ranch takes up nearly the entire north side of the river, between it and Cherry Peak, to Willow Lake and back. From this drive you really see the land in all its wild glory, the rolling hills and the tufts of sagebrush and grass between ponderosa pine. Cattle and horses are scattered dots among the velvet gold. This place was my home growing up and it never ceases to mean something to me.

But for the first time, on this drive I've done a million times, I'm nervous.

It's not just that my mom had that talk with me and now I've got it in my head that I need to talk to him (even though I know I won't). It's that everything feels like it's coming to a breaking point. Maybe it will be something I say. Maybe it's something Fox will do. Or Julie. Perhaps they'll announce she's moving in or they're getting married. Crazier things have happened.

I just know that no matter what it is, something is changing and it's changing for good. There's too much electricity in the air and there isn't even any hint of thunderstorms.

"Here we are," my mother says, as I park the car alongside Maverick's truck, with Fox's forest green Jeep on the other side. She pats my hand. "Things are going to be fine. It's the same old same old at the Nelson's."

But the moment we step inside the house, we know it's not true.

The first person I see is Julie.

Julie with her pixie cut and her cheekbones is standing in the kitchen in one of Vernalee's aprons, a glass of wine in hand. Rachel and her mother, Vernalee, are also in aprons and laughing about something. Julie looks right at home.

In the living room, Fox is sitting down on the couch with a beer, talking to Maverick about something. Shane, Dick, and Hank are all sitting around the table with whisky, while Dick is eating a bag of potato chips as if we aren't all about to eat a huge meal.

The only person missing is Riley.

Regardless, it feels like my mother and I are interrupting a family we aren't a part of and considering I was raised here in the little cabin right next door, that's an odd feeling to have.

I glance at my mother to see if she feels it too, but she's smiling at everyone as she always does and so I'm pretty sure it's just in my head.

"Sorry we're late," she says, even though we're not late at all. Then her eagle eyes spot the chips in Dick's hand. "Dick, what are you doing spoiling your appetite like that? Shane, Hank, you know all that trans fat isn't good for him."

Shane and his father look overly reprimanded with their heads down, which almost makes me laugh.

My mother melts into the room effortlessly while I stand by the door, my eyes darting between Julie giggling in the kitchen with Rachel (traitor!) and then over to Fox on the couch. Neither of them have seemed to notice me yet.

Then Maverick does with a jerk of his chin and I say, too loudly, like I can't control the volume of my voice, "Where's Riley?"

"On call," he says, getting to his feet. "Want a beer or a glass of wine?"

I can't help but notice that it's Maverick who is offering, not Fox. Not that Maverick isn't always trying to make people feel taken care of. He's good at that.

"A beer would be great, thanks," I tell him, forcing my

eyes to stay on Mav as he goes to get my drink. "Too bad she had to work."

"I don't think she minds," Fox says and I wait a moment, pressing my lips together before I look at him.

"What makes you say that?" I ask.

He shrugs with one shoulder, the beer dangling between his fingers. "Our family can be a bit much. She was probably grateful for the break." His eyes narrow as he looks me over. "You look different."

"*Nice* different?" I ask pointedly.

His gaze goes to me again, as if he's giving himself permission to take me all in. I swear my skin heats up as his eyes trail over my legs to my stomach, to my breasts, finally to my face. I can't read his expression; his eyes are glittering with something I'm too afraid to look into.

"Yeah," he says thickly. "Nice, different."

"Here you go," Mav says, slicing right through the moment like a blade and handing me my beer. "Hey, you've got like makeup on and stuff." He grins. "I like it. You're like my sexy sister."

"That's what everyone wants to hear, Mav," I tell him with a laugh.

Mav reaches out and runs his hand over my hair, letting it glide between his fingers. "And...oh my god. What is this? You have...*hair*?"

"Shut up," I tell him jokingly, stealing another glance at Fox. He doesn't look too happy with the way Maverick is touching me, even if it was preceded by the fact that I look like his sexy sister. Then again, I remember a dinner here once, before Riley and Maverick were dating when they were just co-workers, and Fox was dancing with her. Bugged the shit out of me and Maverick.

So maybe that's why I gently touch Mav's tattooed forearm (he's even bigger and more muscled than Fox is) and say, "Jeez, all this attention, I might have to wear my hair down more often."

"And the lip gloss," Mav says, eyes settling on my lips. "Nice touch." He gives me a wink and now I'm pretty sure he's doing it for the same reasons I am. Mav has always had my back.

Not unlike my mother. By now she's in the kitchen talking to Julie and smiling politely at her.

Mav's eyes follow mine and he puts his hand over mine holding the beer and manually forces it up to my mouth. "Drink up buttercup." I can almost see him thinking, *You're going to need it.*

I take a gulp of the beer, my eyes giving him a grateful look, and then Fox gets to his feet, clearing his throat as he brushes past us and goes straight to Julie in the kitchen.

I immediately look away but Mav is still here, staring at me.

"You going to be okay?" he asks gently.

I give him a dry look. "Of course. Why wouldn't I be?"

Mav watches me for a moment, pursing his lips. "It's not often he brings a girlfriend over to dinner. It's not often he has one."

"I'm happy for him." Tight smile. Another sip of beer. I can do this. "Truly. It's about time."

Mav opens his mouth to say something just as I hear Dick exclaim from behind me. "Now who is this stranger?"

I turn around and Mav's grandpa is smiling in surprise. I'm pretty sure he knew it was me, I mean it's not like no one has ever seen me with my hair down and he's not that senile.

Then he frowns at my jeans.

"Delilah, I hate to tell you this but your jeans have holes in them. Did you wrestle with a steer or what?"

"It's called fashion, Dick."

"If that's what constitutes as fashion nowadays, you kids

53

can keep it," he grumbles, giving me a dismissive wave before popping a chip in his mouth that he had hidden in his flannel shirt pocket and heads back to Shane and Hank at the table.

"Delilah sweetheart," my mom calls out to me from the kitchen. "Come over here."

So much for my mother being my rock.

I exchange a quick glance with Mav before I sigh and trudge on over to her.

"You've met Julie, right?" my mom asks innocently, which forces me to now look at the fact that both Julie and Fox are standing in front of her and Fox has his arm around Julie.

Fuck.

I nod while I raise the beer to my lips and start swallowing down the rest of it. God help me.

I also want to kill my mother. How can she do this after everything I just told her? I mean, she saw me crying my eyes out over my feelings for him and now she's forcing me to look at it and confront it and…

Oh…

Shit.

This is tough love, isn't it?

And because I'm not saying anything because I'm frantically finishing my beer, Julie then says, all white teeth and perky lips, "We were all at The Bear Trap on Friday night. I can see why all the locals like to hang out there. It's a great place."

She's nice. I hate that she's nice.

"Del took it over a few years ago," Fox says. His grip tightens around Julie's shoulder while he's simultaneously smiling at me, a smile that would normally make my knees feel weak but now is just flaming the anger and embarrassment inside. "She's done an amazing job."

I finish the beer and clear my throat, trying to shrug. "Well, you know. The peanut shells really class up the joint."

"We like to think of Delilah as the town babysitter," Vernalee says, holding a salad bowl between her hands. "Whenever we don't want to deal with our husbands or significant others for a while we just drop them off there."

Julie laughs and places her hand on Fox's chest. "Good to know." She glances up at him with an impish smile. "Now I know where to put you when you've been misbehaving."

Hurts. This *hurts*.

"Del," Rachel says quickly, gesturing to the cupboards with her head. "Help me set the table, okay?"

I mumble something in agreement, the room starting to feel swimmy, and hurry on over to her. With my back turned to Fox, Julie, my mom, and Vernalee, I feel scant relief. My face is going hot, my heart is racing. Jesus. I need to get a fucking hold of myself here, this is crazy.

"Hey," Rachel whispers to me as she takes out the plates and hands them to me. "Are you okay?"

I really wish people would stop asking me that.

But all I can manage to do is clamp my lips together until they feel bloodless and nod.

Rachel looks over her shoulder and then eyes me. "I know this is weird." She pauses. "And before you can tell me that you're fine, Del, I know you and I know you're not fine. You looked like you were about to faint back there."

"Low blood sugar," I say feebly.

"Come on people, let's get eating or I'm opening another bag of chips!" Dick yells from the dining room.

"Don't you dare!" my mom volleys back.

We make quick work of it, Rachel and I setting the table while Dick grumbles to anyone that listens about how hungry he is and how we'll all find out in a few years that trans fat is actually good for you and how I've finally dressed up by wearing jeans with holes in them, then Vernalee and my mother put out the spread.

As usual with the Sunday roasts, it looks delicious. A rib roast with crackly skin, new potatoes, carrots and parsnips. Even when the weather gets stiflingly hot in the summer, like it is now, the warm and hearty meals never change. Before Vernalee moved into the Nelson's house (and Rachel into the guest house with Shane), it was Hank and Shane who made the meals. They're both good cooks but you can tell the pride and effort Vernalee puts into it, plus the gathering as a whole. For a bunch of people who have lost loved ones and found new loved ones, it's a way of keeping us together like family.

I sit down at the table between Maverick and my mother and try not to wince when Fox and Julie sit down directly across from me.

Needless to say, I spend a lot of the meal with my head down, trying to eat, even though I've completely lost my appetite. I've discovered there's one good thing about having your hair down, it's that you can hide your face, even if it gets in your food half the time.

Maybe it's the amount of wine I've had with dinner but when dessert comes out—lemon meringue pie—I dare to look up and actually watch Fox and Julie together. It's like trying to catch a glimpse of a car wreck. It's morbid that you even want to watch to begin with and it makes you feel like a dirty-person inside, but you can't keep your eyes away.

It's not even anything vulgar that makes my lungs seize up.

It's just the way he's touching her, one arm around her shoulder, his fingers running down the edge of her earlobe.

It's just the way he's looking at her. Tenderly, warmly. Like he's sharing a secret language with her.

A language I'll never know about.

A language from the heart.

I think I'm at the breaking point.

Without thinking, I get to my feet and blurt out, "I need some fresh air."

And with everyone's eyes on me, Vernalee whispering "What's wrong with her? She looks like she's seen a ghost" to someone, I quickly get out of the house and into the warm night outside.

It's dark now and quiet except for the crickets. In the distance, the town of North Ridge glows, the lights giving way to the dark mountain ranges behind it and beyond that, a clear, starry sky.

I immediately feel better but it's not enough. I need to walk, to get my head on straight, to get my heart to stop caving in.

I head down the slope to the barn. It's second nature to want to come here during hard times. Growing up, if anyone in the house was fighting—and it was usually Shane and Fox —this was where you'd find them afterwards, licking their wounds.

Right now the barn is empty, all the horses are either in their paddocks or the pastures. I glance up at the hayloft and contemplate going up there when I hear footsteps behind me.

I immediately stiffen. It's funny how you can feel someone's specific presence without seeing them.

"What's wrong with you?" Fox asks gruffly from behind me. Typical. Even if he's concerned, sometimes he comes across like it annoys him to be concerned.

I take in a deep breath and turn around. "I don't know," I say, my voice measured. "Just felt a bit nauseous."

He studies my face intently, so intently that I look away, my eyes drifting over the empty stalls. "I thought maybe I'd pissed you off somehow," he says.

Is he baiting me?

I meet his eyes. "Why would you think that?"

"You could barely look at me during dinner," he says, taking a step toward me until he's a foot away. "Was it something I did? Is this about Conan?"

He's so damn earnest in that last question that I have to laugh. I fold my arms across my chest. "No, Fox. This isn't about your squirrel. It's not about anything. I'm just...tired."

I can tell he doesn't believe me and the intensity has changed in his eyes. They've become more focused on me, like he's seeing me for the first time and nothing else around us matters.

"I like this," he says, his voice sounding thick. He takes a strand of my hair between his fingers and runs them down. "Your hair is so long. You should wear it down more often."

I roll my eyes and hope I'm not blushing. "You guys are all the same. A girl wears her hair down and puts on some makeup and suddenly you realize that she's actually hot. It's like *She's All That* come to life."

Oh shit. I probably shouldn't have said that last bit out loud since it's a whole bunch of assumptions and I'm not one to flatter myself like that.

But he just grins. One of those cheeky, warm smiles that makes his eyes crinkle at the corners, the dimples appear in his scruff. He doesn't smile like that very often and every time he does for me, it makes me feel...invincible.

"Del, I've always thought you were hot," he says, still smiling. No awkwardness or hesitation. He just comes out and says it.

And now I *am* blushing. "Yeah right."

"What?" he asks, tucking my hair behind my ear and—*hell* —his touch causes warm shivers to wash down my back. "It's true. I mean, look at you."

Don't read into it. Don't read into it.

"Do you remember that birthday party where we played spin the bottle?" I ask him, my voice sounding broken.

He nods. "Kind of." But he doesn't remove his hand, keeps playing with my hair.

I don't know why I'm feeling brave all of a sudden but I am. "Well you spun the bottle and it stopped right at me. No mistake about it. And you got up and said it was stupid and left. Fox, we were good friends and you acted like kissing me was the worst thing on earth."

His dark brows knit together but his eyes stay warm. "You remember that?"

"Fox. I'm a woman. I'm always going to remember when a boy rejects me, especially my best friend and especially at a young age."

"But we *were* young. And I was pretty stupid back then."

"You thought I was gross."

He lets out a soft laugh. "I can promise you I did not think you were gross." His hand then leaves my hair and trails down my arm to my hand. Sometimes Fox holds it and I know I shouldn't think anything of it but every time he does I wonder if he realizes what it does to me. Then again, I'm starting to think he's oblivious to absolutely everything.

"I didn't kiss you," he goes on, "not because I didn't want to. I did." He swallows, shrugs. "I just didn't want our first kiss to be from spin the bottle."

*Hold up…*what?

"What do you mean? Our first kiss?" I repeat, my pulse quickening.

"I don't know, Del. Back then, I kind of assumed that we would end up together at some point. You know all through high school I had just been waiting to make my move and ask you out. At least figure out if you liked me or not. But then you started going out with that guy with the big ears, what was his name, Ryan McGee? And that's when I realized that it was probably all in my head. You were just a friend. A sister, even. And I was just a brother to you."

59

Holy. Fucking. Shit.

This is way too much to process.

Fox thought we'd end up together.

He actually liked me back in high school!

"You look shocked," he says, raising a brow. "I thought it was pretty obvious."

"Obvious?" I blurt out. "No. No it wasn't."

He lets go of my hand and shrugs with one shoulder. "It's funny how life goes, isn't it? It was probably for the best anyway. Could you have imagined us dating? Being a couple."

Yes, fucking yes.

He rubs at the back of his neck, causing the hem of his shirt to rise just a little, showing off an incredibly toned and flat stomach. My cheeks feel like they're on fire.

He goes on. "I'm sure I would have done something stupid to piss you off and you'd dump me and that would have ruined our friendship. If we had gone out, I doubt we'd be standing here like this today."

"Rachel and Shane dated in high school and they're getting married," I say quietly.

"Darling, you and I are not Rachel and Shane. They barely found their way back to each other."

I nod. "I'm sure you're right," I manage to say.

And he probably is. If he had asked me, I would have said yes for sure. But who knows how long our relationship would have lasted. Fox was even more volatile and cranky in high school than he is now and I was drowning in teenage angst. It probably would have ended in many, many tears.

"So does that answer your question?" he asks.

"About what?" I say, my voice barely a whisper now.

"About whether I think you're hot or not," he says, a small smirk on his full lips. "You were the most beautiful girl I'd ever seen back then and I'd be hard-pressed to say that anything has changed."

Oh my god.

"What are you guys doing?"

Shane's voice breaks through us and I take a step back, suddenly aware of how close Fox was standing to me.

"Delilah, are you okay?" Shane stops in front of us, his eyes volleying back and forth between us.

"I was just feeling dizzy," I tell him with a placating smile. "I'm fine now."

He eyes Fox warily and then nods at me. "Okay. Grandpa is bringing out the good whisky and he said if you both don't partake, he's going to be very upset. Honestly, I just think he has indigestion from those potato chips."

I smile at that and the three of us walk back to the house.

But contrary to what I told Shane, I am not fine.

I'm not even close.

Everything I used to think about Fox and our relationship over the years has now drastically changed with this new bit of information.

All this time I thought he saw me as his sister.

It turns out that couldn't be further from the truth.

I was the most beautiful girl in the world to him. I was someone who he thought he'd end up with.

And now I'm wondering if there's even the smallest chance he could want me that way again.

Hope can be so dangerous.

4

FOX

I'VE NEVER LIKED ALTITUDES. FROM THE SLICK MODERN interior to the overpriced drinks and the scantily clad bartenders and cocktail waitresses, everything about this place seems desperate, including the people who come here. Sure, if you're young and hip and looking to score, this is probably more fruitful than The Bear Trap, but you aren't going to find much charm or sincere smiles here. It's all about posturing and narcissism, everything I hate combined in one room and fueled by alcohol.

Which is why I found it a bit odd that Julie would text me and ask me to meet her here.

Then again, things were kind of strange between us on the drive back from the ranch after dinner last night. I asked if she wanted to spend the night but she stiffly declined, saying she had to be up early to start on some stuff for her upcoming classes. And given that we haven't yet slept together, I took that rejection rather personally.

So I decided to keep my distance for the day and it was almost dinner time when she texted and asked if I'd meet her for a drink here. You would have thought she would have chosen The Bear Trap, given how much she'd waxed on about the place and Del, but since she's new in town I decided to give her a pass. She'll figure out the good places and the bad places soon enough.

When I walk in, I'm immediately accosted by shitty music blaring far too loudly for it being only seven p.m. and the bar isn't very busy. I spot Julie sitting at a table in the corner, sipping from what looks like a margarita.

I can't help but smile to myself, thinking about how Del would take it if Julie had asked for that at The Bear Trap. Del prides herself on stocking as few extra ingredients and liqueurs as possible, saying that when it's just her behind there, making a drink for someone is too time-consuming and pisses off everyone else just wanting a beer. Which is probably true, but I also think that Del just likes things as simple as possible.

"This seat taken?" I ask Julie as a joke, hand on the back of the empty chair across from her. Since we haven't been dating all that long, things are still a bit fresh and awkward between us and when she looks up at me, a tight smile on her face, I'm thinking that maybe my lame jokes aren't quite appreciated.

"Have a seat," she says, and I do, just as the waitress comes by.

"Fox," the waitress says, giving me a polite smile. "I never see you around here."

The girl's name is Pam, someone I went to school with who never ended up leaving the town, much like me.

"Hey Pam," I tell her. "Wanted a change of scenery. Can I get a beer?"

"What kind?" she asks and then rattles off a ton of them before I stop her and ask for a pale ale.

"You know her?" Julie asks me after Pam goes.

I shrug. "I know everyone. Went to school with her."

"Did you date her?"

I shake my head. "No. Pretty sure Maverick did for a bit. Then again, if I happen to know everyone, he's happened to date them."

"He's a nice guy."

"Mav? Yeah. He's alright."

"And Shane is nice, too. Very quiet though."

"That would be Shane. Maverick's the playboy, or at least he was before he met Riley. Shane's the quiet, serious one."

"And what are you?"

It's an innocent question and one I'm sure all three of us have been asked more than once. But for some reason, I'm drawing a blank. What am I? I used to think maybe I was the brave one but with every day that passes I'm starting to think I might not be that brave at all.

I clear my throat, trying to dispel the sense of unease. "I don't know. You tell me."

"I don't know you well enough," Julie says before she has a small sip of her drink. She's so dainty and delicate, every movement she makes reminds me of a baby bird. It makes me feel like I can protect her, like she needs protecting even though I'm sure she doesn't.

"But," she continues, "from what I do know, I would consider you brave. There's not a lot of men out there who will head right into a fire to save land and lives. It's selfless too. You're definitely powerful and strong. You're quite smart. Shane might be quiet, but you're a lot like him in that way. You're always thinking and feeling, I can see that, even if I don't know what it is. You keep a lot of things close to your chest. You're guarded and that's okay. It's natural, especially around people you don't know that well yet."

"I don't know," I tell her as Pam hands me my beer, "it seems you might know me quite well already."

Julie leans forward on her elbows, face resting in her

hands. She really is a pretty girl. "I'll tell you one more thing, maybe it's something that you don't even know." Her smile turns crooked, forlorn. "You're in love with Delilah."

I stare at her blankly, just blinking for a few moments as I try to process what the hell she just said.

"I'm what?" I manage to say, my hand tightening around my beer.

She sighs softly and twists the margarita around and around, the ice clinking against the glass sides. "So maybe you don't know it. Or you're in denial. But I've seen the way you are around her Fox and it's not the way you are with me."

I open my mouth to say something that I know is going to sound harsh and then I say it anyway. "No offense, but I don't love you. How could I? I barely know you. You barely know me. That's apparent now."

"Look, I know *we're* not in love with each other. I'm just saying that you're in love with her. And because of that, I don't think we should see each other anymore."

Fucking hell.

"Julie, you can't...don't do this." I lick my lips, feeling panicked. "You have nothing to worry about with Delilah, she's just a friend. She's my oldest friend. She's like my damn sister."

She lets out a caustic laugh and leans back in her chair. "Fox, believe me, you can tell yourself this but you don't look at her like a sister. When I see the two of you together, you're staring at her practically the whole time like...I don't know, like she fascinates you. Last night during dinner, you barely ate. You were just watching her as if you were daring her to look at you. She wouldn't and I have my own theories about that."

"What theories?"

"It doesn't matter. The point is, that I can see it even if you can't. I know she came to your house the other day."

"Because I told you she did," I say, not getting the problem. I've been nothing but honest with her.

"You wanted her to take care of your squirrel friend, not me. And not that I would because I despise rodents, but you didn't know that."

"I didn't think you were the jealous type," I grumble. I feel like everything I had is starting to slip through my fingers, the future, a world of what could have been. A way out. A chance at happiness, at peace.

I start massaging my temples, pain starting to spike inside my head. I'd left my pills at home.

"Fox," she says, softly now. "You're a good guy. I'm a pretty good and understanding girlfriend. I'm not jealous. I'm just telling you the truth. You and I, we aren't going to go anywhere. You might think you can get over her by going out with me but I'm telling you, it's not working. I was even willing to give you the benefit of the doubt until she ran off at dinner. You didn't even hesitate. You let go of me like I was deadweight and went after her and then I knew for sure."

I shake my head, running my hands down my face. There's a ball of fire rising inside my stomach, growing hotter, blacker with frustration. I hate how everyone always says this. I hate how people allude to it. When the fuck did it change? When did my relationship with Del become something that our friends could speculate about? In the past, no one ever questioned the two of us and now…now I can't even keep a fucking girlfriend because of Del.

"If you're asking me to stop being friends with her…," I start.

"I'm not," she says quickly. "I'm not that type of person. I just don't think you'll ever find anyone or be truly happy until you face facts."

"Julie, please, seriously." I reach out and grab her hand across the table, squeezing it. "Just give me another chance. There isn't much I can say to convince you but you just have to believe me."

"No," she says with a sad smile. "I don't believe you. I only believe that you don't know it yourself." She brings her hands out of my grasp and gets to her feet. "I'm sorry Fox. But I deserve to be with someone who can give me a future and your future is wrapped up with her."

"It isn't," I practically cry out, anger racing through me. My fists ball up and it takes everything inside me to keep from pounding them on the table or punching them through a wall. "It fucking isn't."

"I'll see you around, okay?" Julie says and for a moment she looks not just relieved but actually wary of me.

Fuck it. Fine.

She leaves the bar and then it's me, alone.

I don't even want to think about what she said, it will only make me angrier and right now I'm so close to exploding. No wonder she looked a bit scared of me.

Pam chooses this moment to come by with a shot of whisky.

"Hey," she says to me. "That was rough."

"You heard all that?" I ask, slowly looking up at her though grateful for the whisky.

"No," she says. "But I've seen enough breakups in here to know what it looks like. Though I did catch what she said about Del. You know, it's totally none of my business, but I always thought the two of you would have ended up together."

I stare at her for a moment and the words I told Del last night ring through my head. *I assumed that we would end up together at some point.*

I swallow hard. "Thanks for the drink."

"Anytime, Fox," she says and walks off. It's then that I noticed her ring finger. She's married. Of course she is, why wouldn't she be? At my age everyone is either settling down or has already settled down a long time ago.

Obviously, not me though. Obviously, because the entire world thinks something that isn't even remotely true.

I finish the whisky in one gulp and don't even feel the burn.

Then I get Pam to bring me another.

And another.

Until I look and see Maverick standing over me, Riley at his side.

"You okay, brother?" Mav asks, looking me over.

I blink at him. Everything has slowed but at least the anger is buried somewhere under layers of alcohol. "What are you doing here?"

"Pam called me," Mav says. "Says you needed a ride home."

I look back at the bar where Pam turns her back to me.

I sigh. "Yeah I guess I shouldn't drive." I get to my feet unsteadily and Mav puts his hand out to help but I shove him back. "I'm fine. *Fuck*."

"I don't know," Riley says. "Seems you've really cranked that asshole dial tonight."

I glare at her. "You're lucky you're cute." I look at Mav. "I'll leave this godawful place with you but I'm not going home."

"Okay," he says uncertainly. "Where are we going?"

"To The Bear Trap. I need to talk to Del."

He and Riley raise their brows in unison and exchange a glance.

"I need to figure something out," I go on. "I'll pick up my Jeep from here tomorrow."

To their credit, they don't ask me what I want to talk to Del about. Maybe they're already assuming.

"So what happened in there?" Riley asks as we get in Maverick's truck. "With Julie. Pam said she had been in there and now there's all this drunken drowning of the sorrows and shit."

"Anyone ever tell you how eloquent you are?" I ask.

"Shut up."

"Fox," Mav warns. "Be nice to the lady."

Riley laughs. We all know she's proud to not be a lady.

I grind my teeth together, not wanting to say another word about all this. But, eventually, just as we pull into The Bear Trap parking lot, it comes out. "Julie broke up with me."

"Oh no," Riley says softly. "I'm so sorry."

"Yeah, bro," Maverick says, putting the truck into park. "That's a fucking shitty deal. What happened?"

I open the door and get out. "She just didn't see a future with me, that's all."

As we walk toward the bar, Johnny Cash booming through the walls, Mav jokes, "Was it because you equated your dick to a firehose?"

"What?" Riley asks, wide-eyed.

"Nothing," I tell her. "Just that Mav thinks all firefighters have a fascination with hoses."

"When you were young you'd piss on any fire you saw," he points out.

He's got me there. "Not that it's any of your business, but I didn't even fuck her."

"*What?*" Riley says again, even louder than before as we pause outside the front door to the bar.

"Don't look so surprised," I tell her. "I'm not like Maverick."

"Hey," he whines. "That was a low-blow."

"Whatever, man-whore," she says jokingly, then wraps her hands around the back of his neck and gives him a kiss.

"Fuck this," I say, pulling open the door and stepping into the bar, leaving the happy couple to their face-sucking on the front steps.

Then I see her. Del, in her usual place, on the other side of the bar. She's talking to some guy I don't know, smiling at him and it's hard to tell if that's the smile she gives to be nice or the smile she gives when she likes you. With Del you see what you want to see.

And that's when I feel it.

I actually *feel* it.

A pang of jealousy. Hot, like a poker into my chest, causing my heart to pick up the pace. Maybe that feeling has always been there when I've seen Del talk to another guy but now I think I'm recognizing it for what it is.

But so what? Why does that have to mean anything?

And then she sees me staring at her. Our eyes lock and I feel something else between us, a current of fire that flickers and then wanes and then dissolves into ash.

Maybe coming here was a bad idea. Maybe I'm seeing things that aren't really there as a way to make sense of everything that just happened with Julie.

Del mouths, "hi" to me and I'm suddenly hit with the realization that things between us are changing and more than that, they've been changing for some time. In the past I would normally head right into the bar, pull up a stool and start talking to her about who knows what, while she'd hand me a beer and tell me about her day.

Now it feels like that version of us is something I'm not sure will ever come back.

I jump, startled, when Maverick claps a hand down on my shoulder. "Come on," he says to me. "Let's get you a drink."

We head over to Del.

5

DELILAH

One a.m.

I should be home in bed by now.

But I'm not.

Because even though I closed the bar at midnight, it still has one last customer, sitting in a chair by the pool table with a cue in one hand, a drink in the other, staring blankly at nothing.

I haven't seen Fox in such a peculiar mood in a long time. He's drunk for sure, but there's something else affecting him. Tonight was pretty busy for a Monday so I didn't have a lot of time to talk to him. For the most part, he was playing round after round of pool with Mav and Riley and drinking like a fish.

Then, when everyone started to go home, he told them that he'd go later and catch a cab. I totally expected them to insist he come with them and there was something that Riley was trying to telegraph with her eyes that I couldn't quite pick up on, but they left and then pretty soon it was just me and Fox as the last people standing.

Only difference between us is I'm stone cold sober and he is very much not.

As if he can read my thoughts, Fox looks up from across the room and meets my eyes.

"You're off-duty now," he says in a low voice. "Have a drink with me."

I debate this for a moment then give in. "Okay. But just one."

I pour myself a big glass of red wine and then come around the bar, walking over to him. "I'd offer you something but I dare say you've had enough."

He raises his glass of whisky at me and nods, looking me in the eye. "You are quite astute. Cheers."

I go to clink the glass against his, looking down for a moment to aim and he yanks his glass back toward him in objection.

"Hey," he says, sounding hurt. "You're supposed to look me in the eye as you do that. Seven years bad sex if you don't."

I laugh softly and force myself to look back into his eyes. Honestly, it's the most natural thing in the world. I could look at them forever when we're just like this.

Of course I have to fuck it up and make it all awkward by saying, "Well we wouldn't want to mess anything up with Julie, would we?"

His expression falls, looking pained.

I quickly slam the drink against his and then take a large gulp of wine. "You know, because of the seven years of bad sex thing," I add on.

He nods slowly, seeming to think that over and then has a sip of his drink. "Yeah. Well. We broke up."

He says it so easily that I'm not sure I heard him correctly. "What?"

"We broke up." He sighs and sinks back into his chair,

shaking his head. "Or she broke up with me. Just what I fucking needed, you know? One minute you think things are going well and the next…"

I'm not sure what to say to him but I'm not so selfish that I don't recognize he's in pain. No wonder he's drinking like he is. He must have *really* liked her. I ignore the squeeze in my chest and force myself to be his friend right now.

"I'm so sorry," I tell him. I place the wine on the ledge above his chair and crouch down so I'm at his level, putting my hand on his knee and hoping it's as innocent as it seems. "You must have really liked her."

"I thought I did," he says gruffly, his eyes drifting to my hand. Should I move it? Keep it there? "At least I wanted to. I thought maybe…we had a future together. I know that's pretty fucking lame for a guy to say but…"

My heart pangs at that but I give his knee a soft squeeze. "It's not lame, Fox. It's normal. You should want to find someone to love and settle down with. We're not getting any younger and everyone else around us seems to be finding someone…"

He glances at me curiously, his eyes both wired and glazed at once. "What about you?"

"Me?" I get to my feet, hating when this question is thrust on me, no matter who is doing the asking. "I'm fine."

"You really oughta get a tattoo of that somewhere," he says, getting to his feet as well and resting the cue against the table. "Maybe on your forehead." He reaches out and runs his thumb above my brow.

I try to give him a look but he just physically raises my brows instead so I can't frown.

"Very funny," I tell him, though I'm secretly enjoying his touch.

"I'm serious, Del," he says and just like that a switch goes off behind his eyes, the hint of playfulness in them fading to something sharp. "Why are you single? You're so beautiful. So smart. So funny. You make everyone around you feel good. So fucking good."

Then he lets his hand drop from my face, down to my neck. I'm not breathing as he runs his large, warm palm down my arm, then over to my waist. With one hand slipping to the small of my back, he finishes his whisky, his eyes never leaving mine as he places the empty glass on the pool table.

"You confuse me," he says, his voice much lower now, throatier, as the distance between us closes in. His fingers press against my back until I find myself nearly held against him, only a few inches keeping our bodies apart. I can feel the heat radiate from him, smell his heady scent of pine and soap. I'm almost dizzy.

"I confuse you?" I whisper.

He's confusing *me*. What is he even doing saying these things, standing this close?

Touching me like this.

"The way you make me feel," he says, his eyes flashing with his words. "How can anyone not want to feel that way?"

Maybe I don't want anyone else to begin with. But I don't say that. Instead I have the courage to ask him, "How do I…make you feel?"

He peers down at me, thinking it over as his eyes search mine, looking deep emerald in the dim bar lighting. "I don't know," he says slowly, licking his lips. I try not to stare, try not to want to kiss them. "It's like…in my head and my heart, there's fire that I can't control. It's like nothing in this world, nothing that I've seen. The flames are black, sticky, and they rage and it's just this twisting, churning mess inside and I can't see straight, I can't think straight and then, then…I'm with you Del and all of that goes away. The pain fades. You bring me peace. It doesn't last but when I get it…it makes this life manageable. You just make me fucking *happy*, whatever being happy is."

Whoa.

I don't know what to say, what to think. I've never had Fox unload like this before and I'm both horribly flattered that I give him peace and deeply troubled that he needs it to begin with. I mean, I know how messed up Fox can be at times but I honestly didn't think it was this bad, that he has this black fire raging inside him all the time, something he can't put out.

"I had no idea," I finally say, overly conscious of how his gaze has now dropped to my lips.

"I didn't think you would," he says. "But it's the truth. Fuck knows if I'll find that with anyone now."

I swallow hard. "So why did she break up with you? Did she say?"

He gives me a lopsided smile. "She did. She says I'm in love with you."

What?

Did he just say what I think he said?

Holy fuck.

My stomach summersaults over and over and over again.

"That's crazy," I whisper, my words barely audible as I stare up into his eyes, my heart pounding so hard that I feel like I'm shaking inside, that whatever is holding me together is about to come loose.

"I know it is," he says, voice hoarse. "Completely crazy." His other hand slides behind the back of my neck, his long strong fingers applying pressure against my skin. I fight the urge to let my lids droop, to sink into this feeling of him holding me like he's never held me before. "But now I'm looking at you Del, and I'm feeling crazy. I'm wondering what it would be like. I just need to know."

Know what?

But before I have a chance to vocalize it, he's pulling me so I'm right flush against him, our bodies pressed against each other with enough heat to start a fire and then he's leaning in closer and closer, his eyes fluttering closed just before his lips brush against mine.

I melt.

From my lips, down my spine, to my toes I'm dissolving as he kisses me, a slow, gentle press of his lips that slowly opens, deepens, until his tongue slides against mine and my world is forever changed.

My heart feels open and clear and wide as a night sky and fireworks are exploding, lighting me up inside.

This can't be happening, this can't be happening.

But it is.

Fox is kissing me.

He's *kissing* me.

His mouth open, his kiss soft, the easy, wet slide of his tongue, the gentle pressure of his lips. He's holding me tighter and I feel his erection against my hip and I'm just gone, I'm gone.

I can't handle this.

And yet I am.

I'm kissing him back, tentatively because I'm afraid what might happen if I let loose, if I let all these years of pent-up feelings out. I might just devour him.

"Del," he says, voice choked, as he pulls back enough so that his lips brush mine as he speaks. I feel the ache and need in his voice all the way to my bones. "I need you. I need this."

I can't even speak, I can only whimper, my body winding around itself, tighter and tighter as his hand drops to the button of my jean shorts and undoes it.

Wait, wait, wait.

A thin voice echoes through my head.

Rebound. You're a rebound.

76

And I know I should listen to that voice. I know I should put my hand on Fox's chest and push him back. I know that he's upset and drunk and that he's probably not thinking straight and I'm just a rebound, just the right girl at the right time.

But I don't listen to that voice. Because I've wanted this, needed this and never in a million years did I actually believe this would happen.

So I'm taking this for all it is, for all Fox has got.

I grab him, my hand at the back of his neck, the other making a fist in his shirt and I hold him next to me, the massive width of his firm chest pressing against mine, our mouths working against each other as the hunger grows.

Fuck, he tastes amazing. Our kisses are dark magic, this easy rhythm that we both fall into, kisses that burn in my blood and light me on fire. I'm growing wild along with him, knowing that if we continue we'll never be tamed.

I don't want to be tamed tonight.

I want to be taken and let loose, feral and out of control.

"Del," he groans into my mouth. "Fuck...god, I need you."

Each of his words and desperate sounds throttle me, shaking me until I know I'm wet already between my legs.

He knows too as he slips his large hand into my under-wear, the brush of his rough fingers sliding down between my legs causing me to ache with need.

I can't believe this is happening.

He has his hand down my shorts, he's...

My thoughts falter as his thick finger slides along my clit and my body immediately melts into his hand, needing more, wanting more. I'd never had the need to get off strike me like this before, like a match against the striker.

I've had years of playing it safe.

I want him to throw gasoline on the fire.

"Fuck me," I whisper as I pull back and stare into his eyes, his eyes which are drowning with desire, making me feel like he's close to just devouring me.

"Jesus," he swears, biting down on my neck, the pain sweet.

My body is greedy for him. His fingers play gently along my clit, teasing like fluttery wings, before they plunge up inside me.

A gasp escapes my mouth as I spread around him.

"Oh god," he says thickly, bringing his lips back to mine. "You sound like a fucking angel." Then he lowers his head to my breast, pulling the neckline of my shirt to the side until my nipple is exposed and hardening in the air. His lips gently suck at the tip before he draws it into his mouth in one long, hard pull.

My back is arching for more and breathless groans are coaxed out of me. We're still standing in the middle of the bar and I'm not sure how much more I can take like this. I'm getting desperate for him in a way I never thought possible, an aching need that's clawing its way up through my core, turning every part of my body into an addict.

He pinches my nipple between his teeth and, as he does so, plunges his fingers back inside me, three of them this time. I expand around him, needing more. The desire is so acute that it feels like I'm on drugs, like if I don't get off, if I don't get him inside me, I might die.

"Fuck," he growls, yanking down my shorts and underwear, then he's grabbing me around the waist and lifting me up so I'm sitting on the pool table, my shorts and underwear dangling off one foot.

He's between my legs and I'm completely bare for him but I don't feel a hint of self-consciousness. I feel like it was always supposed to be this way, that Fox was always supposed to look at me this way.

And, fuck, is he ever looking. He's gnawing on his lip as

he stares and my skin heats under his carnal gaze and he's slowly sliding both of his hands up along my thighs, my sensitive skin dancing.

"Are you sure you want this?" he manages to say, his voice coated with this huskiness that makes the hairs on my arms stand up, the space between my legs flush with heat.

My "yes" is caught in my throat. I can only nod.

Please touch me. Touch me everywhere.

My whole body moves toward him like gravity, wanting more. Craving more.

He gives me a half-smile that borders on predatory. "You have no idea how long I've waited to do this."

"Tell me about it," I manage to say as his mouth dips toward my jawline, nibbling along it before it slides down my neck, a hot trail of lips and tongue and teeth.

His mouth returns to mine, his lips soft and strong, and I'm melting into his mouth, dissolving underneath his tongue. It's just as raw as sex, and I feel open and bare from just the heat of our kiss, the languid, penetrating way he explores my mouth. It's like he's devouring me, conquering me, and I've never been happier to give in.

"Del," he says, our mouths parting for a moment, my name an urgent hiss on his lips. His hands are now moving down to my shirt, sliding over my skin. His hands feel so warm, so possessive as they glide over my waist and stomach, slowly making their way up to my breasts.

I help him out by grabbing the hem of my shirt and pulling it up and over my head.

He lowers his head to my breasts, kissing the swell of them while he quickly reaches behind my back and deftly undoes my bra, discarding it on the peanut shell-covered floor beside us.

My nipples tighten in the air, begging to be touched. He cups one breast and brings his mouth to them slowly dragging his tongue around it in circles, over and over again, before giving it a hard flick.

I moan, my head back, as his tongue continues to flick my nipple, hard and fast. It pulls every nerve ending into a tightened knot. I'm growing more turned on and desperate by the minute. My back arches, and I push my breasts up to him, craving more and less at the same time.

I don't have any time in my foggy brain to think about it being Fox.

But it is Fox.

It's his teeth now razing over my nipples, causing me to gently cry out.

It's his hands sliding up my legs to where I'm warm and wet.

It's his cock that presses against me, pushing against the fabric of his pants.

Lust hits me like a rush. I want nothing more than to come. I want him to make me come, I want his clothes off, I want to be fucked silly on this pool table until I'm screaming his name.

If he wants to spank me with the cue stick, I wouldn't complain.

My god.

This is actually happening.

"Lay back," he murmurs gruffly, putting his hand on my chest and urging me down.

I lie back, the soft green felt of the table pushing into my shoulder blades while he takes his hand and slides it between my legs, his fingers skirting over my clit, before one finger slowly makes its way inside of me. He leans forward, gazing at me, drunk on lust. "And so very, very wet."

His eyes are unnerving. I don't think I've ever been looked at so sexually before and never by him. It's almost too intimate. I have always been lost in his eyes but never like this.

Not even close.

I close my eyes and try to control my breathing as he slowly pushes another finger inside me. I gasp, clenching around him, while the pad of his thumb grinds against my clit.

It's fucking bliss.

"Are you ever going to get naked?" I ask breathlessly, looking up at him.

"When I put my cock inside you and fuck you on this pool table, yes," he says, his voice hoarse. "For now though, I want to taste you."

Then he gets to his knees and puts his head between my legs as I'm hanging halfway off the table. His hands spread my thighs wide before he presses his fingers into my hips, holding me in place.

I'm not ready for this, for him to go down on me. It was something I fantasized about daily, but I never imagined it would happen with me completely naked on this pool table in my pub, him fully clothed, head between my legs.

I try and sit up to watch, utterly fascinated and turned on by the sight, but as his tongue languidly slides over my clit, washing over my nerves, slippery and wet, I have to lie back down. The feeling is too much and I feel like a sponge trying to soak up stars and lightning and everything beautiful, and it's too overwhelming for this world.

And Fox is relentless.

I mean, good lord, the man can eat pussy. He's at me with messy precision, his lips, tongue, and occasionally those long fingers of his working me into a wild frenzy.

I can't think.

I can't breathe.

I can only feel as my blood runs hot, my nerves tying up

in knots upon knots, pulling, pulling, pulling, until he's groaning against me and I'm digging my nails into his hair and his tongue is pushing *into* me in hot, quick stabs.

I'm so swollen, so desperate, that when he brushes his fucking nose against my clit, the knots all come undone at once.

I come. Hard.

I am blasting through space, groaning, writhing on the table as the orgasm rips through me, feeling like I've had a million swirling stars being born inside me.

But the relief is short-lived.

As I catch my breath, my limbs still loose, and peer up at him as he stands between my legs, he's taking off his shirt.

Undoing his belt.

Letting his pants drop.

He's just in his grey boxer briefs.

Damn.

He might as well be naked.

I can see every hard, rigid detail of his cock.

I swallow hard, amazed how quickly I've gone from spent and sated to hungry and, well, a little afraid in a matter of seconds.

Fox is a big man and so my fantasies always took that into consideration but the real thing is blowing all my fantasies about him out of the water.

He's huge.

Beautiful.

Perfect.

Somehow I manage to pry my eyes away from his underwear and take in the rest of him. As I'd known, Fox is fit as fuck with a body sculpted by hard and dangerous work. He's all firm angles and long planes, from the wide breadth of his tattooed shoulders and chest, to the definition in his abs and the way they lead to the sharp V of his hips. A dusting of chest hair thins out before becoming a treasure trail again. I've seen his body so many times over the years but never ever like this. It's like seeing him for the first time.

He's so manly, and his posture suggests he's completely at ease with his body. I want to get to know that body better, like I never have before. I want to run my lips and fingers and breasts along every lean, hard-earned inch of him. I want to feel it press against mine, damp with sweat.

"Are you just going to stand there?" I say to him, feeling just a tad bit vulnerable that I'm still naked and spread eagle and *waiting*.

He flashes me an assured smile and pulls down his boxer briefs, letting his cock, swollen and thick, jut out in front of him.

Damn. This is now an urgent debilitating lust he's stroked within me. The kind that wants it all hard and fast and *now*.

He steps between my legs, the dark, wet tip of his cock rubbing against my sensitive clit before he pauses. "I don't have anything. But I'm clean."

"I'm on the pill," I tell him, impatience running through me, hot and tight. "Now hurry up."

His eyes gleam with intensity. It's something dark and deep, like he's not just after my body but my soul. I can feel it in his gaze, in the way he keeps sifting through the layers, searching for something to satisfy him.

He's seeing me for the first time.

"Sit up," he murmurs, sliding his arms around my waist and pulling me up. I wrap my legs around him, place my hands behind his neck, already damp with sweat. Our faces are inches apart, but he's not kissing me. He's fucking me with his eyes, the way they simmer over my mouth, as if he's thinking of all the things my mouth could do.

I want to show him.

I bring my face closer, take his bottom lip between my teeth and gently suck.

I feel a rumbling groan build through his chest, like he's barely holding his lust in check, a million wild mustangs waiting to be unleashed.

"I'm trying to have patience with you," he whispers hoarsely, kissing the corner of my mouth. "I can't have this over too fast. I need to savor," he kisses my jaw, "every," he kisses my neck, "part of you. Who knows if we'll have this again."

Oh god.

Oh god, I hope we do.

"Savor me later," I tell him, as a sudden surge of adrenaline rockets through me. I grab the back of his neck, wanting, needing him to kiss me hard. His cock is this hot, stiff pressure rubbing against my clit, and I'm desperate, so desperate, for him to come inside me.

His mouth continues along my collarbone, nipping and licking, and my legs pull him closer. I'm whimpering, his lips ducking down to my nipples, so swollen and sensitive.

"Please," I beg, my voice ragged in my throat. "I need you inside me."

He brings his head up, his eyes wild with this hazy, heavy kind of lust. "I've always dreamed of you saying that," he says thickly. He reaches down, positioning his cock against me. His eyes hold mine at knifepoint, and I'm unable to look away as he slowly pushes himself inside.

I stretch around him, my breath hitching tight in my throat.

"Oh, fuck," Fox gasps against my neck, his hands dropping to the small of my waist and pulling himself deeper into me. "Fuck. *Delilah*."

My name has never sounded so good.

Meanwhile, my body is still adjusting to his size, feeling absolutely stretched and full. Thank god I'm drenched.

He pulls back—so fucking deliberate, like he's trying to feel every centimeter—and I'm ravenous.

I'm crazed.

An animal.

I need more.

Crave more.

My hands move to his shoulders, and I dig them into his skin, wanting all of him.

As Fox pushes back in, I expand around him, accepting him as if he's always belonged in me, as if he's always been home.

Because he has been,

From the start.

The connection between us is tight and frightening, and the intimacy is nearly too much for my heart to swallow. Our eyes dance with each other, glancing through lowered lashes, through the sweat and haze, searing deep and then moving on to other parts. He takes in my mouth like a glass of water, and the carnality in his gaze snaps a million strings inside me.

He murmurs my name again, his voice sliding over me like rough silk, and I am enraptured by his surrendering, his pleasure, lost in the hot, ragged draw of his breath against my skin and his raw grunts in my ear.

I can't believe this is happening.

Fox Nelson.

Inside me.

I'm on a pool table in The Bear Trap Pub.

Being thoroughly fucked by a man I had only dreamed about.

A man who has my heart.

This is unlike anything I've felt in this world. This is

holding fire and electricity in your burning hands. This is magic and light running through your veins, a switch being turned on, turning you into everything primal and basic and real.

This is the us we always should have been.

The table starts to shake underneath me. An earthquake of his doing. My legs grip him harder. I reach down and shrug his toned, round ass between my hands, pulling him into me. His grunts are hoarser now, loud from lust, and I still can't believe this is my reality, that this is my moody, brooding, wonderful Fox, and he's so deep inside me I can't breathe. I can't do anything but hold on.

His pace becomes frantic. A drop of hot sweat rolls off his brow and onto my collarbone. His lungs gasp with exertion, because this is a workout to fuck me like this, so fast, so deep, so thorough.

I never want it to end.

Then his hand slips between my legs, his thumb finding my clit, and now I'm frantically chasing my release until I'm at its mercy, on the edge, ready to fall.

I groan loudly.

I'm opening, I'm opening, I'm opening, legs falling apart, wider and wider.

I'm coming.

I'm coming.

I'm…

And then I'm off like a bomb.

Crying unintelligible words.

My body convulses violently, spasming around him.

It's so good, it's too good.

I never want anything else. Anyone else.

Just this, this, this.

Him.

All the time.

Forever.

His neck cranes, head back, jaw tense as he grinds his teeth together. He comes, and I watch with a sense of relief and wonderment that I'm doing this to him.

Me.

This is all my doing.

His face is pinched in a mix of rapture and anguish, and he's swearing in a low guttural voice, his grip on my hips so hard I think he's going to leave plum-colored bruises.

"Fuck," he swears as he slows his pumping. He's shaking. I'm shaking. His eyes flit over my body in a daze, sex-soaked and spent. I stare up at him, and it's like looking through a dream.

It hits me slowly, like dissipating smoke, what exactly we've done and what it means to me.

Everything.

He pulls out of me, and I'm immediately hollow. I want to keep him inside. My terror builds as he retreats, pulling up his briefs, and I want reassurance that the world isn't ending. I need to feel that this wasn't a one-time fling, that I'm not alone and adrift. The urge for his contact is unbearable.

Fox's chest rises and falls as he stares down at me in a mix of worry and amazement.

"Hey," he says gently, his voice thick. He reaches down and slowly pulls me up by my waist and shoulders like I'm a ragdoll. His longer fingers press against my cheeks as he holds me in place, searching my eyes. "Are you okay?"

I can't speak. I can only swallow, though it's like bread crusts are lodged in my throat. I nod.

He rubs his lips together, looking worried. I don't want him to be worried, I don't want him to regret anything.

"I'm more than okay," I manage to say.

"Good," he says, his eyes gazing over me. Lazy, sated,

glimmering at what we've just done. He reaches behind my head, pulls me into him and kisses me.

My emotions won't stop swirling.

I'm not sure if I'll ever come down from this high.

He pulls away and gives me a lopsided smile. "Can you give me a ride home?"

I laugh, glad that things are back to being easy between us. "Of course."

Easy but forever changed.

6

DELILAH

F<small>LAMES</small>.

I'm dreaming of fire.

Of two bodies writhing against each other, a wild, hot, sweaty race that's creating fire out of friction.

I'm being burned alive and I'm smiling.

Laughing.

Until I'm reborn in the ashes.

Phoenix rising.

Knock knock.

I blink. Awake. My eyes open. A ceiling. I have a hard time trying to figure out where I am. Nothing seems real right now and I can't tell what's a dream and what isn't.

But this is my bedroom ceiling.

And only my heart is on fire.

"Delilah sweetheart?" my mother asks from the other side of the door. "Are you okay? It's almost ten thirty."

Oh my god. I reach over for my phone and press the home button. She's right. I've slept way in.

"I'm fine," I yell back. "I, uh, forgot to set the alarm."

Which isn't a lie. I forgot to do a lot of things last night when I got home after three a.m. I must have crawled into bed after dropping off Fox. He had invited me in to spend the night at his place and I honestly don't know how I had the discipline to turn him down but I did, telling him I didn't want my mom to worry.

I mean, how stupid is that, a woman my age worrying about her mom but the truth is, I wanted the distance between us. I had a hard time processing what happened and am having hard time now and that would be a million times more complicated and difficult if I woke up in Fox's bed.

Though, fuck. I also wish I had woken up in his bed. I wish I could have slept with his arms around me, wish I could have had sex with him again this morning if only just to finally realize what the hell happened.

I had sex with Fox.

In my bar.

On the pool table.

I had sex with him and it was better than my wildest dreams.

Which makes me feel like maybe it could have been a dream. I mean, how does something that you've wanted for so damn long finally happen like that?

But then I get up and I'm sore between my legs and I think I pulled a muscle and I swear I can still feel his lips at my nipple, that harsh delicious tug, and then I know it wasn't a dream at all.

It was all very, very real.

Holy shit.

My phone beeps and my heart races with hope, thinking it's Fox.

I glance at it. It's Rachel.

Are you ready? I'll be there in five.

What on earth is she…oh damn. I had totally forgot about

her last dress fitting today. Riley and I are supposed to go with her.

I jump out of bed and race to the washroom to get ready. I don't bother with makeup, pull my hair back in a ponytail and slip on jean shorts and a T-shirt. But even though I've done nothing to myself, my reflection makes me stop and stare. I look like I'm glowing. My eyes are bright, lips seem fuller, my cheeks have a hint of pink. I totally have the look of someone who just had hot sex.

Scratch that, not just hot sex but hot, wild, sweaty sex with someone I've been in love with my whole life. That takes the concept of sex to a whole other level.

But what does it mean? a quiet voice says from somewhere deep inside me.

I don't pay it any attention, not now, not while I'm riding this high, feeling this joy like I'm made of champagne bubbles and sunshine. I'll worry about reality another time, *that* I can count on.

I practically skip into the kitchen and kiss my mother on the cheek goodbye, then leave her startled as I go out the door to Rachel's truck.

"Where's Riley?" I ask her as I get in.

"She's meeting us there. I think her and Mav are a bit, well, tied up."

I roll my eyes though I can't keep from smiling. "Oh, those two."

"I know, right?" Rachel says, then she squints at me. "Did you do something different? You look great."

"You mean I normally don't look great?" But I'm still grinning from ear to ear. "So, you must be excited."

She cocks a brow at the subject change but lets it slip. "I am. Actually I'm nervous. Not about getting married, don't worry. It's just...I don't know. I kind of wish that we had just eloped."

"Your mom would have killed you. *I* would have killed you."

"I know, I know," she says, kneading the steering wheel as we head toward downtown and the bridal salon. "It's just so much to think about, you know? I swear my mother keeps adding to the guest list, even though we've already given the final number in to the caterer. So what are they going to eat? Dick says he can make some of his famous ribs but that's going to be a disaster. Ribs at a wedding? All that sauce over all those clothes." She takes in a deep breath. "Then there's the fact that my father won't be there, which is why I think my mom is inviting so many people over, to prove that we both are doing fine."

Rachel's father used to be the town Sherriff who sexually, physically and emotionally abused both Rachel and her mother. He's been in jail for a long time but the scars he left on them both, even on Shane, the whole town, isn't something that will ever go away.

"I know you're stressing out but everything is going to be fine," I assure her. "It will work out, even if the whole town comes. Your mother is just proud of you, that's all, and I am too. You and Shane…you have a real life love story going on. A love that battled the odds. You found your way back to each other no matter what wrench life threw at you. You're fated."

She steals a glance at me with big blue eyes. "You're awfully sentimental today."

"I'm always sentimental," I say with a shrug. "So I know it's hard, but don't stress. Today you'll get to try on that dress for the last time before the wedding. You won't have these moments again so live in the present and enjoy them. Be grateful that you get to marry your best friend. You have no idea how lucky you are." I think normally I would get sad reflecting on how I don't have that, but considering what happened with Fox last night, my mind is not going there for once.

She pinches her lips together and nods, her eyes getting watery. "You're right. I know I'm lucky. I just want to be married to him, that's all, and forget all the rest."

"You're going to have an amazing time at the wedding, believe me. How can you not? All your friends and family on the ranch, it's going to be one big wild party."

"Hopefully not too wild," she says, smiling. "I better get Riley to keep an eye on Maverick. He's the best man and all and the person most likely to start doing a striptease on top of the table." She pauses, looks to me. "You know what would make the wedding even better?"

Her tone is serious. I brace myself. "What?"

"If you could talk to Fox about Shane."

Oh. "What…what would I say?"

"I don't know. I just…you know how it is between them and this is a new chapter in Shane's life and I think he just needs the closure. The two of them, they need to talk shit out, whatever problems they have with each other, they need to put it to rest for once and for all."

I twist in my seat to face her. "First of all," I say, checking off my fingers, "every time I've tried to talk to Fox about this, he clams up. Second of all, I'm just friends with Fox and he doesn't necessarily listen to me. I have no sway over what he does. Third of all, you're going to be Mrs. Nelson soon and Fox will be your brother-in-law. You are family. You should be talking to Shane and if that doesn't work, *you* talk to Fox."

"You think you have no sway over Fox?" she asks, ignoring everything else I just said. "Man, you both are so damn blind."

"We are not," I practically snap, then quickly add, "And anyway, the point is, this is something they both have to sort out on their own."

"Yeah right. You know how stubborn they both can be. Plus, they're men. Nothing would ever get done if it wasn't for their women setting them straight."

"I'm not Fox's woman," I say and look out the window watching the colorful storefronts go past as we pull into the parking lot of the bridal salon. A tiny smile creeps up on my lips. I may not be Fox's woman right now but I was for sure last night.

The memory of him floods my brain, creating a hot flush from my cheeks and down over my chest. I can almost feel the way he slid inside me, the way I parted for him, took him all in with no hesitation, as if it was something that was waiting to happen, that needed to happen. That look in his eyes as they burned into mine, watching me come, the quick, hurried way he fucked me, barely speaking, just making those beautiful little noises like he'd die without getting his fix.

"Hello? Del? We're here."

I snap out of it and notice the truck has been parked and Rachel is already half-way out the door. We head inside.

Riley still hasn't shown up yet so Rachel goes ahead and gets changed into the dress.

When she steps out, she takes my breath away.

"Isn't she darling?" the tiny old seamstress says, clapping her hands together. "You're going to make such a beautiful bride, my dear."

The dress is strapless with many flowing layers, reminding me of a cake, with intricate beading along the hem. Rachel gathers up her black hair high above her head to mimic the way her hair will be styled and the seamstress hands her a short veil.

"I still haven't decided, veil or no veil," Rachel says, trying on both in the mirror. I think she looks gorgeous either way so I'm no help.

The bell above the shop's door rings and Riley appears, bottle of champagne in one hand, three glasses in the other.

"I'm sorry I'm late!" she yells and with an apologetic grin raises the bottle in the air. "But I brought champagne."

"Then all is forgiven," Rachel says, turning around to face her.

"Oh my god," Riley exclaims, stopping in her tracks. "Rachel you look *gorgeous*. That dress! Shane is going to fuck you senseless on your wedding night."

The seamstress clears her throat and looks away but Riley pays her no attention.

"And oh my god," Riley says looking at me now, pointing the bottle accusatorily. "You had sex."

"What?" Rachel says. "Del?"

The seamstress clears her throat again, mumbles something about counting stock and disappears into the back room.

"Yeah what?" I say to Riley, putting on my best poker face. "What are you talking about?"

The thing is, I'm not purposely trying to lie to them. It's just that I don't know how to make heads or tails of what happened last night. I mean, this is huge. This is bigger than huge. My life was following one specific path and I just derailed it, putting it on another track and I'm not sure where it's going or what the outcome will be.

If Fox will be a part of it.

So the plan was, until I figured out how I felt about everything, until I talked to Fox and found out where we still stand with each other, I would just keep it to myself. Even if it kills me.

Too bad Riley is amazingly perceptive.

She narrows her eyes and inspects me. "Well, you look different. Like, happy. Relaxed. Your eyes have got that spark. Basically you look like me all the time. Thoroughly fucked."

"Ugh." Rachel moans. "Must you always work how much sex you have with Maverick into every conversation? He's like a brother to the both of us, we don't want to hear it."

"Whatever," she says with a dismissive shake of her head. "So who is it Del?"

"Nothing, no one," I say quickly, trying to laugh it off. "I just had a good sleep, that's all."

"So you mean nothing happened after we left Fox at the bar with you?"

"You were with Fox last night?" Rachel asks me.

"Yeah, nothing unusual about that."

"It is when he was just dumped by his girlfriend," Riley points out, sitting down in one of the waiting chairs and peeling the foil off the top of the bottle.

"Julie dumped Fox?" Rachel says, wide-eyed. "When? I mean she was just over for dinner."

"Yesterday," Riley tells her, now wrestling with the cork and gripping the bottle between her thighs. I know I work out but Riley's somehow both curvy, lean and muscled, her biceps are looking fierce in her tank top. No wonder her and Maverick are always fucking. They storm up the mountains to save people and then storm each other in bed. "Poor guy ended up at Altitudes of all places, drinking alone. Mav and I had to go get him."

"And you brought him to The Bear Trap?" Rachel asks, putting on the veil once again and eying herself in the mirror.

"We wanted to bring him home but he was insistent we go there. He said he needed to talk to Del," Riley says just as she pulls the cork off with a loud *pop*.

Rachel lifts up the veil to look at me. "What did he want to talk to you about?"

I throw out my arms. "Beats the hell out of me. This is the first I've heard of this." And that's true. I didn't know that

Fox made them bring him to the bar just so he could talk to me. Because, honestly, we didn't do a lot of talking.

Now they're both looking at me expectantly.

I swear, I'm this close to confessing what happened. I know I should talk to someone about it. But I think I need to talk to Fox first and because of that I somehow manage to lock this secret in.

Then, like serendipity is meddling with me, my phone beeps.

It's Fox.

Can u come over?

That's it. That's what he texts me. I have no clue what that even means. Come over when? Now? Why? For a booty call? To talk?

I quickly text back, aware that that both Riley and Rachel are staring at me.

What's up?

Three flashing dots.

I need to talk to u. Can u come over?

That doesn't help me at all and now my insides are twisting, not sure what's going on.

I'm with Rachel getting her dress fitted. I can come over after.

I wait, but there's no response yet.

"What is it?" Riley asks, pouring the champagne into the glasses. "Shit, was it rude of me to bring only three glasses? Do you think the shop lady wants one?"

"It was Fox," I tell her and crane my neck to look toward the backroom. "And I'm pretty sure she's okay with skipping the champagne. In fact, I don't think she's coming out until Rachel asks her to."

"What did Fox want, how is he?" Rachel asks, stepping away from the mirror and plucking a glass of champagne out of Riley's hand.

"Yeah is he okay?" Riley asks, leaning forward to hand me my glass.

"He just wants me to come over. I'm sure he's doing okay." I raise my glass to Rachel. "Enough about that though, here's to you Rachel. The beautiful bride-to-be."

"Here here," Riley says.

We clink our glasses against each other's and I'm reminded how I did this with Fox last night, how I didn't look him in the eye and how that alone made everything else that followed spiral out of control.

"You okay?" Rachel asks before she takes a sip of champagne.

I blink and straighten up. "Yes. Yes." I have a few gulps, the bubbles tickling my nose.

I'm not sure if they believe me.

After we've finished the bottle and Rachel packs up her dress to take home I ask her to drop me off at Fox's. I know I should probably go home first and take my own car but since I'm apparently giving off weird vibes today, I'm pretty sure my mother will be able to deduce what happened if she gets a chance to talk to me.

"Are you sure you're okay?" Rachel asks again as she drops me off in front of the chalet.

I glance up at the house and see Fox on the balcony above, dressed in grey sweatpants and a white T-shirt, watching us. "Yeah I'm fine," I tell her, opening my door. "I'll talk to you later."

"Okay," she says warily before she drives off. I have a feeling she's eyeing us in the rear-view mirror the whole time.

"Hey," Fox says from above. "Come inside."

Oh shit. Not only am I now nervous to be alone with him but he's wearing grey sweatpants *and* I now know he has a big dick. That's a dangerous combination.

I hurry through the door and once inside take in a deep calming breath through my nose. Even though I've been over here a million times, everything looks different to me, feels different. There's anticipation in the air, a change.

I go up the stairs to the main level and see Fox leaning against the entry to the kitchen with a cup of coffee in his hand. He's not smiling but he doesn't look annoyed either. And, I know, why should he, he's the one inviting me over. But you just never know what you're going to get with him sometimes.

"Coffee?" he asks.

"Sure," I say, reaching for his cup.

But he holds it far away from me. "Let me get you a fresh one."

He walks into the kitchen and I admire his ass in those sweatpants and the firm muscled plane of his back and those gorgeously sculpted shoulders and it hits me once again that I know what all of that feels like under my hands. I dragged my nails down his back last night. In fact, the more I stare, the more I think I see faint pink marks I made.

My face flushes. The reality of what happened is now between us like something real and big and palpable.

He pours me a cup and hands it to me, then asks, "So how was the dress fitting?"

His voice is easy, his eyes are holding mine like they always do, curious and inquisitive and like...nothing has changed.

"Uh, it was fine. She looks great." I chew on my lip, wondering if he's going to bring it up or if I should. You know, the whole best friends fucking on a pool table thing.

"I'm sure she'll be a beautiful bride. I can only hope I make the wedding," he says, taking a sip of his coffee. I catch a whiff of it. Somehow it smells more abrasive than mine.

I frown, bringing my attention back to what he said.

"Why wouldn't you be able to? You're able to schedule work off, aren't you? I know you've been able to before."

"I am usually. Sometimes. But it's not like a normal job, you know that. I have to leave tonight."

"Tonight?" I grip the coffee mug tighter.

"There's a fire just south of the border, near Wenatchee. They've been fighting it for a few days now but it's out of control and big as fuck. They need us to come down. That's why I asked you to come over."

"Oh." I see.

"I need you to take care of Conan. I spent the morning setting everything up so it's easier for you."

"Okay," I say, kind of wishing I hadn't agreed to this whole thing. I mean, I love all animals, even squirrels, but this is so not part of my job description.

That said, there is something completely adorable and captivating about watching Fox try and care for a baby squirrel. I follow him into his room and he starts laying out all the supplies and essentials next to the cage, going over everything and meanwhile I'm staring at his bed and trying to reconcile the memories of last night with the reality of us right in front of me.

He's acting like nothing had happened. I mean, he did remember how deep he was inside me, right?

He did remember the words he said, the way he kissed me, the way he looked at me, like he was too hungry to make up for lost time that he could barely control himself...*right*?

"Of course I understand if this is too much for you and you end up taking him to someone else," he says as he turns to face me, one arm leaning on the cage.

"I'll play it by ear," I tell him. "So, you think you might not be back in time for the wedding?" Shane's going to be crushed if Fox doesn't make it and will take it way more personally than perhaps he should. Or maybe he has a right to take it that way.

"I'm going to try my best. Believe me, I don't want to miss this. I'm hoping our team will be in and out fast. No longer than two weeks. But it's a big fire and so many aux crews are fighting some of them in California right now." He closes his eyes, scrunching up his forehead.

Without thinking I reach out and delicately touch his forehead. "Are you okay?"

He nods slowly and opens his eyes one at a time. "Yeah. Migraines or something. Anyway everything is so fucked right now. The world is just spiraling out of control."

Actually it sounds like his thoughts are spiraling out of control and I remember what he said last night about how I bring him peace. I wonder how much of that was really true, how much was drunken Fox speak. I don't see him open and vulnerable enough to really draw any conclusions.

"This doesn't have anything to do with last night, does it?" I ask. Point-blank. Because, shit, someone had to bring it up. I couldn't go on pretending even if I wanted to.

He stares at me, frowning. "What? My migraine?"

"Your whole world spiraling out control thing," I say, wishing that I didn't feel so awkward in bringing it up.

He shakes his head. "No. Del, that's just...that's just the world now. Don't you see that? Feel it? It's like...the very bedrock beneath our feet is in flux. Fires are breaking out more and more, they're getting more extreme. Even California has a year-round fire season now. There are no off-times anymore. The planet is getting angry and violent and she's fighting back against us."

I lick my lips, slowly nodding. "Well good. I mean, I thought it had something to do with us and not global warming. We are going to talk about last night, aren't we?"

He blinks at me. "What's there to talk about?"

My brows raise to the ceiling. *Excuse me?*

"What's there to talk about?" I repeat. "I mean...that wasn't all in my head, was it? We did have sex last night, didn't we?"

He relaxes into an easy smile. "We did."

I wait for him to elaborate but he doesn't. "And?" I say.

"And what? It was...it was a long-time coming, I think."

"You don't think it changes things between us?"

He tilts his head, eying me curiously. "Why would it?"

"Because we had sex, Fox. That was a..."

A big deal. A huge deal.

It meant fucking everything to me.

But those words will not come. They know they'll fall on deaf ears. I don't know what fucking mood Fox is in right now or where his head is. Probably far away already, fighting the flames. This sometimes happens right before he goes out, like he has to mentally prepare himself days before. I don't blame him, considering the things he must do.

But still, right now, in an entirely selfish way, it hurts. I want him to know how big this whole thing is, what it meant to me.

And if he doesn't feel the same way...

"Hey," he says, putting his hands on my shoulders and giving them a squeeze, the rough calloused feel of his palms shooting lightning through my skin. "Last night meant a lot to me, Del. I needed a friend and you were there for me. Don't worry, this doesn't change how I think of you, it doesn't change our friendship at all. I promise."

Ow.

Ow.

That was not what I wanted to hear. I can understand, I guess, why he might think that would be a good thing to say to me right now but fucking hell, it's *not*.

But I smile anyway. He's about to head out to fight fires in the middle of a forest somewhere. He's about to risk his life. I'm about to take care of his god damn baby squirrel. Now is not the time to tell him that I don't want things to stay the same between us. At the very least, I want what happened last night to happen again.

Now that I know what it's like to have him kiss me, to have his hands run down my body, how he so easily makes me come over and over, I can't possibly go back to the us we were before.

But apparently *he* can.

"Good," I tell him. Lying my ass off. "I just wanted to make sure that nothing was weird between us."

"Nothing could ever be weird between us. That's why we work so well together."

Then with a wink, he goes over the instructions for Conan again and this time I force myself to pay attention.

I know there will be time later for me to dwell over and analyze everything else.

He's going to be gone for a while.

FOX

"You know why I like this job?" Roy says to me as he pulls the meat away from the sparerib he has in his hand.

"Is it something to do with the food?" Davis asks, smirking. This guy is always smirking.

"Damn right it's something to do with the food," says Roy as he tears into another section of meat. "Becky doesn't cook this good at home. She tries, believe me she tries, but hell. This stuff is *always* good. Don't tell her I said that."

A little known fact about these stations they set up for us wildland firefighters in the middle of nowhere, is that we eat like kings. We have to put down six thousand calories a day here to compensate for the work that we do out in the forest. But even with all the gourmet food that's served in the mess hall, we still usually lose weight while we're here. You're on twelve-hour shifts, you're hand digging firelines, you're running hoses up and down steep and rugged terrain, all while carrying packs that weigh fifty pounds.

It's tough, punishing work.

But sometimes, at least to Roy, the food can make up for

it. We even have our favorite caterers whose primary job is to serve top-notch meals to wildland firefighters.

It's actually pretty surprising the way that these camps operate—with military precision. Makes sense when you think about how many people here have a military background. Whether it's in a baseball field on the outskirts of town or on some farm's pastureland (like we are right now, in the tinder dry mountains outside of Wenatchee, Washington), these massive camps are erected in twenty-four hours and become a sea of tents.

Our crew, the North Ridge Hot Shots, normally wouldn't be down here across the border, but this fire is just too big and back home there's a brief respite in terms of fires. That could all change in a day or two with the lightning strikes coming this time of year, but for now, we're here.

Aside from Roy and Davis, there are twenty other men in my crew, the head honcho being Captain Frank "Mad Dog" Rogers, who ironically used to work with my cousin River in the Coast Guard on Canada's west coast. All of us work together all summer long and often do training in the off-seasons as well. As a result, we're a pretty tight-knit team and even though there are many familiar faces at massive camps such as this one we tend to stick together. These guys are as much my brothers as Mav and Shane are.

Our crew is also different because we are inherently smokejumpers, and the only smoke-jumping hot shot crew in Canada. There are only seven or eight in the US itself. But because that part of our job is only useful when fighting remote fires before they get a chance to really start, we spend most of our time helping out other crews, sometimes as far south as California.

After dinner is over, we head out to the debriefing with 200 other firefighters as captains stand on a makeshift stage and go over what to expect tomorrow.

We've only been here for a few nights now and you can tell that things are changing. When we first arrived, the visibility wasn't that bad. Now the smoke has moved in, obscuring our sight, making our eyes water, singeing our noses. The blacker the smoke, the worse the fire and this one is already 400 miles across, the biggest on record in Washington state.

"Sounds like we might get spiked out tomorrow," Roy says to me as we head back to our tents. Getting spiked out is when you don't get to return back to base camp and end up spending all hours of the day and night out on the line. There are supposed to be upwards of 600 firefighters here though at any given time, half of them are here and half are out.

I nod, ready for it. I've had this restlessness inside me ever since I left North Ridge, like there's something clawing to come out of me and I don't know what it is. To be honest, I'm almost afraid to let it out. Plus, I swear my headaches are getting worse, and I need more pills.

Fire has always been my greatest distraction. When I'm with the team, when I'm out here in the wild and I'm staring the flames in the face, racing against the clock, inhaling smoke until I can't breathe, then I'm really living. Then I'm really someone. Then I don't think about all the shit at home, the confusion, the guilt. I don't think about any of that.

It's like I have to risk my life in order to feel like I have a life worth risking.

"So how is that girl you started dating?" Roy asks as we head between the rows of tents, twilight settling in. "I forget her name."

I was hoping that Roy wouldn't bring her up. Out of all my teammates, Roy is the funniest, crassest, and yet the biggest lover ever. Despite his comments about her food sometimes, he's absolutely head over heels in love with his wife Becky and their two young daughters Sara and Elena.

He loves to talk relationships and sex and everything else in-between. When Riley first came to North Ridge, she reminded me of him.

I sigh, raising my hand in a wave to some guys we know as we pass them by. "It didn't work out. She broke up with me."

"Aw, I'm sorry man," Roy says and he sounds sorry. "Most women just don't understand this job. Even Becky still has her moments where she wants me to quit."

"Really?"

"Oh hell yeah, man. She tells me that she doesn't want our babies growing up without a father, you know all that guilt-ridden stuff. But then she's also proud of me so I don't know what the fuck to think. I get it, though. If I were in her shoes…"

"Yeah. Well. It wasn't that. We were barely together."

"So what was it?"

"There was someone else." He raises his brows. I pause. "On my side."

"Oh, you dawg," he says slyly.

I give him a tight smile. I wasn't prepared to open up about Del with him, not in this way. "It's not like that. She's a friend. I've known her since I was six years old. She's practically a sister to me."

"Except that she's not."

I shake my head. "No. She's definitely not. And I've got to be honest with you man, I'm a bit messed up from it all right now."

"Well if you've known her for that long, I can see why. I'm guessing she feels the same way about you?"

"That's just the thing. I don't know how she feels and I don't know how I feel. We had sex the other night and…I mean I was drunk and upset and I needed someone and she was there but I had no idea how much it would mean. How good it would feel. It was like I had waited my whole damn life for that one moment and I had it and...fuck man, it scared the shit out of me."

I don't even think I could admit that to Maverick, but Roy is nodding like he completely understands.

"You know, my Becky and I, we were high school sweethearts. We were the couple everyone wanted to be. Prom king and queen...you know if we celebrated prom in Canada. We split up when we graduated though. She went to university in Montreal, I stayed at home in Fernie. When she came back though, we went right back to the way things were. There was no other way and we didn't want there to be any other way. It was all or nothing with her. Maybe this girl is all or nothing for you. And believe me, that shit is scary. Scarier than these fucking fires, that's for sure."

I take in a deep breath. Even talking about this, thinking about it, is making my heart beat a little faster, a little harder. "I just don't want to disappoint her, you know? I don't want to fuck things up between us. I mean she knows me, she really does. She knows this job. She knows it all and she's there for me and yet I know that...I'm a fucking mess. What if I ruin what we have?"

He gives me a wry grin, totally amused. "First of all, you will disappoint her. Because you're a man and that's what we do. Sooner you accept that the better. Second of all, it takes two to tango. You said you slept with her? I have no doubt she wanted and waited for that to happen as much as you did. I mean, she did enjoy herself, didn't she?"

I think of the way Del looked at me, the lust that burned in her gaze, like I was all she'd ever wanted. I'd never seen her like that before and on such a level. It reached a part of me I didn't know existed, brought out this primal urge, need, to keep that look in her eyes going.

Then the way she moaned as she came around my cock.

The way she squeezed me so perfectly, her body melding with mine, the way her neck arched back, her tits pushed up. She bit her lip and it nearly undid me at the seams.

Delilah wanted me that night. Not just as a friend, but as a lover. Whether she wants anything more, remains to be seen.

"I take it she did enjoy herself," Roy goes on, reading my face. "Anyway, then you're good. It sounds like this had to happen. Be glad it did. And when you go back, figure your shit out. Figure out what you want, then let her know. Be honest. But for fuck's sake, no matter what you do, don't go into this whole thing thinking you're going to fuck shit up and that you're a fucking mess. That doesn't help anybody. This girl, if she's your friend and she's known you that long, she knows all that about you and is still wanting you, still by your side. Don't you dare sabotage yourself, because I know you too Fox, and I know you have one hell of a complex."

I frown at him. "Complex?"

"Oh, don't act like you don't know what I'm talking about."

I shake my head as we come to a stop beside our tents. "I don't have a complex."

Roy raises one brow and looks me over. "I could argue with you all night but I think we need some sleep. Or at least I need to Facetime my Becky and the girls while I have reception. Maybe you should think about doing the same."

"Facetime your wife and kids?"

"Don't get smart, *Foxy*. See you in the morning."

He crawls into his tent and I crawl into mine.

I get into my sleeping bag and rest my head on the pillow, knowing that this might be the last time I'll have a comfortable place to sleep for a few days. Despite the fact that it's not entirely dark out, the tent city is a quiet place around the clock because of the crews coming in and out at all hours of the day and night. We try and get quality sleep whenever we can because once we're out there on the line and spike out, we're often running on empty.

I think about what Roy said and take out my phone. One bar of reception.

I should text Del.

I haven't since I left.

Ask her how she is.

How Conan is.

Ask her if we're going to be okay, whatever "we" is anymore.

But before I can decide whether I'm going to or not, my eyes grow heavy and then I'm asleep.

* * *

MY SLEEP IS DREAMLESS SO when my alarm blares at six a.m., I'm not even sure if I've been asleep or not. I'm both tired and wired, even after I get a couple of cups of strong coffee inside me, standing with Roy, Davis and the rest of our crew at seven a.m., when the morning briefing starts.

We're a motley crew, a gruff bunch of men and women sipping coffee, yawning, trying to prepare for the day which is always more grueling than you anticipate, no matter how many times you've done it before.

Today there's a sense of unease in the air, which seems to thicken along with the black smoke. I've rubbed my eyes raw by the time the section chief talks about fire growth and injuries before moving on to the weather update for the day, team assignments, then division leaders are identified, safety is addressed, air support is run through and there's an update on the medical situation.

There's only been one injury so far—a snag, which is a fallen tree and one of our biggest hazards—which is pretty amazing considering what we're doing and the size of this crowd and how common snags are and while that seems like good news, it makes me feel worse, like there's another shoe out there ready to drop.

We meet with Mad Dog and the hot shot team from Medford Oregon whom we'll be working with today and are given our assignments. Anticipating a possible wind change, they want us to go up north of the fire, over a dangerous ridge that should take us all day just hiking. Once there, we'll be either chopping down trees or setting them on fire in order to stop the fire's progress. Sometimes a line in the dirt just won't cut it.

After breakfast—where we filled up as much as possible on eggs, potatoes, meat and grits—we are suited up and packed into the convoy of F-250 trucks.

"So did you call her last night?" Roy asks me as our truck bounces up and down along an old logging road, the smoke getting deeper and deeper as we progress closer to our jumping off point.

I fidget with the collar of my jacket and glare at him. This is not the place to be talking about this, surrounded by everyone. I know they're like family, but just like with family, I like to keep some things to myself.

"Call who?" Simon, the youngest guy in our troop, asks. "This that new girl of yours?"

"No, he's done with her," Roy says. "This is someone else."

"Fox, I didn't know you had it in you," Davis jokes, elbowing me in the side. "So who is she?"

"None of your business," I tell everyone. "And definitely no longer Roy's business."

He puts on a mock-offended look, clutching his chest.

It's a long drive so by the time the trucks reach the destination at the foothills of the ridge, we're more than ready to get hiking.

"Five kilometers straight up," Mad Dog says to us. "Pace

yourselves. The air is only going to get worse and the heat isn't letting up. Let's pray that this is all in vain and that the wind doesn't switch direction because if it does we won't have a lot of time. We don't have a lot of time as it is."

I ease on my dusty backpack, grab my Pulaski axe, a hot shot's best friend, plus a can of gas for the chainsaw in Roy's hand, and we start up.

There is no time to catch your breath, just a water break here and there. I keep my eyes focused on Davis's boots in front of mine. My lungs burn, my calf muscles are cramping and the pack is feeling heavier with each passing second. I'm soaked with sweat.

But I keep going. We all do. Even though we are marching straight up to do one of the things I hate the most about this job.

Our job while we're spiked out is to work in "the black" or the burn. It's a firefighting tactic that has worked since the 70's, even though it rests in total destruction at our own hands.

We cut down the trees or burn them before the fire has a chance to reach them. We destroy beautiful pristine forest. We ravage large swaths of forest for the greater good and the what ifs.

That's the worst part to me. The what if. Many times I've taken a torch to a beautiful stand of trees and watched squirrels and birds have to abandon their nests and their babies are burned to death. The ground becomes alive with rattlesnakes and deer and mice as they race away past us and I swear I see the blame in their eyes, wondering why we're doing this, destroying their homes when the fire never ends up coming their way to begin with.

But it's what we do. It's the ugly side of trying to save animals and people and forests and buildings. Sometimes you really just lose more than you should.

Once we reach the top, we get to work.

I have the drip torch, setting the back burn.

The trees in front of me, tall, stately, their needles a vibrant green not yet touched by this summer's drought, go up like a row of roman candles. They pop one by one. Crackle. Whoosh. They roar. Heat sears the air and smoke billows up above the rising flames. I'm facing an inferno that I created.

I watch, leaning against my shovel, and as I often do, wonder just what the hell I'm doing. A snake slithers over my dirty boots as it flees but I don't pay it much attention except to mouth "I'm sorry."

I'm so sorry.

I've always tried to prevent death.

And sometimes I have to cause it.

We do this for the rest of the day.

The wind holds.

We do more digging than burning, which is harder work, especially when we're working fast, but it's better.

At three a.m. we hunker down in a circle on the ground away from the line and up further on the ridge for a few hours to get some sleep. Mad Dog watches over us, our supplies and equipment, and the fire that never stops raging.

As dawn breaks the sky, a dull pink glows through the smoke that sits on top of the pines like a layer of strawberry foam, we're shoveling instant coffee in our faces and are back at it.

Another day of digging, burning.

Scrambling against time.

Monitoring the wind, the weather, working harder and harder while being extra vigilant.

My body is exhausted but somehow it still feels strong. It's my mind that feels weak, tired. Everyone is in the same boat.

"Fox," Roy says beside me, patting me on the shoulder. "Have some water."

It's two in the afternoon and I know I'm dehydrated. He hands me a canteen and I taste dirt and salt on the lip as I get the water down, spilling some over my chin. My helmet is hot from the flames, my brain feels like it's melting. My headache wants to come back with a vengeance but I won't let it here. It never happens here.

"Davis says the fire below isn't burning on the ground," Roy says to me when I give him the water back. "Climbing ladder fuels now, bunch of trees going up all at once. There's a hot shot team from Idaho, the Red Eagles, they're below us on the ridge and their line is fucked, it's torching right by it. If the wind switches, we might have to evacuate."

And as if Roy's words have power, I feel a subtle change in wind. Just a push of heat against my face, coming from the side. The low, loud rumble that's been building beneath us suddenly gets louder. Compared to the roar of the trees we had set fire to yesterday, it sounds like a jet taking off. Both of us look up and see embers and ash float past in the air.

Not good.

One of the embers goes over our heads and floats down onto the branch of a blue spruce. Dry as sand, it goes up in flames so fast that it takes Roy and I a second to react.

"Shit," Roy says as we jog over to it. The tree is in the unburned section that we're trying to protect, beyond the black matchstick forest of back burn, and we immediately try to put it out. It's a strange feeling trying to quell a fire so close to the stand of trees you just purposely set flames to.

Roy coughs into his sleeve. I'm coughing too. Fresh air seems like a dream at this point. We've been doing this for twenty-four hours straight now on little sleep and I'm wondering if we're beyond the point of fatigue. Somehow our muscles keep going though, our instincts and adrenaline propelling us forward.

Then more embers come, delicately floating in the air. We all stop what we're doing and watch. It's like watching snow-fall in Hell.

They land and trees ignite. Not just one or two but three or four, then batches, then stands.

Pop.

Crack.

Hiss.

Roar.

Fuck.

We all start scrambling, even though I know that it's too late, that this is going to get worse, that sometimes when you punch the fire, the fire punches you back.

Davis runs over to us with a hint of panic on his face. At thirty-five, he's been with the hot shots for a while and he's usually as cool as a cucumber, having done a few tours of Afghanistan with the Canadian army, so to see him look worried makes me extra worried.

"Garrett, the division supervisor, said they lost the line," he says breathlessly, soot streaked across his face like war paint. "The Red Eagles are trying to get out. We all have to evacuate, now."

As if on cue, Mad Dog gets on his bullhorn. "We've lost the line. Gather your tools and evacuate *now*."

We get our stuff, everyone running everywhere. This isn't anything new to us, to have to leave like this, but the forest around us is now going up like sparklers, section by section. The smoke is unbearable.

Roy is trying to get his chainsaw and it keeps slipping out of his hands and then his helmet keeps slipping over his face. He's tired and showing it.

I start coming over to him when someone yells, "Snag!"

I look up.

A charred tree from the back burn is falling over.

It happens in slow motion or at least it does in my mind as I struggle to make sense, to realize what's happening. It moves slowly, the long, blackened weight of the dead tree just tipping, tipping, tipping.

The tree is falling straight over Roy.

"Roy!" I manage to scream and start running toward him, my boots, pack, gear, everything has never felt heavier, my lungs burning from smoke, eyes stiff with fear.

Roy looks up at me, the helmet slipping over his eyes.

He doesn't look up to see the snag yet.

It's falling.

And I'm almost there.

My arms are out, ready to shove him out of the way, to take the hit if I have to.

Then he looks up.

Sees nothing but black tree trunk.

It comes down like a hammer and smashes Roy into the ground.

The blast nearly knocks me backward onto my ass and I'm staring, frozen, unable to think, to move.

Then, "Roy!" I scream again.

Others from the crew join me as I try and lift the tree off of him.

He's not moving.

I can see one arm out, fingers curled in. Everything else is buried by the massive burnt trunk that's still hot to touch.

The forest around us is igniting and yet we're all staying amongst the flames, six of us spread out along the trunk, trying to lift it just a few inches.

With grunts and cries of strain and sorrow and frustration, we do and Mad Dog drags Roy out from under the tree.

We let go, dust flying from the impact.

But one look at Roy and we all know we're too late.

Our helmets protect us from small snags, from rocks.

They don't protect you from entire trees.

Nothing does.

Just luck.

And luck wasn't on Roy's side this time.

I'm beside myself.

Disconnected.

This can't be happening.

Somehow we get Roy on a stretcher, even though Mad Dog just pronounced him as dead, and we head down the hill.

Foot after foot.

As quickly as we can.

The forest burns behind us, all our hard work for nothing.

Roy's death for nothing.

The fire won this time.

It took more than maybe it meant to take.

It's certainly alive. A living breathing thing.

It's supposed to be neutral.

But when it takes my good friend, a man that was like a brother to me, how can I not think that it's evil.

Or maybe it isn't evil at all.

Maybe I didn't get to Roy on time.

Maybe the tree should have taken me out.

Maybe a lot of things.

All I know is that he's gone.

A part of me inside is gone too.

Now the flames are twenty-feet high in the sky, shooting up columns of smoke and ash and we lost and we failed and he's dead.

8

DELILAH

"Where the hell is Fox?" Rachel yells. "Where is he, where is he, where is he?"

We're currently in the upstairs bathroom of the Nelson farmhouse and she's seconds away from slipping into a panic attack. It might have something to do with the fact it's her wedding day and there's not only a thunderstorm approaching, but the bartender called in sick, her makeup artist got the dates wrong, and Fox is nowhere to be found. Also the fact that the wedding starts in about thirty minutes and Rachel just tore a hole in the bottom of her dress as she walked past some brush.

Suffice to say, she's just in her strapless bra and underwear now, panicking, fluttering her hands around her and I'm doing my best to dab the tissues under her eyes and keep her mascara from running down her face. "Honey, I don't know. Damn, I wish Riley had used waterproof mascara on you."

"Oh my god, it's being ruined isn't it?" Rachel sobs, trying to turn to get a look at herself in the mirror.

I hold her tight in place. "No, I'm fixing it, you look beautiful and everything is going to be fine."

"Okay," she sniffs. "Wow, you have like kung-fu grip man hands."

I narrow my eyes at her. "They are not man hands, they're just strong from opening so many bottles and throwing losers out of the bar. Now hold still or I'll poke your eye out."

Because the makeup artist didn't show, Riley had to do her makeup this morning instead. Honestly, she did an amazing job considering she doesn't wear too much makeup herself and isn't a pro.

But that's not making Rachel feel any better.

"This is horrible," she whines.

"Everything is going to be fine," I reassure her just as there's a knock at the bathroom door. "Come in."

It's Riley, also looking gorgeous in her bridesmaid dress, with a stain remover pen in hand. "I found one. Actually it's your mom's, Del."

Oh yeah, the stain remover is for me. I was drinking red wine earlier, trying to calm my own maid-of-honor nerves and I spilled it on myself, which didn't help Rachel's stress level.

"How's the dress?" Rachel asks her.

"She's almost done." My mother has Rachel's dress and is in the living room downstairs trying to sew up the parts that ripped, meanwhile Vernalee is running around the Nelson property trying to keep the circus together. "It's going to be fine, Rach," Riley adds. "Dress looks perfect." She hands me the stain remover pen and looks at me, impressed. "Your mom is all sorts of genius, Del."

I take it from her and start dabbing the pen on the bodice of the dress, right over the red wine stain. I've already blotted out most of it with warm water and luckily Rachel put us in navy dresses so it's not as bad as it could have been. "My mother was a professional nanny taking care of me and three rambunctious boys. She's fucking Mary Poppins."

"Wow," she says softly.

It's rare for Riley to say *anything* softly so I pause my pen in mid-dab and look at her. "What?"

"Nothing. It's just...I know I haven't been here all that long but being with Mav and you guys, it's just sort of amazing that your mom was able to raise them and they all turned out to be such normal, good dudes."

"To be fair, Hank raised them too. He did most of it. My mom was just there."

She has this dreamy look in her eyes. "Still. To think of all three of those boys being here growing up, to see them get bigger, smarter, stronger. I envy you both, you know. You both got to grow up with them, see them how they were and how they are now."

Rachel snorts. It's the first time today she's sounded remotely amused. "Riley, you're seeing Maverick's highlight reel. Believe me, you wouldn't have wanted to be there through all of their awkward boners and voice changes and sibling dramatics."

"I don't know," she says with a sigh. "You all have this history and it feels like I'm starting from square one." She goes to the window and looks down at the fields as if she's imagining our childhood. I glance over and see the crowd, hear their murmurs float up. All the chairs have been set up for the ceremony, the altar by a lone pine tree with the backdrop of the river and town behind it. Tents are currently being erected for the reception, which is adding to the chaos. They should have been set up before but, well, that was another thing that went wrong. Now people are hustling trying to beat the oncoming storm.

"But that's just the way you and Mav found each other," I tell her, grabbing a hand towel and blotting the rest of the stain remover from my dress. "You wouldn't have worked if you had met him back then. I mean, the other day Fox told me that he had a crush on me in high school and that he thought we would end up together but in the end it just didn't work out."

A thick silence falls over the room, the only sound the dripping tap. I look up to see them staring at me.

"What?"

"Fox told you that?" Rachel asks in disbelief.

"I am so not surprised," Riley says, folding her arms across her chest and making her boobs practically pop out of the V-neck halter of the dress. I definitely don't fill it that well. "When?"

I tell them cautiously, not sure how much to share, "Here, the other night. When I acted like an idiot and ran to the barn because apparently I'm not very good at hiding my emotions."

"What did you guys talk about?" Riley asks. "Like, how did it get on *that* topic?"

"And wait a minute," Rachel says, holding up her hand. "Wait a minute. You just said you were hiding your emotions. What emotions, Del?"

Ah shit. I did just say that, didn't I? Sometimes I forget what I've admitted to people other than myself. The list is very short.

I sigh and lean back against the wall, dabbing my dress out of habit now. "I, uh. I wasn't a fan of Julie. Let's put it that way."

"Because..." Riley coaxes me.

"Because... I was jealous."

"Because..." Rachel adds.

I take in a deep breath and exhale noisily. I look at the both of them and display my hands. "Because I like Fox and I want to be with him. I mean...I love him. I'm in love with him. I'm hopelessly, terribly in love with that man and I think I'm losing my mind every fucking day."

In unison they both make this little squealing sound, stamping their shoes on the bathroom floor, big, smug smiles on their faces.

"You guys, this isn't a good thing," I tell them quickly. "This is in fact a very bad thing."

"Love is never bad, Del," Rachel says.

"Easy for you to say! You're getting married in like, shit, ten minutes to the love of your life. Love is great for you." I point at Riley before she can say anything. "And you, missy, you're standing here complaining that you didn't get to grow up with the love of your life. I mean, talk about looking for something to get upset about. You guys just bought a place together, it's only a matter of time before you guys get married too, or whatever."

"We're not getting married," Riley says and though she's rolling her eyes, there's a hint of tension in her voice. "Maverick isn't that type."

"Yeah right!" I exclaim. "He's crazy for you and you know it. Whatever way Mav was before, he's a different man with you."

"But this isn't about me," she says.

"No, it's about Rachel."

"No, it's about you and Fox," Rachel says. "What the hell, Del? Do you know how long we've been waiting for you to finally admit that you like him? This is huge!"

"It's not huge." At least, that's not the part that's huge.

"So he's now single…" Riley says innocently.

"So?"

"So go and make your move."

"Riley, you don't just make your move on a guy you've been friends with forever."

No, in my case, they apparently make the move on you.

Then act like nothing happened.

Then disappear.

"You know Fox feels the same as you," Rachel muses.

"Why? How?" I say, a little too quickly. "Did he say anything to you?"

She shrugs and pulls up her strapless bra a little higher. "No, he didn't say anything to me. I doubt he'd say anything to anyone. I doubt he even knows it himself. But you know we've all thought you guys have had the biggest, maddest crushes on each other and if you're finally admitting the way you feel, then you should maybe admit it to him."

"Or at least tell him you want to jump him and get yourself laid," Riley says.

"That's a terrible idea," Rachel chides her.

"Why?" I ask, my skin growing hot.

"Oh come on," Rachel says. "You sleeping with Fox would be a major mistake."

"Why, why, why would that be mistake?"

"You can't just sleep with him, not when you've been in love with him your whole life."

"But if he feels the same way…"

"Guys get confused when sex enters the picture. It makes them feels things in a different way. I just think you should sort your feelings out for each other first before you do that. Otherwise, you might be setting yourself up for heartache. I mean, can you imagine if you have a fling with him and it doesn't go anywhere? How awkward that would be for you guys. And us."

I press my lips together, feeling like she just dumped a whole vat of ice water on me. Thank god I didn't discuss this with her earlier, before I had spoken to Fox and thank god Fox seemed to want our relationship to go back to the way it was. Okay, well maybe I'm not thanking god for that because I do want more but I guess it could have been worse.

"Del," Riley says slowly as she peers at me. "Del, did you sleep with Fox?"

"Oh come on," Rachel says but her smile fades when I don't immediately say anything. "Oh my god. Delilah Gordon, did you have sex with Fox Nelson?"

"It sounds extra weird when you use our full names," I admit quietly.

"Oh my god!" Riley and Rachel exclaim in unison, their eyes bugging out of their heads, mouths dropped.

"Rachel!" a voice yells and the door to the bathroom starts shaking from someone pounding on it. "You have to go now! Wedding is starting, like, fucking *now*."

It's Maverick.

Riley flings the door open which causes Rachel to scream and grab a towel from the rack and attempt to cover her bra and underwear.

"Oh like I haven't seen that before," Maverick says as he steps in the bathroom. He looks handsome as hell, clean-shaven, wearing a well-fitted tuxedo.

"Rachel needs her dress before she can go out there," I say, gesturing to her.

Riley grabs his arm. "Did you know that Fox and Del fucked?"

"What?!" Mav exclaims loudly, staring at me with the same expression Riley is. "When?"

"Is he here yet?" Rachel asks Mav, tugging on his other arm.

He shakes his head, blue eyes focused on me. "No, he's not. Del where is he?"

"I don't know!" I throw out my arms. "I haven't talked to him at all since he's been gone."

"Did you guys fuck before he left?" Mav asks.

"Oh stop being so vulgar," Rachel says, smacking him

now. Then she looks to me. "But, did you? When did this happen?"

"Rachel, I'm done!" my mom yells, suddenly appearing in the doorway with the wedding dress in hand. "Are you guys having a party in here? I smell booze."

"Delilah and Fox slept together," Riley tells her.

"Riley!" I cry out.

Oh my god!

"Not cool, babe, not cool," Mav mutters under his breath.

"What?" my mother asks, brows raised, as Rachel takes the dress from her. "Delilah?"

"Okay everyone out," Rachel says, waving her hands around, "I have to put this on."

"What in tarnation is going on up here?" Dick says, also appearing behind my mother. Rachel yelps again, this time covering herself with the dress.

He looks at all of us with utmost disapproval. "Enough with the lollygagging in the bathroom, get yourselves downstairs and out that door to the damn wedding!"

"Everybody out!" Rachel yells, grabbing the edge of the door. I'm about to leave the room too but she pulls me back by my elbow. "No, Del you stay. I need your help."

"Is it true?" I hear my mother whisper to Mav on the other side of the door. "About Fox and Del?"

"Is what true?" Dick asks.

I groan and lean back against the sink, resting my head in my hands.

"Hey," Rachel says softly, putting her hand on my arm. "It's okay. But first, as maid of honor, you have to help me into this dress. Then, as my best friend, you have to tell me everything."

My hands drop away and I look at her. "You just said it was a colossal mistake."

"I know. I'm sorry. I didn't know. Just talk to me. And help me get this damn dress on!"

She's starting to go into panic mode again and it doesn't help that I'm hearing the soft strains of the wedding march come through the window.

I quickly unzip the dress and help her get into it. My mother really did an amazing job with the hem, you can't tell that it ripped at all.

"It happened the night of the breakup. He came to the bar like Riley said, all drunk and damaged and one thing led to another…"

She holds her boobs together so I can get the bodice on properly while I start to zip up the back. "What, you guys had sex at The Bear Trap?"

I can't help but grin. "Yeah. On the pool table."

"Oh my god."

"I know."

"So what…what does this mean? I mean, I want to hear the details and all but…"

"But we need to get you downstairs and to your wedding," I fill in as I snag the hook and eye closure together. "There, you're in. You're done." She slowly pirouettes around. "And you look beautiful."

She smiles sweetly and then says, "But are you guys okay?"

I nod. "I think so. Next day I went over to talk about his squirrel—"

"His what?"

"Long story. Anyway, he acted like nothing had happened and when I wondered if things were weird now, he said nothing would ever change between us. That we'd always be friends. I never said otherwise but I guess…things are just back to normal. Like we both got it out of our system."

She looks me closely in the eye. "Del, you just don't get love out of your system. Not like that."

I swallow, nod. "I know."

"So you really haven't talked to him? You don't know where he is?"

"I wish I did, Rachel. You know how he is when he's away. I'm sure he would have made it if he could have."

"Shane is going to be so upset."

I put my hand on her cheek. "He'll get over it. Right now, all he cares about is you. Now come on, let's go make you his wife."

We head out of the bathroom and down the stairs, and then go around the corner of the house to wait for our cues. Maverick is already here, as is Vernalee, Hank and Dick. I peek around the corner and already see Shane standing at the altar with the minister.

"Rachel," I say in awe. "Shane looks *so* handsome."

She grins at me. "I'm so nervous!" she whispers harshly.

"You're going to be fine," Hank says, holding out his arm. Since Rachel's father is thankfully absent and tucked away in prison somewhere, both Hank and Dick agreed to walk Rachel down the aisle together. Vernalee is here to walk Riley down the aisle in the case that Fox doesn't show up, and so far that seems to be what's happening.

"That's our cue," Vernalee says, putting her arm out for Riley. I know that traditionally, if there's an uneven number, then the person walks alone, but I have a feeling this is more for Vernalee than it is for Riley.

She and Riley walk down the aisle between the rows of chairs, Vernalee's grey dress and fancy hat a nice compliment to the navy blue of Riley's dress. In the background that thunderstorm keeps churning closer and closer and just as Riley takes her place at the altar and Vernalee sits down in the front row, the sky flashes with fork lightning.

Everyone goes "ooooh" and Mav takes my arm. "Talk about a dramatic entrance, huh Del?" he says to me as we start heading down the aisle toward them, the thunder now rumbling through us, a hot, electrically charged breeze ruffling my up-do. "I can't believe you slept with Fox," he adds.

I keep the smile pasted on my face for the guests and talk to him out of the corner of my mouth. "I can't believe it either."

I take my place at the altar beside Riley and give her hand an excited squeeze for a moment, then look at Shane and grin, mouthing "yay!"

He's looking handsome, he's also looking wired. Not scared exactly, but anxious, nervous, a whole mess of things. I know the spot beside Maverick burns with Fox's absence but so far Shane seems to be keeping it together.

Then Maverick leans into Shane and whispers something in his ear.

Shane's eyes widen and he looks right at me. "You and Fox did what?" he cries out softly.

Oh my god.

Fucking Maverick!

I'm glaring at him for telling Shane now of all times, but then Riley is poking me in the side. "Hey, it's Fox."

I glance at her and see where she's staring. Fox is coming out from around one of the tents, straightening his bow-tie.

I can barely believe that he's here, he made it.

Like the rest of his brother's, he looks devastatingly handsome, if not a little out of place, in a tux.

"He's looking rough," she whispers to me. "Did he just jump out of a plane to get here or what?"

He is looking a little rough, she's right. His face is pale and ashen, eyes are hard and intense and accented by dark circles. He walks right over to the altar and takes his place beside Maverick, giving him and Shane nothing more than a nod.

He doesn't look at me or Riley, or anyone else in the crowd, just kind of pretends that he's always been standing at the altar like he's supposed to.

He's *here*.

And yet, I can tell in his head, he is so far away.

The music grows louder and I tear my eyes off of Fox to look at the end of the aisle where Rachel appears, Hank and Dick on either side of her as the three of them proudly walk down the aisle.

I can't help it, I'm tearing up already from the sight of them. Dick won't stop grinning, wearing a black cowboy hat and shiny black boots to go along with his suit.

Even though I had just helped Rachel into her dress moments ago, it's like I'm now seeing her through new eyes. Seeing her through Shane's eyes.

I steal a glance at him and see his eyes watering with love as he gazes at her, unable to keep the smile off his face.

Rachel, too, is having a hard time keeping it together as Dick and Hank drop her off in front of Shane and go back to their seats. Riley is sniffing from beside me and muttering something about waterproof mascara.

Shane takes Rachel's hands in his, squeezes them and they gaze into each other's eyes and I'm seeing a love that I can only dream about having for myself.

I can't help it. I look past Shane to Fox and for a moment, just a moment, I meet his eyes. It's like looking at a lover, looking at a stranger, looking at a friend.

Then he looks away.

I look back at the couple.

The minister says, "Shall we begin?"

9

DELILAH

THUNDER RUMBLES, CAUSING EVERYONE TO ERUPT INTO nervous laughter.

"I'm not sure how much time we have," the photographer says to us. "Let's get a few more shots before the rain falls."

I glance up at the sky. The clouds are high and billowing and dark as sin and the wind has been steadily picking up. Somehow the rain managed to hold off for the entire ceremony and the photos so far. It's weird because it's almost as if the storm has split around us, half of it skirting above the river and obscuring the town with sheets of rain, while the other half is sliding along the base of Cherry Peak. It's a matter of minutes before the two halves converge.

With my arm linked around Riley's in our current pose, I pull Riley tighter to me and we smile in unison at the camera. Rachel and Shane are between us, out behind us are Mav and Fox.

I haven't been able to say anything to Fox since he joined the wedding except a nod, "hey" and that's it. It doesn't help that everyone else keeps watching our every move like the two of us are just going to start fucking right here.

"Delilah, can you smile bigger?" the photographer asks, and I quickly oblige. Who knows what kind of expression I just had on my face. I'm pretty sure whenever I'm thinking about Fox now I just look totally confused instead of love-struck. Maybe a combo of both.

"All right," he says after he's snapped a few more. "One more with the wedding party and family."

We're all posed by the barn leaning back along the fence, so Dick, Hank, Vernalee and my mother, who were waiting anxiously behind the camera, all come out to join us.

"When this is done, can we start drinking?" Dick asks, rubbing his hand over his weathered face.

"Hell yeah we can," Shane says with a laugh.

Then Dick takes off his cowboy hat and tosses it to Shane who catches it with ease. The photographer snaps away, getting the hat in the air and then as Shane puts it on his head and gives Rachel a joyous smile.

The first drop of rain falls right down my cleavage.

Time is up.

"Okay that's a wrap for now," the photographer says staring up at the sky before quickly putting his camera away.

"It's going to be a doozy!" Dick yells. "Shane, give me my hat back!"

All of us start to head up the hill to the house and the tents that were luckily set up before the oncoming deluge. The sky flashes with lightning and the thunder rumbles again as the rain starts to fall more steadily. I know we're going to get soaked soon but I hang back behind everyone else, the end of my dress in my hand so I don't tread on it, until I'm walking beside Fox.

"Hey stranger," I tell him with a wary smile, looking him up and down. "I don't think I've ever seen you in a tux before. You didn't even go to our high school grad."

He nods, hands in his pockets, eyes focused straight ahead. "Are they mad that I'm late?"

I stop walking and he stops beside me. "Who? Your family?"

"Yeah."

I frown at him. I can't tell if he's drunk or what he is, but he's cagey, fidgety, liking he's fighting something internally. "Honestly, I think they're all just glad you're here. They know your job, they knew you not showing was a possibility." Boldly, I reach out and grab his hand, squeezing it tight. "But I'm glad you're here."

He blinks at me, as if seeing me for the first time since getting here. He squeezes my hand back. "How is Conan?"

I smile. "He's good. He's growing more and more every day. I took him to the wildlife center, by the way, but they're booked up. Said maybe they can take him next month when the fire season calms down."

"I don't think it will ever calm down," he says, his voice grave.

And just like that, the rain comes down in sheets, slamming into us, bouncing off the dirt. "Shit," I say.

"Come here," he says, pulling me toward the closest shelter, which is the barn.

It's pretty much too late though, my dress is already soaked through and sticking to me.

And now I'm in the barn with Fox, the rain pouring down just outside and echoing off the roof.

He lets go of my hand, as if knowing what I'm thinking, what I'm feeling, realizing he's alone with me, and he walks off to the first stall, leaning back against it with a sigh. He opens his suit jacket and pulls a flask out of the pocket.

He holds it out offering it to me with a shake of his hand. "You want some?"

"What is it?" I ask, coming over to him. Normally I

wouldn't, but because of the rain and the wedding and the tension between us, I think I just might. Besides, it reminds me of being teenagers, sneaking Hank and Dick's alcohol out here and drinking it.

"Rye," he says gruffly. "It gets the job done."

I take it and have a sip, wincing at the burn as it goes down my throat, then give him a sheepish smile as I give it back to him. "Thanks. Do you always carry this with you?"

"Sometimes," he says, not smiling, eyes locked on mine as he has another large swig and I can't tell if he's joking or not. Then he looks around the barn. "This reminds me of stealing Dick's whisky and coming here. Then filled his bottles back up with water, of course."

"I was just thinking that," I say to him, and he hands me the bourbon again. "Some things never change."

"No, not really. And then all at once, everything does. Isn't that life though? One minute becomes a million minutes and you're just living every day like it isn't your last and then another minute more and it is."

Oh dear. He's definitely in a mood. I study him as I take another shot, this one going down easier. "Are you okay?"

"I don't know. Am I ever okay?"

He exhales, looks down at his feet. It's then that I notice he has ash and twigs in his hair.

"You have, like, a forest in your hair," I tell him, taking a step so I'm right up next to him and running my hand through his hair. I pick out a twig and toss it to the ground, brush away some ash.

"I didn't even have time to shower," he admits, still looking down, still letting me touch him. "I knew Shane and everyone, you especially, would have slaughtered me if I didn't make it on time. I did my fucking best."

Whoa. He's volatile tonight.

"You know it's because you and Shane have issues you

need to work out," I tell him, proceeding carefully as I remember Rachel's plea. "That's the only reason why anyone would think anything of it." He just grunts in response and I know he's not going to elaborate on that one. "But you're here and that's all that matters."

I keep running my fingers through his hair even though all the ash and twigs are gone, enjoying the feel of it, feeling this close to him. He smells like pine, and smoke, and heat and all those things I associate with him, things I've grown to love. Occasionally his eyes droop closed, which means he must be enjoying this too.

Finally, he looks up at me with a pained expression. "Hey. I'm sorry about the other night."

I look at him curiously. "What other night?"

"At the bar. What happened between us."

Oh. Oh, this isn't good...he's *sorry*? *Sorry for the sex?*

Brave face. Put on your brave face.

"Okay..." I slowly take my hand away but he reaches out and grabs me by the wrist, holding me.

"I'm sorry that I left things up in the air," he says, his eyes flashing with intensity as his grip on me tightens. "And I'm sorry I had to leave right away. I didn't want to do that. I didn't know what to do."

"It's okay, Fox. We're friends and we just happened to..."

"I have to leave again," he says quickly. "Tomorrow night."

The intensity in his gaze deepens, holding me hostage as the air changes around us like we're our own thunderstorm in the making. Meanwhile, the one outside the barn starts to rage.

He puts his hand at the back of my neck, his palm hot, his grip possessive. He holds me in place as he searches my face, his nostrils flaring slightly. "I don't want to be alone tonight, Del. I don't want to go home without you."

Our storm has reached another level. I can practically feel

the lightning striking between us, making my hair stand on end, my heart to be jolted again and again. We're charged, more alive than ever before.

"Okay," I say softly.

He slips his other hand around my waist and pulls me right up against him. The flask falls from my fingers as I reach up and grip his jacket.

"I'm wet," I warn him.

I meant from the rain, but he just grins at me and says, "Good."

Then he kisses me.

It's even more electric than the first time.

Maybe it's the rain, the way my dress sticks to my body, or it's the fiery taste of rye on his lips, or it's the storm building outside, or the overall romance of Shane and Rachel's wedding day. Or it's just how Fox is kissing me right now, with a wild, unbridled intensity, like he's been starving for me for weeks. Either way, this kiss feels like it might be the end of me.

"Del," he whispers against my lips.

But he doesn't have to say anything else.

He kisses me, wet, hot, then grabs me and pulls me into the nearest stall, the ground covered in hay, his grip on me tight, dominating, commanding.

"Get on the hay," he says, his voice husky and rich.

Bossy.

I like it.

I drop down to my knees in the hay-covered stall, staring up at him while he quickly unzips his pants. His cock bobs free between him and I'm breathless once again.

I can barely tear my eyes away from his cock to look up at him. Of course he looks smug—why shouldn't he—but there's a sense of awe in his eyes, like he can't believe this is happening again.

That makes two of us.

I close my eyes and tentatively slide my tongue along the sensitive underside before circling his crown, dark and lush, licking at the precum. The salt hits my tongue, revving my desire for him to another level.

His hand goes into my damp hair, pulling lightly, and he groans as I try and take him all into my mouth.

"Del," he whispers hoarsely. "It's been too long." He pulls away from me, his cock wet and bobbing from my mouth and glances down at me with heavy-lidded eyes. "I hate to make you stop sucking my dick because you suck so well but I need to be inside you. I need to fuck your brains out right fucking now. I need you like nothing else."

Since I'm already on my knees (and totally ruining my dress), I grab his ass with one hand, my fingernails digging in as I tug him toward me. With my other hand I grasp his cock at the base, making a circle around it

He jerks his chin at me. "Turn around."

My heart is pumping hard in anticipation as I pivot around on the hay so I'm on all fours, my ass raised in the air. He drops to his knees behind me and I hold my breath, waiting for his touch.

Swiftly he lifts up my dress until it's bunched around my waist and slides my underwear over.

"God, I need you, need this," he says gruffly, moments before he grabs my ass, squeezing hard so I stay in place. I flinch, the pressure from his fingertips is firm and yet the moment he yields, I want it even more.

He pulls me toward him as he positions himself and with one swift jerk, pushes into me. I gasp.

"You good?" he asks, shuddering the words as he pushes himself fully inside.

I try and nod, get my breath. I can't think. Can't talk.

This is *good*.

His grip around my ass tightens. "I won't be gentle, not now, not when I need to fuck you this much."

Holy hell.

I've never seen him like this.

He's lost to a wild, burning place and I'm carried in the undertow.

"How badly do you want me?" he asks, his voice thicker now.

I whimper my response.

Badly.

He sucks in his breath and then he's pounding into me, fast and deep and relentless. Over and over and over again, this breakneck pace that has me trying to hang on to the hay for dear life, my breasts jiggling with each quick, hard thrust.

"I've missed this, missed you," he says through a husky groan. His pumps become quicker, deeper, and messy, like he's losing control and going over the edge and taking me with him.

"I want you to come," he growls, grabbing the back of my hair until it's gathered in his hand, totally ruining my updo.

Jesus. He's out of control. He's become someone else, an animal, a beast, as relentless as the flames he fights. I'm at his mercy and I don't think I've ever wanted something more than for him to take such control and just fuck the living hell out of me.

Hell, heaven, whatever this is, I know it's something I'll never come back from. I know I'll never want to. In my wildest, kinkiest dreams about him, it's never been *this* good.

While he yanks back at my hair and then holds me down in place, he slips his other hand under my stomach, his fingers finding my clit.

I'm so wet, slick and ready for him, it doesn't take long for him to push me to the edge. I can feel the fire raging inside me.

I don't even have time to tell him I'm coming. It just happens, quick and swift, and I'm swept away, tumbling and turning, over and over as the orgasm churns through me. I'm burning up in flames, I never want it to let me go. My body quakes and shudders from head to toe as I pulse around him. I am light and heavy and my heart has dove wings, flying into the rafters.

"Delilah," he groans out my name and then I feel him as he comes, the pressure in my hair, the slamming of his hips into my ass. The sounds coming out of his mouth are crude and I'd give anything to watch his face as he empties into me. "Yes. God, yes."

His thrusts slow down, his hand in my hair slowly letting go, releasing the pressure from my head. He's breathing hard. Drops of sweat fall onto my back, making me shudder.

Then, as the orgasm starts to slide away into the background, the reality of what we'd just done hits me.

Fox just fucked me in the barn. From behind. My head pressed—no, *held*—to the hay.

He was animal.

He was wild.

He dominated my every move.

Just as he dominates my heart.

I get to my feet, my hands are marked with deep indentations from the hay.

I pull down my dress which isn't any drier now and take some hay to wipe him off my inner thighs, then turn around to see Fox zipping his fly back up.

I give him a lazy, sated grin. "Well we certainly never did that as teenagers." I pause. "Unless you had sex in this barn with someone else and if that's the case, I don't want to hear about it."

"Don't worry about that," he says as he picks up his suit jacket and shucks it on. "Do I look acceptable?"

I walk over to him, feeling unsteady on my feet and smooth down the front of his shirt, straighten his bowtie, and tug on the lapels of his jacket. "You look ridiculously handsome."

He gives me a small, almost sad smile before he runs his thumb over my bottom lip. Then he grips my chin between his fingers and kisses me softly. It's still enough to make my toes curl, my body melt slightly into his.

Is this us now? Is this what we do? Or is this just for here, just in private?

He pulls away and says, "You don't think they suspect anything between us, do you?"

Oh. Shit.

"Uh," I begin awkwardly. "I'm pretty sure they've figured it out."

He cocks a brow and reaches over, picking a strand of hay out of my hair. "You told them?"

"It was Riley. She guessed it. And then after that…"

"After that I'm sure even the neighbors knew."

"Are you mad?"

He runs his hand through his hair. "Mad, Del? No. I just wish it was between us because this feels like something very…I don't know. New. Special. *Private*."

"I'm sorry," I tell him, feeling like shit. "I didn't think everyone would know."

He sighs. "Well, at least I don't have to lie too much when we go back up there and they're asking where we were."

"Honestly, we don't have to say a thing."

He steps out of the stall and picks up the fallen flask from the floor, finishing the rest of it. Then he puts it back in his inner pocket and from his other pocket he takes out a couple of round white pills and throws them back in his throat, swallowing them dry.

"What are those?" I ask.

"I get headaches," he says.

"Like, after sex?"

He smiles softly. "Like, often. Not during sex though, thank god." He holds out his arm for me. "Come on, the rain has died down. Let's go eat and be social. If you're lucky, I might even ask you to dance."

I put my arm in his and we head out of the barn.

10

FOX

THERE IS NOTHING IN THIS WORLD BETTER THAN WAKING UP IN your own bed after weeks sleeping in tents and on cold, hard ground.

Actually, that's not true.

The one thing that's better than that is waking up in that bed, with a beautiful naked woman next to you.

My eyes are open, the fragments of a horrible dream slipping away into nothingness, and Del is lying beside me sleeping on her stomach, her gorgeous face at peace, her thick and shiny hair sprawled out around her.

I have to take a moment to let it sink in.

There are feelings rushing through me that I'm not sure what to do with, that are catching me off-guard. I feel so much for her at this moment, and I'm momentarily breathless.

I can't believe this is happening.

That this did happen.

Me.

With Del.

All my life she's been there. I was lost after my mother

died, unmoored and angry and reckless and sad, so horribly sad, and then she came along and changed my whole fucking world.

The truth is, I never thought of her as a sister. I may say that to people and I certainly get why Shane and Maverick might think that way about her, but I never did. She was always something separate, the girl next door, a light that would always lead me out of the black. She was my saving grace and the one constant thing I had in my life, the one person who could turn things around.

I've never told her that. I'm not sure that I can. What I feel for her has always been so deep and complicated that I still don't quite know what it is.

What I do know is that sleeping with her has injected a little chaos into my life. Not in a bad way, just in a way that I can't seem to wrap my head around. Roy died last week right before my eyes. The first member of our hot shot team to go and…I haven't been myself since then.

Fuck, I don't think I've been myself ever. I don't know if I even know who my true self is.

But I do know that the moment I laid eyes on Del at the wedding yesterday, looking impossibly stunning in that dress that showed off her tanned smooth skin, the curve of her breasts, the slope of her shoulders, all that sorrow was diverted. It didn't stop, it was just sent in another direction, far away from us.

It's stayed away. Being deep inside her brought me peace. It made the war in my heart come to a cease-fire. It made me feel a fire that didn't burn from hate and shame but from another place, a pure place.

Though to be honest, what I'm feeling for her right now is anything but fucking pure.

I reach over and pull back the covers so her ass is exposed and take a good long minute to drink her all in.

Del has a fantastic body. She's tall, with lean muscle and these perky breasts that drive me crazy every time she's not wearing a bra. But I'm pretty sure her ass is my favorite part. Of course, I've seen her in a bathing suit numerous times. Sometimes, when I'm home during the summer, we'll be down at Willow Lake with a cooler of beer and she'll be wearing some retro bikini that makes you stop and stare.

But everything is different now that I actually have her in my bed, now that I've had her in my hands, that I've touched and licked and tasted every part of her. I can't stop wanting her. I can't believe my luck.

She groans softly, turning her head over on the pillow and I smile at her, her lithe tanned body against the white sheets. I'm sure she'd think I was a total creep for just staring at her like this.

I don't care. I'll take her scorn. The more I look at her surprising beauty, the more the darkness is banished, somewhere, elsewhere.

"Are you staring at my ass?" she says, muffled into the pillow.

I bite my lip to keep from laughing as she turns over onto her side, her hair spilling over half her face.

"I was," I admit. "Now I'm staring at your tits."

I'm pretty sure her face is slowly turning red under that hair. I reach over and brush it back off her face, cupping her jaw as I stare into her eyes. Green and gold and bronze all swirling around. I used to say she had mood ring eyes as they always seemed to change color, especially while growing up. Now, even in certain light, like the bright morning sunshine coming through a gap in the blinds, they look as gold as a field during sunset.

"Now I'm staring at you," I say, licking my lips. "Because I'm having a hard time believing that you're in my bed,

143

naked. I'm waiting for that moment when you evaporate between my hands and you were never here to begin with."

"Oh, Fox," she says.

My name sounds so good.

I unleash myself on her neck, licking and sucking just the way she liked it before, until soft moans fall from her mouth. Music to my ears.

My fingers slip between her legs and I'm instantly hard

"God, you're so wet for me," I whisper to her, my voice catching in my throat. "Can I make you wetter?"

She gives out a breathy "yes" as I slip my finger along her cunt, the sensation making me delirious with lust. She lets out a lengthy moan, her hands tighter in my hair. "I want my cock to slide into you, just like this." I add an extra finger and move them in together. "In and out, in and out," I whisper as my fingers go along. "You want it harder, deeper?"

She groans and I look up to see her arch back, her breasts pointed forward, her sweet, pink nipples tight and hard.

What a fucking sight.

"Do you want my cock?" I ask softly. "My tongue? How would you like me to fuck you?"

"Anything, Fox, anything," she says through another moan as I drive my fingers even deeper.

"I want to fuck you from behind, darling," I tell her as I slip my arm under her back and flip her over.

I press my hand down on her shoulder for leverage, slowly pulling myself out, then back in, trying to find the rhythm without crushing her. My thighs are doing most of the work, shaking slightly, the muscles popping as I move faster and faster, my cock disappearing entirely inside her, the base shiny from her desire.

My hips circle and I shorten my thrusts so I don't slip out. She's wet down to the middle of her thighs and I want to stay inside her deep like this, tightly packed. It's such a fucking squeeze that a sweat is breaking out at my temples, my muscles wound too tight.

Delilah is moaning something deep and desperate.

"Do you want to come, darling?" I whisper hoarsely. "Will you come on my cock? Make my cock so fucking wet. You'll make it so fucking wet."

She's groaning, whimpering for something.

"I'm going to make you come," I say. Breathless. Rough. "I'm going to make you come so fucking hard."

I move one hand down to her waist and grip her while the other squeezes in between her hips and the mattress until I reach her clit. It's soaked and my finger slides over it with ease.

That's all it takes.

Her body tenses and then starts to quake beneath me. She pulses around my cock, her clit throbbing under my finger. A cry leaves her lips, then softens.

I come immediately after, exhale loudly, my breath elsewhere, my heart thudding to a marching beat inside my head. I lean back on my thighs, absently run my hands over her bottom while I remember how to breathe. Then, when it doesn't feel like I'm having a heart attack, when the sweat stops rolling off my brow, I gently pull out.

Leaning forward, I put my lips to her ear. "Did you like that?"

She turns her head, her eyes closed and makes a noise that I think means *yes.*

I brush the hair off her face and kiss her cheek. Then place tiny, soft kisses on her neck, shoulder, down her spine, until I finally get off of her.

We take a few moments, lying next to each other, trying to bring our breath back into our bodies and calm our racing hearts. We might even fall asleep for a bit. The sun seems to have shifted.

"Guess it's time to feed Conan," Del says with a yawn, getting out of bed. I watch her walk completely naked, that fantastic ass on display, all the way to the cage. She doesn't care if I'm watching. Hell, she probably wants me to watch.

She manages to get out the syringe and the baby food, then she glances at me over her shoulder. "On second thought, I should probably put on some clothes before I do this. Don't want Conan to think any of this is weird."

"He'll get over it," I tell her. "Stay naked."

But she slips on one of my T-shirts she finds on the floor and somehow that's even fucking sexier.

Something inside me flinches, just a bit. It's suddenly scary how much I'm loving this, watching Del fish that damn fucking squirrel out of the cage, how easy all of this is. I'm not used to finding this kind of peace, this softness in my life and now it's here and it's all Delilah.

And what happens after this? What happens when I have to leave again tomorrow? What happens when I come back? Every time I head out there now, I feel like I'm coming back with missing pieces. I used to fight fires to banish the doubt, to make myself feel like I was someone and worth something. But ever since Roy died, I'm afraid that I'll come back changed yet again.

"Are you okay?" Del asks softly when she's done, putting Conan back in the cage. He's so much bigger now that it nearly takes me by surprise. Another sign of time passing, life changing while I'm gone.

I give my head a shake and feel the pressure increasing inside my head again. I'm almost out of pills and I'm not sure if I'll be able to get anymore from my supplier. "I'm fine, I'm just…"

Suddenly she's sitting beside me, hand on my knee. I should be quite aware that I'm naked and she's not but I feel any sense of self-consciousness slip away.

"Talk to me," she says. I find the courage to meet her eyes and I see the Del that's always there, the one that cares, that wants to hear what I have to say, the one that never judges.

"It's nothing."

"Fox…it's something. I've been waiting for you to tell me because I know when I pry you usually clam up, but I want to know. I need to. Talk to me."

I take in a deep breath. "You know Roy Smith from Fernie?"

"The Roy from your team, Roy?"

"Yeah. He, uh, he died."

"Oh my god," she gasps, covering her mouth with her hand. "I'm so sorry, Fox. I know you talked about him all the time. How did he…?"

"A snag. A dead tree we had burned the day before. We were high up on the ridge and the fire had crossed the line. We all had to evacuate. We were scrambling, panicked, so fucking tired. You know that's when you make the mistakes and Roy was struggling. Trying to pick up the chainsaw, deal with his helmet. I should have gone over to him right away, I should have helped him. I saw the tree coming down and I didn't react in time, it was like a dream…"

"Fox, please. You know none of this was your fault."

"If I had reacted when I should have, if I helped him, he would be alive."

"But you would be dead."

I shrug. "He has a wife. Two daughters. It's better me than him."

Silence fills the room. I glance at her warily and see her lips pressed together, a rare kind of anger in her eyes.

"Don't you ever fucking say that," she says, her voice hard. "Don't you ever fucking say that Fox. Okay?"

I have to admit, I'm both flattered that she cares this

much and surprised that she's getting this worked up about it. "Okay."

She sighs, running her hands over her face. "Fox, I know that what you do is terribly hard and it sets you up for things like this, but you need to…look, you once told me that I make this dark and sticky and terrible thing go away. You were drunk when you said it, but you said it. That's not normal, Fox. What you feel, that's not normal and I'm glad that I can bring you peace but I can't be there all the time. I worry about you so much when you're out there fighting fires. So much. And it's not because I think a snag is going to take you out. It's because…"

I try to swallow, my throat feels like I've got sawdust inside. "What?"

She rubs her lips together, eyes roaming the room, thinking. Finally, she says, "You've got a big heart. You don't always show it, but it's there. It goes above and beyond for the people you know and don't know. It's like you're always trying to make up for something and that's fine, we all are. We're all feeling like we're lacking something and we do whatever we can to fill that void. But with you…I worry, Fox. I worry you don't care enough about yourself. And that one day, you will pay that price."

Del is not wrong. But even so, her insight surprises me. Most of all, I don't want her to be right.

"You don't know what you're talking about," I tell her as firmly as I can. "You're just making shit up on the spot."

"Fine," she snaps, getting up. "I'm making coffee."

And at that, she quickly leaves the room and goes down the hall.

Fuck.

I just fucked up a nice little moment, didn't I?

I shouldn't punish her for being observant. It's not her fault she knows me this well.

I get up, slip on a pair of boxer briefs and follow her.

She's standing in the kitchen, the light illuminating her hair, making her look like an angel in just my T-shirt. It's both the most heart-warming and sexiest sight I've ever seen and for a moment it hurts somewhere deep inside of me that I wasn't having this side of her sooner.

As she scoops coffee into the filter, not turning around, I come up behind her and wrap my arms across her chest, hugging her, my chin nuzzled into the smooth crook of her neck. She smells like soap and lilacs and summer mornings.

"I'm sorry," I whisper, holding her close to me. "I didn't mean that."

She pauses with the coffee, sets the scoop down on the counter. "What?"

"What I said. That you didn't know what you're talking about. You do know, Del, you always have. Better than anyone. I guess…" I take in a deep breath. "I guess I just don't like to hear the truth sometimes. Not from someone I care about."

She sighs, relaxing into me and I place my lips on her shoulder, slowly leaving kisses along her skin. I lift up her hair and run my lips up her neck, sucking just behind her ear until she moans audibly.

The sweetest fucking sound.

"I don't want to leave tonight," I tell her, turning her around until she's staring up at me. I cup her face in both my hands. "I don't want to leave at all. Not so soon, not after all of this. I feel like I'm not getting enough time with you, all I want is days like this with you over and over again."

"Me too," she whispers.

I kiss her, taking her bottom lip in between my teeth and tugging, and then push the coffee maker aside, spilling the grounds everywhere.

I don't give a fuck. I put my hands at her waist and lift her up until she's sitting on top of the counter, her legs open and on either side of me.

I hunch over, sliding my hands slowly up the soft smooth skin of her inner thighs, pushing up her T-shirt until it's around her waist and she's all bare and exposed, just for me.

My head sinks between her legs, licking up the soft sides of her thighs, tasting her, tasting our sex from earlier.

I honestly can't get enough of this.

Enough of her.

What are you doing? A voice flits through my head.

But I ignore it.

I'm lost to her again and there's no place I'd rather be.

FALL

DELILAH

"Well, well, well, look who it is. Mr. and Mrs. Nelson," Riley says over her shoulder at Shane and Rachel who just walked in the bar holding hands.

They grin at each other, then at us. They just got back from their honeymoon in Maui and are looking more tanned and rested than I think I've ever seen them.

"Get a lot of baby-making done?" Riley adds with an exaggerated wink. "And by that I mean, fucking."

Rachel rolls her eyes.

"We always know what you mean," Shane says. "You never need to clarify. And yes. Lots of that."

Rachel elbows him, blushing.

"I guess I should give you a welcome back beverage on the house," I say with a sigh, though I'm glad to see them. It's been a bit of a lonely three weeks, especially with both them and Fox being gone for most of them. I've been hanging out with Riley when I can, though she's often busy with work and Maverick.

I get Rachel a glass of wine and Shane a cold beer, then I pick up the bottle of water I was drinking out of and raise it.

"Here's to the newlyweds. May there be plenty of babies in your future."

We all cheers and Rachel smiles shyly. "Jeez, you'd think I wasn't getting enough pressure already with my mother."

"She's really laying on the grandchild guilt, isn't she?" Riley asks.

Rachel nods. "Yup. It's a lot of 'but I want to be a grandmother while I'm still young, don't you want me to be able to babysit and run around with the kids?'"

I laugh. "Kids? You better turn into a baby-making machine, Rachel, stat."

"Well at least making the babies is the fun part," Riley says.

"You don't want kids?" I ask her, though I won't be surprised if she says no.

She shrugs. "Not really on my radar. I'll adopt all the dogs in the world with Maverick but kids are something that I don't think is in the cards for us. If we change our minds, great, but for now…nah." She looks to me. "What about you, Del? Does your mom get on your case?"

"No, probably because I don't have a guy in my life." All three of them look at me expectantly. "What?" I go on. "I don't."

"Sure, and you and Fox were in that barn because you were bailing hay," Riley says.

"Bailing hay, is that what we're calling it now?" Shane says, grinning at me like a smug bastard.

"Whatever. I don't have anyone."

What I do have is a lot more complicated.

"So how is Fox?" Rachel asks.

"Still away," I tell her. "I haven't talked to him much, just a text here and there. He was supposed to maybe be home last night but it could be tonight. Could be tomorrow."

"I heard about what happened to his teammate Roy," Shane says in a low voice. "That's got to be hard on him."

I nod, not wanting to get into it. What Fox told me felt intensely private and I already fucked shit up by telling everyone we slept together in the first place. "He hasn't been taking it that well. I wish his team had some sort of mourning period, you know, where they could just pay respect and deal with their feelings instead of being trucked off again to fight yet another fire."

"It's hard being here and worrying about him," Rachel says quietly. "The not knowing."

"Well I should be used to it, shouldn't I? The only bright side to all of this is that the fire season should be ending soon. It's already mid-September somehow, and by October first they should be going into off-season training which is a lot more manageable."

"And so…" Rachel starts, pausing to take a sip of her wine and think before she continues. "Are you two…you know? Fuck buddies?"

"Ugh, please don't use that term about my brother," Shane grumbles.

"Don't worry, *I* won't use that term," I tell him, then address Rachel. "And I don't know what we are. All I know is…I'd be happier if he were here. That's all."

Rachel, Riley and Shane stay for a couple of hours and then head on home, leaving me alone in the bar. Now that September is half-way through, the town has become a lot quieter, and as a result, so has the bar. There are still some tourists around since the autumn foliage can look really photogenic against the brightly colored shops of the down-town area. There will be more tourists when the ski hills get snow, but for now, I should probably enjoy the downtime, even if it means less money.

I've just shut off the OPEN sign when I get a text from Fox.

Just one look at his name flashing on my phone and my heart does flips inside my chest. I feel giddy, an immature sort of happiness like I did when Fox was just a schoolgirl crush.

I just got back a few hours ago. Come over?

I grin. I know this is a booty call now but I don't care.

Okay be right there

I close up the bar, get in my car and ten minutes later I'm parking outside the chalet. There's a cold nip in the air as I walk to the front door, signaling that fall is truly on its way now.

The house is warm and cozy as I step inside. Even though I've been spending a lot of my days here while Fox has been gone, taking care of Conan, it already feels different now that he's home. There's a charge in the air wherever Fox is, something that reaches deep inside of me and rearranges the molecules, making me feel more vibrant and alive and electric.

I go up the steps and see Fox in the kitchen, the lights on low. He's holding out a glass of a champagne in one hand, a rose in the other.

"Are we on The Bachelor?" I whisper as I stop in front of him.

He gives me the rose. "I'll pretend I've seen that show."

I smell the red rose and smile, though it never smells as strong as you think it would, and my eyes happily rest on Fox. He is looking insanely handsome tonight. Maybe it's because I haven't seen him in weeks, maybe because I'm so happy just to be here with him, maybe because I'm just so fucking in love with him, but he honestly makes my skin hot just looking at him.

He's got a cut on his forehead, which is a bit concerning,

but in a way, it adds to his rugged charm. He's got a full-on beard going, his eyes are shining at me in an easy way. He's wearing those deadly sweatpants of his again with a thin, worn white T-shirt with the North Ridge Hot Shots logo on it.

"What happened to your head?" I ask, as he gives me the glass of champagne. "Are you okay?"

"Oh, I'm great," he says in such a way that makes me wonder how much champagne he's already had. "Even better now that you're here."

I take a sip of the drink. "I have to say, the rose and the champagne are quite the surprise." I pause. "A good surprise. So, what happened to your head?"

"A branch," he says rather sheepishly. "Jumped out and got me as I was running." He jerks his head toward the living room. "Come on, let's sit down."

Well I'll be damned. I'm as nervous with him now as I was the day after the two of us got together. Nervous, anxious, excited. I feel like every time he comes back, we have to spend a bit of time together getting our groove back, finding out how we fit. The only problem with that is the fact that by the time we do find this new rhythm with each other, he's gone again.

I settle down on the couch beside him and finish the rest of the glass in a few gulps.

"Maybe I should be asking if you're okay?" he asks and I swear he slurs his words just a bit.

I frown. "I'm fine. Say, how hard was that hit on your head?"

"Not hard. They gave me pills, I'm fine."

"The same pills you took in the barn at the wedding?"

He shrugs and seems to think about that for a moment, a flash of clarity coming across his eyes. "No, different. But I'm fine. Are you?"

I nod and sit back in the cushions and he puts his arm around me. "I'm good. Things have been good. I guess I'm just…can I ask you a question?"

"Always," he says, peering down at me. "What is it?"

"Well, one is more of an observation than a question," I say, twisting a little on the couch to see him better. "And that's just…well, I'm fine and all, but if you're ever wondering why I'm acting strange, it's just that I'm, uh, nervous around you."

"Nervous?" His dark brows knit together. "Why?"

"No real reason," I tell him, my cheeks growing hot at the admission. "It's just a change. We were a certain way before and now we're this way. We're…intimate. Physical. And it's a whole new Fox and Delilah, you know? And every time I think I'm adapting and getting used to the new us, you leave and I feel like we're starting all over again. Which isn't necessarily a bad thing, it's just that it's something I'm realizing. Perpetually catching up."

He nods slowly, chewing on his lip for a few beats. "Okay. Well, I get that. I guess it's different from me because the entire time I'm gone, all I can think about is seeing you, being with you. Like this. And by this, I mean sex."

I laugh. "That was almost romantic, Fox. Almost."

He reaches over and cups my cheek with his hand. "I'm new at this too, you know. With you. So things might sound more romantic in my head. But honestly Del, you're the one thing that keeps me going through those hard days."

I think I'm melting a little inside. Whether he means it or not, *that* was romantic.

But still I have to ruin it.

"And the other thing," I go on, "the question I had for you, is…" I take in a deep breath, finding it easier to stare at his beautifully full lips instead of the quiet intensity of his eyes. "What are we doing? I mean, where is this going? Are we…

friends with benefits? More? Is there even a potential for more? I hate to get all, I don't know, clingy or pressure you for a commitment, because I'm not like that, but…"

But I'm in love with you.

And I have to know exactly how much this is going to hurt down the line.

He sighs and closes his eyes, leaning back against the couch.

"I'm sorry," I tell him, "if I ruined this. I just want to talk about it, that's all. And if you don't know, then you don't know and that's fine."

"But that's the thing," he says, eyes still closed. "I don't know. I don't know what I want in general or where my head is. I don't know what the future holds. I'm too…I don't know, scared, to even look. I'm just…" he opens his eyes and they focus on me, holding me in place. "I'm a mess, to be honest with you. And you're the only thing that makes sense. That's all I know. I need you right now. I want you right now. And I'm just playing it day by day by day."

It stings, like tiny papercuts on my heart. To know that he's not willing to commit yet. To know that I'm needed for now but maybe not for later.

And I know I should think about protecting my heart. I should probably take a step back and call all this off and try and salvage our friendship or what remains of it because I want him body and soul and I'll never be happy until I have all of him. I mean, I *love* him.

I love him.

More and more.

Every day.

But that's also the problem.

Love makes you foolish. Love makes you choose love.

This is the first chance that I've ever had to be with Fox and I'd rather have him like this than not have him at all.

"Then I'll play it day by day with you," I tell him.

I just want you right now, like you want me right now.

I'll take whatever you can give me.

I'll take every part of you for as long as I'm able to.

"You're alright with that?" he whispers, his expression growing both soft and wanting all at once.

I nod. "More than okay."

I wish I wasn't lying.

12

DELILAH

"Delilah, dear," Dick says. "You are looking absolutely glowing lately, you know that?"

"It's true," Vernalee says, rather suspiciously. "What's your secret? I want to be the best-looking grandma in town."

While Rachel gives an exaggerated rolling of the eyes (because, no, she's not pregnant), I give everyone at the table an embarrassed smile. "It must be the company."

The truth is, I've been feeling anything but glowing lately, though if I do look good at all, it's probably because of Fox. You know, how love changes the way you see the world and thus changes the way you look. That and sex. All the sex.

On the other hand, every shitty thing I'm feeling is probably because of Fox too.

He's been gone again. This time for just a week, but it's enough. It's October, it should be the end of the forest fire season but this year things don't seem to stop. Not only is he fighting one over in Alberta but there's a massive fire raging in Northern California. Wildland firefighters are being pulled from all over the US and I know that the minute the

Alberta fire is under control, he's going to be called out to the California one.

It's hard. It's obviously harder on him, but it's hard on me too. Just the not knowing. I know the last time we were together we talked about it and I was okay with being Fox's fuck buddy, friend with benefits, whatever we are but at the same time…

Fuck. I want more. I want to be with him. To have all of him, not just his dick. The sex is amazing, better than I could have ever imagined and I don't think I could ever stop with him but I want his heart. I want his heart and his mind and his soul. It's a lot to ask of anyone but he has mine, whether he wants it or not. I mean, it's a fair trade.

But love isn't a trade at all. It's something else. It's a gamble. And right now, I'm close to laying it all on the table and hoping for the best.

So, while he's gone risking his life, I'm left wondering, hoping, that when he comes back we'll have something to work with, something to develop. The longer I'm with Fox in such an intimate, physical way, the deeper and more obsessed I become.

Then there's the fact that I've just been feeling off lately. Pretty sure a flu is coming on, though I just hope it doesn't strike when Fox is next in town.

Once dinner is over, I'm in the kitchen helping Rachel clean up. Fox, Riley and Maverick were all absent tonight, the latter two out on a special search and rescue call, so there are less dishes.

Even so, I'm starting to feel a bit dizzy after bending down to load them in the dishwasher and have to lean against the counter for the moment.

"Are you okay?" Rachel asks, putting her hand on my back.

I nod frantically, pressing my lips together as a wave of nausea comes over me.

"Are you sick?" she goes on. "Was it the food?"

I make the motion for her to wait a moment and I close my eyes, breathing through it. Then, after a few deep breaths, the moment passes.

"I don't know what that was," I admit. "I think I'm getting the flu. I haven't been feeling well the last couple of days."

"Well it is cold season," she says, watching me closely with concern. "And you do work in a bar. Maybe you should close one of the nights this week. You know I don't have much to do but run the Air B&B out back and that's a pretty do nothing gig. We don't even have anyone booked. Why don't I bartender for a night or two?"

"That's really sweet of you," I say gratefully. "But honestly, I'll be fine."

"I'll do it though, I'd love to. So as long as I get to keep the tips. I can get Shane to help me too."

"I'm sure after long hours on the ranch, working at the bar instead of drinking at the bar will be the last thing on his mind. I'll be fine, really. Maybe I ate something off."

"Well it was your mom and mine who made this roast," she says raising her palms, "so I'm absolved of all the blame here."

After that the feeling sort of goes away. I'm a bit out of it, a bit on edge for some reason, but other than that, I'm okay. Then the next morning when I go to Fox's house to take care of Conan, I have to put the guy down on the bed while I run to the toilet to throw up.

I don't know how long I'm on my knees, just puking and puking, feeling drained, until I realize that in my haste I didn't put Conan back in his cage.

I flush the toilet, rinse out my mouth with mouthwash

and splash water on my face before turning around to go on a panicked hunt for Conan.

Luckily, I don't have to search very far because the squirrel literally followed me into the bathroom and is standing on its hind legs, little T-rex arms hanging in front of him, watching me with big eyes.

"Hey," I say to him. "You didn't run off."

Conan tilts his head and then runs.

Toward me.

Up my leg, his little claws digging into my jeans as he scampers up and up, all the way to the crook of my arm.

Well, fuck. Ain't this just the cutest, coolest thing. He's...tame.

And he thinks I'm his mother.

"Hey there Conan," I say to him softly, and he looks like he's hanging on to my every word. "I was just a little sick there, but I'm better now. Don't tell your father I puked in his toilet, okay?"

I put him back in his cage which he's starting to outgrow and make a point to ask Fox if maybe the squirrel should stay with me, since I'm the one pretty much taking full responsibility for it. I just have to run it past my mother since I do share a house with her and who knows what her stance on squirrels is.

Even so, I feel bad when I have to leave him all alone and head to the bar to open up. Then I feel bad, physically, when it's ten minutes until opening and I'm feeling sick yet again.

I run to the bathroom and throw up, surprised that there's even anything left in me since I barely ate today, just some bone broth chicken soup with my mother.

I don't think I have a choice. I can't bartend from the washroom. I pull out my cell and call Rachel, asking if she'll do that favor she mentioned last night. Being the good friend she is, there is no hesitation and both she and Shane come by to run the place while I go home to try and sleep it off.

I should have felt more nervous than I did about leaving the bar with them but Shane especially has been here every single weekend for the last ten years, so he knows how to run the joint and Rachel is pretty efficient as well. The place is in good hands.

As for me, I feel better when the morning rolls around, though maybe that has something to do with my mother spoiling me like I'm ten years old. Lots more soup, cold medicines, hot water bottles, anything I want, she's taking care of me. It feels good for once to be on the receiving end.

Then when evening rolls around again and I think I'm ready to take over the bar, the sickness strikes again a few hours after opening. Shane is already in the bar with Rachel and Shane offers to drive me home while Rachel takes over.

I get into Shane's truck, taking deep breathes with the window down, the cold night air making my head feel clearer.

"Can you take me to Fox's?" I ask him as we pull out of the parking lot.

"Why, is he home?"

"No. I have a squirrel to take care of."

Shane frowns at me. "Sure," he says slowly. "But we're stopping somewhere else first."

Before I have a chance to ask him where, he's pulled up alongside the entrance to a pharmacy. "Stay right here," he says and then leaves the truck running with me in it as he jogs into the store.

He comes back out a few minutes later with a small white paper bag, gets in the driver's seat and thrusts it in my lap. "Here," he says. "Now I'll take you to Fox's."

I open up the bag, expecting some sort of anti-nausea medicine.

Instead I gasp.

It's a pregnancy test.

"Is this for…is this for Rachel?" I ask, trying not to get too excited. "Oh my god, do you think she's pregnant?"

He shakes his head, face grave. "No. It's for *you*, Del."

"Me?" I repeat, laughing. "I'm not pregnant."

He just glances at me for a few long hard moments before turning his attention back to the road.

"What? I'm not!"

"You've been sick," he says.

"That doesn't mean I'm pregnant. I'm on the pill."

"Do you use anything else besides the pill?"

"What are you, my doctor? And no, we don't. Not that it's any of your business. Fox is clean. So am I. So it works well for us."

"*That* isn't my business," he says, scrunching up his nose for a second. "But you know if the pill isn't always taken correctly, that there's a chance. So let's just be sure."

"Okay," I say eventually, shaking my head. "But it's not going to be positive. I'm pretty good about the pill and try to take it the same time every day."

"*Try*," he repeats. "And when was your period?"

"Shane, no offense, but it's weird to talk about this with you."

He shrugs. "It's only weird to you. I've had damn pregnancy on the brain ever since Rachel and I officially started trying, so I've been reading up and I know all the signs and well…"

"Well for your information, my period is late," I tell him. Before he can say anything I wave my finger and quickly add, "But it's always late. That's why I've been on the pill to begin with for so many years, even when I wasn't having sex. It's to keep me regular and sometimes it just doesn't work."

Shane glances at me, looking me over. "I have to say, Del, but I have a funny feeling about this."

I roll my eyes. "You're just all hopped up on the newlywed goofy hormones or something. I'm *not* pregnant."

I keep saying that to myself as we get to Fox's chalet.

My period is often late, *especially* when I'm stressed.

I just have a flu.

I'm only getting sick at night so it's not morning sickness.

I'll be better tomorrow.

I've been so good with the pill.

I'm in my thirties.

There's no way I'm pregnant.

No way.

No way.

No.

Way.

And yet another wave of nausea rolls through me and I have to run to Fox's poor toilet once again.

Once I'm done, I make quick work of feeding Conan, which at least distracts Shane for a little bit.

Then when I'm done and Conan is back in the cage, Shane waves the pregnancy test at me. "Get it over with," he says. "Don't you want to know for sure?"

"I do know," I tell him uneasily, snatching it out of his hands. "I just want you to shut up."

So I go in the bathroom and take out the stick, making sure I read the directions properly. The only other time I've had to do this was in high school when, thankfully, the test was negative, though there was a five-minute end of the world freak out period where I read the thing wrong.

I sigh and concentrate and try to pee on the stick.

All I can think about is…god, I hope this is negative.

This has to be negative.

I am not ready for a child.

I am not ready to have Fox's child.

It just wouldn't be right.

It's just not what's supposed to happen.

I figured I'd have children and a family one day, even though that one day is getting more and more unattainable. I just know it wouldn't be like *this*.

When I finish peeing, I place it on the counter and I hold my breath and I wait.

I wait for that one pink line to show up.

It does.

I pray that the other line doesn't show up.

But…

…it does.

I gasp, trying to breathe.

No.

No.

No.

"Oh my god," I say softly. No, it has to be wrong. This is a false positive. It's false.

"What is it? What does it say?" Shane asks through the door.

I can't even speak. I shake the stick, stare at it some more, read the instructions again. But those two lines are stubborn.

Eventually I open the door and all Shane has to do is look at my face.

"No, are you serious?" he asks me.

I swallow hard and nod, showing him the stick without any gusto.

"Shit. Del. I don't know what to say," he says softly.

"Well this is your fault," I tell him, panic clawing up my throat. "You're the one who made me get the test. If you hadn't I wouldn't have known. If I wouldn't have known, this wouldn't be happening right now."

"Easy, Del, take it easy," he says, putting his hands on my shoulders.

"Easy? I am taking it easy. The test is wrong. It's a false positive. It happens. Look, look I'll google it." I hand him the stick, which he takes and cringes, and then bring out my phone, trying to find out how many false results happen and the odds of that.

Only I'm panicking so much, borderline hyperventilating, that I can hardly see straight. "Please, please, please," I say quietly.

"We need to do another test."

I look at Shane with pleading eyes. "Another one?"

"Look, are you seriously just going to pretend it's a false positive without knowing the truth? Tell me you'll be able to sleep at night."

"But I know it's false and I'll sleep fine," I lie.

Because I am not sleeping. Ever again.

"I'm going back to the pharmacy. You stay here. They'll think I'm just getting it for Rachel anyway. We'll get you another test. Then we'll see. And depending on what that says, then you go see a doctor. Tomorrow."

"Shane, please, you're making this out to be such a big deal." I'm hanging onto his shirt, practically crying.

"Delilah, you're my sister. Blood-related or not, you're my sister. And Fox, well, he does happen to be my brother." He pauses. "And now I realize that whatever else I'm going to say is going to sound extremely wrong, but if you're having my brother's baby, then we have to know about it. For your sake, for his sake. Del...believe it or not but this is not something you just ignore and it will go away. It's very real. It's very big. And it's here in your life, right now. So let's just deal with it, step by step, okay?"

I nod and he leads me by the shoulders over to the living

room where he sits me down on Fox's couch, makes me a cup of tea and then flicks on the TV.

"I don't want to be alone," I tell him.

"I know," he says gently. "I'll be twenty minutes at the most."

"You're just going to the store? You're not going to see Rachel? Please don't tell Rachel."

"I'm not and I won't but why?"

"I don't know. I just… I know you guys are trying so I'm not sure if it would be weird for her. And more than that, I've technically known you the longest, Shane. And I trust you more than anyone."

"More than Fox?"

"That doesn't really apply to this situation right now. You promise, no matter what happens, to keep all of this a secret. I don't want anyone to know."

He gives me a sharp nod, his expression earnest. "I promise."

I breathe out a sigh of relief. "Oh, hey. Can you open the cage and let Conan out?"

He pauses at the top of the stairs. "You want me to let the squirrel out of the cage?"

"Just lift the top latch. He'll come out on his own, I'm sure. He likes hanging out with me and I need the company."

Shane just rolls his eyes and heads down the hall. I hear him open the cage door and then he's going down the stairs and out the front, muttering to himself about how the hormones have made me a crazy squirrel lady.

It takes a bit but eventually Conan hops down the hallway and finds me in the living room where he promptly settles in my lap. I know he probably sees me as a giant feeding machine but…

And then it hits me. Again. But with more terrible power this time.

I can barely take care of this baby squirrel.

Fox can barely take care of this squirrel.

How the ever-loving fuck are we going to take care of a baby?

I mean, what are we going to do?

Don't panic, don't panic, don't panic, I tell myself. *It's a false positive, just a false positive.*

Oh, god, please, please.

It feels like an eternity has stretched past with me sitting there with Conan, just trying to breathe, just trying to keep my mind clear, just trying to hang on to every last second I have in this life that I know. Because when I pee on that stick again, everything might change forever.

Then I hear Shane park outside the house.

He comes back in with another bag.

I take the test into the bathroom.

I pee on the second stick.

I make a silent prayer and do the sign of the cross, as if that's really going to help me right now.

"Are you okay?" Shane asks, knocking at the door. I'm having déjà vu though I haven't opened my eyes yet.

"Give me a minute," I tell him, taking in the deepest breath I can.

I open my eyes.

Stare at the test.

Two lines.

Positive.

That does it.

No mistakes here.

This is final.

I'm pregnant.

I'm pregnant with Fox's baby.

I'm absolutely, positively…screwed.

13

DELILAH

IT'S BEEN THREE WEEKS SINCE I TOOK THAT PREGNANCY TEST with Shane by my side.

Three weeks since I went to the doctor the next day and was right away confirmed that, yes, I was in fact *pregnant*. With a capital P.

Three weeks of dealing with my morning sickness that seemed to come at night, trying to make sense of everything, grappling with the fact that my life has been changed forever.

And, of course three weeks since I've seen Fox. He never even came home after the Alberta fire, instead he was sent directly from there to Redding, California to help fight the big blaze down there.

I've talked to him here and there. We text. He even Face-timed me once for a few minutes before he lost reception. The sight of him, a dirty yellow helmet on his head, his beard scruffy, his face marred with soot, was like a punch to the heart.

I haven't told him the news. I can't, not over the phone and certainly not over text. This is something I have to tell him in person and in some ways, I think I'm more scared about that than the actual pregnancy.

Almost.

I know he should be home tomorrow. He's on a bus right now with his team and they just passed through Bend, Oregon. I know I need to start preparing myself for what to say to him.

I just don't know what that is. I don't even know how I feel about it yet, other than being scared to death. Maybe there is no other way to feel about this. Some women are happy, excited, full of joy. You hear about those people all the time. You never hear about the women who are terrified to the bone.

"Hey," Shane says to me, leaning against the bar. "How are you?"

I saw him come in earlier while I was dealing with a customer and already got his beer out of the fridge for him. I slide it toward him. "I'm...okay, I guess. Considering."

"Sorry I wasn't able to come by yesterday, I had to help with the calves," he said, raising his beer at me in gratitude.

I give him a quick smile. "It's fine. You don't have to be here all the time."

"You trying to get rid of me?"

"Never."

The truth is, I feel a bit guilty at the amount of time and attention that Shane has been giving me. I still haven't told anyone, not Rachel, not my mother, and Shane knows that. He's been by here almost every night, sometimes with Rachel, sometimes not. Even though I've gotten better at managing my "morning" sickness, he's been here just in case.

Part of me is flattered to have someone like Shane taking care of me, someone I consider to be a brother. Another part of me feels that maybe it has something to do with Fox instead. I'm not carrying just anyone's baby—this is a Nelson inside me. And as much as the two of them have their issues, I know that Shane wants closure with Fox, wants the two of them to get along. Perhaps, to Shane, this baby is a fresh start.

It doesn't really matter though. The fact that I'm even thinking in terms of "this baby" and "a Nelson inside me" sounds positively alien. I'm not sure when any of this is going to seem normal or real but it doesn't seem to be happening any time soon.

"So Fox is coming back tomorrow, huh." Shane looks at me expectantly.

"Apparently."

"I know this isn't any of my business but…" he glances around him. It's quiet at the bar tonight with only Old Joe at his booth, talking to one of the regulars, Finn, plus a middle-aged couple playing darts. Satisfied that no one can hear him, he leans in and whispers, "you have to tell him about the baby."

I give him a steady look. "Shane. You think I don't know that?"

He sighs, taking off his ball cap and running his hand through his light brown hair. "I know. I know." He pauses and looks up at me warily. "Do you know what you're going to tell him? I mean…now I know this also isn't any of my business, but do you know if you're going to, you know… keep the baby? Or not?"

"Of course I'm keeping it," I say quickly, keeping my voice low.

"I had to ask…I didn't know. You're quite liberal and…"

"Look, Shane. I'm totally pro-choice. But pro-choice only means that…pro-choice. I respect anyone's decision to do what they like with their own damn bodies. And maybe if this had been some random guy's, some one-night stand, I would be singing a totally different tune. But this is Fox's. And…I love him."

And that's all I'll say about that. I couldn't imagine not having it, I couldn't imagine giving it away. I might be scared to death and completely unprepared but I love Fox and this baby is a product of the two of us. He may not love me, but he's still my friend and…

Oh god.

Oh god.

What if he stops being my friend after this?

What if whatever progress we've made as a couple gets completely reversed?

What if I'm not even allowed to want him anymore, to care about my own personal feelings when I've got a baby at stake?

Now I'm scared shitless all over again.

"Hey, it's going to be fine," Shane says, briefly putting his hand over mine as I lean against the counter, barely holding myself up. "Del, you're going to get through this."

I stare at him with wide, horrified eyes. "What if Fox doesn't want anything to do with me and the baby?"

"Please. I know Fox is…I know he has problems but he's a good guy. I can say that, I grew up with him. You did too. You know he's not the type to leave you when you're high and dry. He wouldn't do that to any woman but he especially wouldn't do that to his friend. To you."

As sincere as Shane sounds, it doesn't do a thing to ease the panic crackling in my chest. "But it might drive a wedge between us. And then what? What happens to *us*?"

Shane sighs and stares at me with sad eyes. "Del, unfortunately, I don't think you get a chance to worry about that anymore."

"What?"

"Fox. How he feels about you...I think that's something that has to be worked out later, if you know what I mean."

I know what he means. A month ago, my whole world was revolving around Fox and how he felt about me. The sun rose and the moon set by my love for him. The future was filled with possibilities, silly little hopes that you wish upon shooting stars and blown-out candles. Now that was all gone. As it should be. Now there's something so much more important to think about than love.

And yet, my heart keeps demanding I pay it attention, as if it's more important than what's to be.

Love still rules everything.

"I know Fox will probably do the right thing," I say slowly. "But I'm afraid he might just freak the fuck out."

His mouth tilts up into a wry grin. "I'm going to level with you Del. Fox is most definitely going to freak the fuck out. But you never know. This might be the best thing that ever happened to the both of you."

I can only hope that's true.

"But," Shane goes on, "and again, I'm probably overstepping my boundaries here, but I think maybe you need to tell Rachel. Or Riley. Or your mother. Or someone other than me and your doctor."

He's right. I know he's right. "Is the burden of secret-keeping becoming too much for you?"

"I just think they'll be hurt, that's all," he says gently. "I know Rachel will be when she finds out that I've known all this time and yet she didn't. She'll think you don't trust her and the longer you keep it a secret, the more hurt she'll be."

"But that's not it at all. I wanted to tell Fox first," I tell him.

"I know," he says just as the door opens and Rachel and Maverick walk in. "Hey," he says to them, raising his hand in a wave. When Shane looks back to me, he's giving me a look.

You know, the look that says that I have an opportunity here and I better not waste it.

"You're looking better," Maverick says as he settles down on a bar stool and looks me over. "Less like you're going to vomit everywhere."

"Good," I tell him, slinging my dishrag on my shoulder. "Because that's not a good look on a bartender. Where's Riley?"

"Saving lives and looking sexy while she does it."

I roll my eyes.

"I'm guessing you don't need any help this evening?" Rachel asks.

"Not really," I tell her, pouring Mav his usual draft beer. As it is, the tap sputters and flat foam comes out. I didn't plan on that but I guess that settles it. "Sorry Mav, I have to change the keg."

"No worries," he says, "Kokanee is fine for now."

I get him a bottle of beer from the fridge and look at Rachel. "Rach, can you help me with the keg?" I jerk my head toward the door to the back room.

"I'll help," Mav says, about to get up.

"No," I tell him quickly. "It's fine. We've got it. Can you guys watch the bar?"

"Of course," Shane says, grabbing Mav's shirt and pulling him back down. "Always trying to be a hero, aren't you Mav?"

"For beer, yeah."

I duck under the bar-top door and beckon for Rachel to follow me.

Once we get inside the back store room, I shut the door behind us and face her.

"Uh oh," she says with big eyes. "What happened?"

I sigh and rub my lips together anxiously, trying to find

the words. It's so much harder this way than actually discovering it along with someone like Shane.

"Okay, I have something to tell you and I...I'm not even sure how to tell you."

A flash of terror comes across her eyes. "Oh god. What did Shane do?"

"No, don't worry," I tell her. "It's nothing to do with you or Shane. It's all me. Well, me and Fox."

She looks relieved for a moment then hurriedly tucks a piece of hair behind her ear. "What about you and Fox? Oh my...are you getting together? Or...not? Did you break it off?"

"There's been nothing to break off," I correct her and take in a deep breath through my nose. "Okay. So. Here it goes..."

"Del..."

"I'm pregnant."

She stares at me, blinks. Then, slowly, "Whaaaaaat?"

"Yeah. So that's what's happening."

I watch her carefully. She looks like she's going to faint. "Are you serious?"

"Oh yeah."

"And it's...Fox's?"

I nod. "Couldn't be anyone else's."

"Oh my god. Del...I...do you know what you're going to do?"

"Keeping it."

"Okay. Have you told Fox?"

"He's been away. I was planning to when he gets home. Telling him is going to be even harder than telling you."

"How long have you known...oh wait. Your flu!" she says with a gasp.

"That was nighttime morning sickness. Or something."

Shaking her head, she says, "Del, it's been weeks. You didn't tell me?"

She looks hurt. Shane was right about all this.

"I know, I'm so sorry," I tell her. "I wanted to talk to Fox first."

"But still…does your mom know?"

"No. Only you." I pause, cringe. "And Shane."

"Shane!" she exclaims. "Why does Shane know?" She seems to think that over as she's saying it. "He's known from the start, hasn't he? That's why he's always here."

"He's just been concerned."

"I know. Because that's the kind of guy he is. But why does he know?"

"He was with me. It was his idea. The pregnancy test. He says he's had babies on the brain since you guys started trying."

Her face softens. "He has?" she asks in a dreamy tone.

"Yeah. Really. So he went to the drugstore to get me a pregnancy test. And then another one when I didn't believe the results of the first one."

"Fuck."

"Yeah. That's pretty much what I've been saying every moment of every day. Fuck, fuck, fuck. I am so fucking fucked."

She exhales slowly. I have to say, it does feel good to get it off my chest, to be able to talk about it with someone else other than Shane. It also feels good that she's as shocked and confused about the news as I am. Misery loves company and all that.

"You know, whatever happens, we'll be here for you," she says, coming over and putting her hand on my arm. "So you're not fucked."

"What am I going to say to my mom? To Fox?"

She lets out a soft laugh. "Your mom is going to be fine. I bet she's going to be more excited than anything, definitely more excited than you."

"And Fox?"

Her forehead wrinkles with worry. "Fox loves you Del."

My heart physically hurts to hear it. "Not like that. Not like I do with him."

"Well then, have you told him how you feel?"

I lean back against the wall. "No. I was going to at some point. I think. I definitely won't now."

"Why not?"

"Ha!" My smile feels bitter. "First I have to break the baby news to him. The whole 'I've been in love with you my whole life' news can wait."

"You could tell him at the same time. I mean, I think he deserves to know both, don't you think?"

Rachel looks completely earnest, but she doesn't know what she's talking about. She doesn't know Fox like I do. She doesn't know how hard this is going to be already.

"One step at a time, Rach," I tell her and head over to one of the lager kegs that Maverick likes and try to hoist it up.

"Don't you need help?" Rachel says, rushing over to me.

"I'm strong like bull, I can usually do this myself," I tell her but she crouches down and scoops up the end.

"Not when you're pregnant!"

"I'm barely pregnant," I tell her. "About six weeks or so."

"Can you pinpoint when...you know...what time you had the sex that he knocked you up?"

I almost laugh at her less than eloquent words. "I've been trying to figure that out," I tell her as we carry the keg over to the door. "Honestly, I think it might have been the wedding."

"I hope so. I'd like to think I had something to do with it."

I undo the door with my elbow, about to open it. "But please, don't tell anyone else yet. Not Mav or Riley."

"Your secret is safe with me."

* * *

THE NEXT MORNING after I finally told Rachel, I decided that I might as well be on a roll with confessions and tell my mother. After all, out of everyone, I figured she might actually be the most understanding.

It took most of the day to work up to it, though. I made several attempts but then changed the subject at the last minute, my nerves getting the best of me.

Finally, I decided to go for a drive.

"Hey mom," I say to her, shrugging on a light leather jacket that matches my chestnut Sorel snow boots. The snow hasn't started falling yet but there's definitely some ice around. "Want to go for a drive?"

She doesn't look up from her crochet. "Where?"

I feel kind of bad since she doesn't do needlework much anymore because of her arthritis and is always taking advantage of it on days she feels good.

"Never mind. I don't want to get in the way of what you're doing."

She puts it down and looks up at me. "To be honest, it's starting to burn. I was just hoping I could push through it." She gets up. "I'll go anywhere with you, sweetheart."

Minutes later we're both in the car, the radio is playing the CBC talk show that she likes, and I'm driving us around town. She's taking in the beautiful fall foliage, lost in the gregarious voice of the late Stuart MacLean telling one of his stories. It's such a nice moment, I almost don't want to ruin it.

"Listen, mom," I tell her.

"Are you happy?" she asks me suddenly.

"What? Where did that come from?"

She glances at me, her eyes bright and curious and just a little sheepish at the bluntness of her question. "I worry about you Delilah."

"I know. And we've been over this."

"Looking around at this town, I can't help but wonder... what is there here for you? Don't you want more than this town can give you?"

This really isn't how I wanted this to start off. "I have everything I need here. I have my friends, I have you, I have the bar."

"And love?"

My mother knows about Fox and I hooking up, thanks to Riley and crew at the wedding, but even so, she hasn't asked too much about him. She knows that if there is something to say I will talk about it in some way. Though she hasn't said as much, I do get the impression that she greatly disapproves, probably because she knows how much is at stake personally for me.

Oh boy, is that about to change.

"Look," I tell her, taking one of the roads that lead up to a mountain viewpoint, "this is a conversation for another time."

"Because you don't know how you feel about things?"

"Because things have changed. And yes, okay, so I have been wondering lately if this is all there is to life. To my life. To stay here and keep on doing the same thing and never discovering whether there's more out there. I'm not saying you can't live a rich and fulfilling life in a small town, especially the same one you grew up in. Maybe those lives are more fulfilling than most. The sense of, you know, community and all that. But I just don't know if I would end up finding something that soothes my soul out there, far away from this place."

She watches me carefully and then nods. "I just wondered. Wanted to hear it from you."

"Well what about you then?"

"Oh no," she says with a dismissive shake of her head. "This is about you. And while we're on the subject of you, how is Fox? How is that going? You said things have changed? All I know is that damn boy better start paying you for taking care of that squirrel."

I laugh. "Ah shit, that reminds me. We better stop by his place and feed him."

"Who, Fox or the squirrel?"

"Very funny."

Still, I bring the car to the view point and, as we're leaning against the guardrail, the wind in our hair bringing the scent of pine and snow from some faraway mountain top, I turn to her and say, "I'm pregnant."

Like Rachel, she appears to be stunned by the news.

And then...

She shrugs.

She just fucking shrugs.

"What?!" I exclaim. "Why are you *shrugging*?"

I didn't expect her to freak out, but I didn't expect her to be all "meh" either.

"Delilah, you think I didn't know?" she says, chuckling to herself. "A mother knows everything."

"Mom. There is no way you could have known."

"Oh please. You were sick and I knew. I can tell. Mothers can tell. I was just waiting for you to tell me." She pauses, a small smile on her lips. "Also, Anita Chang was at the doctor's and told me she saw you there. Looking nervous. I just put two and two together."

Shit. That's the problem with small towns, everyone else knows your damn business. I saw Anita too, one of my mother's friends, but I thought maybe I was being overly suspicious.

My mother puts her hand over mine. "I'm not going to tell you how to live your life. I haven't been very good at making decisions, especially when it comes to love and men. You know your father had some good qualities and that's why I chose to stay with him, because I wanted to believe the good ones outweighed the bad. They didn't and he left, and I have a million regrets, but I never regretted having you. I know you and Fox aren't together, but I have faith that this might be the thing that will make him realize what you mean to him."

"Isn't that selfish though?" I ask quietly, my eyes following a raven that has left the branch of a fir and is gliding down the mountain slope and over the valley. "To want that from Fox when I'm pregnant. Shouldn't that go on the backburner?"

She sighs, giving me the look that says I just don't understand anything. And I'm starting to think I don't. "You can have a baby without love. But for that baby's sake, you need to strive for it. You need to try. It's as important as the air we breathe, as important as anything else. A child should be a product of love, it's the greatest gift of all."

All her words don't change a thing for me, even if I agree with them. They don't make it easier, less scary, or less complicated. In fact, if I didn't have feelings for Fox, it would be easier. If I didn't love him and he chose not to be a part of the child's life, I would be disappointed, but not heartbroken. If he did choose to take part, then I would be grateful for the support. But when it comes to love…

I'm still mulling that over when we get back in the car and I drive down the hill, and I guess because Fox is on my mind, we end up driving past his place. He hadn't texted me back today so I'm not sure where he is, so I probably should go feed Conan and pay him a visit. My mother can stay in the car since she thinks the whole wild animal thing is strange.

But when I pull down Fox's street, I see a car pull out of his driveway.

"He must be home early," my mom says.

But it isn't Fox's Jeep that's leaving his house.

It's a red Mini Cooper.

Driven by a blonde woman with a pixie haircut.

She waves at me uneasily as she goes past.

"Oh my god," I whisper, feeling rage start to boil up inside me. Somehow I manage to keep everything under control until I'm close to his place.

I see him walk into his house, shutting the door behind him.

Fox is home.

Either he just got home and she dropped him off (from where?) or he was home already and she came over for a visit but…

Julie was over at Fox's.

Fox is home already.

And he didn't even tell me.

"Delilah," my mom says quietly. "You don't know the facts. Don't jump to any conclusions."

But how can I not?

I quickly drive past, hoping he doesn't look out his window and spot my car, and then head back home.

My knuckles are white from gripping the steering wheel.

My heart feels like it's been pricked with a million needles, over and over again.

14

FOX

THE BODY IS SOMETHING THAT'S CONSTANTLY KEEPING SCORE. You might think you're young enough that it's on your side, think you can get away with some things, might think you can even trick it. Part of the problem is that your body will go along with you too, it will let you think that you can just push and push and push and it will take it.

But it won't do it for long.

After three weeks away fighting two different fires, being spiked out more often than not, I pushed my body to the limit. I survived on little sleep, on not enough food, I lost ten pounds, I rubbed my eyes until they bled and inhaled smoke until I was sure I'd never breathe properly again. I watched countless forests burn and burn, had a million close calls. I did it over and over again because I had to. I had to survive and adrenaline dragged me along.

But even on the bus ride back from California, when the fight was over, sleep didn't come for me. I thought maybe it never would. That long monotonous journey on the I-5 sitting back in my seat, head against the window and trying to nod off, all I could think about was Del. I'm pretty sure I thought about her in a million different ways.

I'd missed her more this time than any other time. When I had to rise from the dirty ground at five a.m. and everything hurt, I'd think about her smile, the way it feels like it's shooting joy right into you, like sunbeams to your heart. When I watched deer running from the forest, smoke billowing off of them, I'd think about her laugh, how loud and freeing it is, the kind of laugh that makes you laugh in return. When I set fire to the back burn and my ears roared with the fire's rage, I'd think about her eyes and the way she looks at me sometimes.

Sometimes she looks at me like I'm her king.

There is no better feeling in the world than that.

The only problem is, I know I don't deserve it.

And as much fun as it is to be with Del, I'm not sure how long it can keep going on as it is. I don't want to think too much about it, about what we're doing. I can't imagine stopping and going back to the way things were but I know it's probably the smartest thing to do. The last thing I want is for Del to develop feelings for me, feelings that will get us both in trouble, especially because I don't know where I stand.

I *should* know where I stand. But I don't.

Or maybe I'd rather be forever confused, in limbo, because the longer you're in that state, then you don't have to make any decisions and nothing can be your fault.

And that's what my mind was running over the entire ride back to North Ridge. How much I love being with Del, how good the sex is, how badly I want to rush back into her arms, throw her on my bed and have my way with her. Feel that peace she gives me, that rush of contentment that no one else can, that nothing else can.

And I'd also think about how ill-equipped I am to deal with a relationship, especially me, especially with my job. I know, at least I hope to god, that if we do break things off and go back to being friends, that we can do so like nothing happened. I just know that if we became something serious, and then broke up, there would be no fixing us.

I would lose her forever.

We've known each other almost our whole lives and it would be gone.

No more future in our friendship.

I can't imagine a life without Del in it.

Back and forth, back and forth my mind raged, being sweet on the present and worrying about the future, until finally I was dropped off at my house and then, then it all hit me at once.

My body finally gave up. I had plans, I wanted to text Del and tell her I was home but I couldn't even pick up my phone and dial. My brain started to disconnect and the moment I got into the house, I collapsed on the couch.

I was in deep sleep for the night and then into the next day. Like I was in a fucking coma. I couldn't wake up even if I tried.

It was a knock at my door that somehow managed to rouse me. When I finally got up and looked at the clock in the kitchen, it was already the afternoon the next day.

I automatically assumed it was Del at the door, though since she had been taking care of Conan daily, she probably would have walked right in. She didn't even know I was home yet.

To my surprise it was Julie.

With a bottle of whisky.

It was like an angel appeared at my door since my house was completely dry and I didn't have the strength to go out and get any.

She'd said she saw the bus come into town last night and wanted to offer me a token of appreciation for all my hard work. Said that the local paper had even done a story about us and Roy dying and the fires we've been fighting non-stop and she felt bad that I was having to go through all of that.

I think she just felt guilty for dumping me like she did. It was so long ago, or at least feels that way now. Either way, it doesn't really matter. Even though I had hopes for the two of us, now that I'm with Del, being with Julie again isn't on my radar.

Still, I invited her inside and we both sat on the couch and had a glass of whisky. I was still a bit out of it so I didn't do much talking—not that I do anyway— and she went on about her job at the high school, and how she's fitting into the town and that sort of thing.

It was completely innocent but I still felt a strange cloud of guilt over me. Maybe it was because I hadn't contacted Del yet and I already had Julie in my house. I know that Del and I are just fooling around and it's nothing serious—we haven't talked about being exclusive, though I think it's because it's assumed—but it still felt wrong.

And yet I had Julie over anyway and even had a glass of whisky with her. I don't know what my problem is but then again, I never have.

After she left, I texted Del to let her know that I was back in town but Del didn't respond which was odd. So I decided to have some more whisky.

That's where I'm at right now.

The whisky stage.

But I've sat on this couch for too long and I'm starting to see those flames creep up behind my eyes, feel the smoldering blackness building inside my soul. It happens slowly sometimes, catching you off-guard, sneaking up on you. I should have seen it coming, predicted it. This almost always happens when I return from a brutal shift and even though that was probably my last deployment for the year, it did its number on me.

If I was a better man I would have better ways to cope with this. To cope with everything that I am. I'd go to a counsellor, for one. Hell, majority of the guys on my team go to one to try and cope with the demands of the job, the things they've seen. A few of the smart ones do yoga, eat healthy, meditate, find ways to cope with the stress. Almost everyone is medicated. I was for my stress headaches until my doctor decided to cut me off, leaving me to get my pills via other ways.

And me, I just choose to wallow in it because that's all I've ever known. And sometimes I'm not just wallowing in it, sometimes I'm being swallowed whole.

I'm out of pain meds now. All the bottles and baggies are empty. I could just sit here drinking but the house seems to be getting smaller, the walls closing in. I need the weight to lift, the sky to open. I need peace. I need to feel nothing.

I contemplate going by The Bear Trap to say hi to Del, but I feel like I might not be welcome. I don't know why really, maybe because she still hasn't texted me back. I should probably ask her about Conan, I really would have thought she would have come by today to feed him, but I guess if she got my text and saw I was home, there was no need for it.

She just saw my text and didn't respond.

Before I have a chance to stew on it anymore, I get in my Jeep and roar toward Ravenswood Ranch. My father hurt his hip earlier this year after he fell from his horse and though he's almost fully healed, I know he was given a fuckload of drugs to help him manage the pain. I also know that because my father is such a hardass, he didn't rely on the pills for too long, so he might have some left over.

I haven't told anyone that I'm back in town yet, so I'm

hoping that I'll be able to get into the house without much fuss. It's seven o' clock at night which means there's a good chance that my father and Shane are out at the cattle barn sorting through hay. Fall is a busy time, especially when the threat of snow is around the corner. There's always my grandfather to think about, but more often than not he's sleeping on the couch with a glass of whisky in hand and as spritely as he is, he's not one to pry too much, at least not with my life.

But when I carefully open the door and step inside the house, I see Shane in the kitchen drinking a glass of water, dressed like some grunge cowboy in battered jeans and a dusty, faded flannel shirt.

Great.

"You're back," he says to me in a strained voice. He looks like he's seen a ghost.

"Yeah," I say, stopping in the middle of the living room. "Where's dad and grandpa?"

He finishes his water, swallowing it down, his eyes studying me carefully. "Dad's down at the barn, Gramps is at the grocery store with Vernalee. Why? When did you get back?"

I'm not sure what it is about his tone that I don't like but I don't like it.

"No reason. And I got back last night."

"Have you talked to Del?"

I frown. "Why would I talk to Del?"

He shrugs, rinses out the glass in the sink. "No reason other than the fact that you always talk to Del."

I narrow my eyes at him. I don't like his tone, I don't like him mentioning Del. In fact, I hate the fact that everyone knows about us. I've had to endure so much ribbing and speculation from my brothers for years about our relationship and now that it's actually become the damn thing they'd been harassing me about, I feel like I'm unable to live it down.

I know I shouldn't blame Del for telling people but I wish she'd kept quiet about it. But maybe it's my fault for not facing it head on and having a discussion about it before it was too late.

"Are you okay?" Shane asks. "You seem edgy."

"You try battling a couple of monstrous forest fires non-stop for three weeks and see how you feel," I snap. "Makes your prancing around the ranch look like kid playing with their ponies."

It's hard to get under Shane's skin. This is probably why he aggravates me so much, he just is so fucking noble and austere that he never lets anything get to him. And he thinks of me as someone lesser than him, that I know for sure.

He rolls his eyes slightly. "Sorry for being concerned."

"Yeah, *concerned*," I repeat slowly, turning around and heading up the stairs.

"Where are you going?" he asks after me.

I don't bother responding. Not sure when Shane decided he was in charge of the damn place but last I checked this wasn't his ranch, nor was this his house. Until our father is gone, it all equally belongs to all of us and not just Shane because he's the rancher around here and the apple of my father's eye.

I head down the upstairs hallway, my head feeling heavy, this weighted anger in my chest, like cement blocks tied to a sinking dead body. I rarely come up here. I don't like the vibes, the feeling I get. Things in this house changed after my mother died, as things do with time. But this hallway, my old bedroom, everything looks and feels like it did before.

Even though I know I shouldn't, I pause by my old bedroom and lean against the doorway looking in. It's pretty much empty, just my old bed in the corner and a dresser. At one point I had posters on the walls, of cars and pretty girls and the usual teenage thing, but those have been taken down by someone at some point.

But it's not my teenage days that I'm remembering when I'm here.

It's when I was a kid.

It's always the day when my mother died.

It's always what I said.

"I hate you."

I close my eyes, take a shaking breath through my nose.

I hate how much the past still has a hold on me, has its claws in me, serrated and razor-sharp. I hate that I've not been able to move past it, that no matter what I've done in my life, it won't let me go.

I see that little boy and I know I could have done more to save her, to help her. If I had been better, she wouldn't have killed herself.

If I hadn't told her I hated her…

The world seems to swim and I open my eyes, refusing to sink again, refusing to feel this pain.

I keep going down the hall until I'm in my father's bedroom.

It's strange now that he shares it with Vernalee. I don't dislike her by any means but I guess it's strange to see him with anyone. Thankfully Vernalee has redecorated the place enough and my father remodeled the bathroom so it doesn't feel exactly like I've stepped back into the nightmares of my childhood.

I open the medicine cabinet, rifling through the large collection of prescription pills that all old people seem to accumulate over time and never throw out.

Finally, I find the prescription opiates and open it, shaking two out into my palm and popping them into my mouth. Then I decide to just pocket the whole bottle. He won't even notice.

"What are you doing?"

Oh, for fuck's sake.

I turn around and see Shane staring at me, standing in the door way.

"What does it look like I'm doing?" I ask him snidely.

"Like you're stealing pills," he says. "What was that?"

I shrug. "Something for my headaches. I ran out of my prescription."

"What headaches?" he asks suspiciously.

"The ones I get," I tell him, heading toward the bedroom door. "From stress. From people like you."

To my surprise, he doesn't get out of the way. Just folds his arms and stays where he is.

"Get the fuck out of the way," I growl at him. I'm having a flashback to one of many times when we were younger and our arguments usually ended in a fistfight. Or at least my fist striking him. He could be passive even when I was slamming him to the ground.

"What the hell is your problem Fox?" he asks and finally, finally there's an edge to his voice. I'm actually getting under his skin.

"You, being in my way," I tell him, taking a step closer until I'm right up against him. "Now move, or I will make you move."

But he doesn't move. The fucker stands his ground. I shift tactics.

"How is it that you can still live here?" I ask him, staring at him point blank, scrutinizing every movement of his face.

He gives me nothing, his features impassive. "What do you mean?"

"Here, Shane. On this ranch. After our mother died, I couldn't wait to get out of here. Neither could Mav. But you,

you Shane, you didn't seem to care. You never even moved. You just stayed. Why is that?"

The muscle ticks along his jaw. "You're not yourself Fox."

"I wish that were true," I tell him. "I wish I were anyone else but me. Do you know why that is? Because she died, Shane. And maybe you don't understand that because you have no memories of her. Maybe that's why this house doesn't mean anything to you, because she didn't mean anything to you."

Something dark comes over Shane's eyes and for a moment I think I may have taken it too far. I swallow, my body primed in case he tries to punch me.

"Are we actually talking about this now?" Shane asks, his voice hard and steady.

"Talk about what?"

"About her. About us. About your fucking problem with me."

I can't help but grin and I know it's coming across as bitter as it feels.

"I have problems Shane, but they aren't with you. Now, if you don't mind, get the fuck out of my way."

He stares at me, nostrils flaring, and then, just as quickly as the anger came over him, it leaves. His face goes blank and he steps to the side.

I step past him as he says, "You have problems with everyone Fox. That's why you're turning into a drunk and a druggie."

I freeze in my tracks, not believing my ears. Turn around to look at him.

"Excuse me?" I'm nearly whispering and it's hard to hear my words over my heart throbbing in my head.

"You heard me," he says, the shadows from the lights above falling on his face, making him look sinister, like someone else. For a weird moment I think that maybe this isn't even Shane at all, that he's been replaced. He's not even making sense.

"Stealing fucking medication from our father," he says, practically spitting. "You're in your thirties, Fox, you need to grow up not act like a fucking emo teenager anymore."

My fists curl, the muscles on my forearms popping as I try to rein in the need to punch him in the face. "Do you know what I do for a living?"

"I know. Everyone knows. You're the hero of the town. You're out there risking your ass to save everyone. Then you come back home and you're miserable. You're closed in, shut-off and angry all the damn time and you're constantly lashing out and pushing away the people who matter to you the most."

I shake my head, my jaw grinding down. "You have no idea what it's like to be me. No fucking idea. I remember my mother—"

"She was my mother too!" he interjects.

"Well you fucking don't act like it!" I yell right back. "You were just a fucking baby and it was because of you that she became depressed."

"So it's my fault she died?"

No. It's my fault.

I swallow, my throat feeling tight, thick, while the hot coals of anger simmer inside. "You just don't know. You never had to experience loss like I did, like Mav did."

"Then explain why Maverick is a fucking saint compared to you. Huh? Tell me why Mav has his shit together and you don't. That means it's all on you, brother, you're fucking up your own damn life."

I reach out and poke him squarely in the chest, hard enough for him to stumble back a step. "And it's my own life to fuck up. It shouldn't affect anyone but me, it shouldn't be anyone's business but mine. So keep your head down and fuck off."

"It's no longer just your life, Fox," Shane growls, regaining his balance, his eyes glittering with dark menace. "It's Del's and your baby's. And you have to get yourself under control for the both of them."

I blink, staring at him blankly. "What?"

I'm not sure what he meant by that.

I think I know what he said but…

And for a moment it looks like he doesn't know either. He straightens up, raises his chin, mouth clamping together. He doesn't explain. He looks…scared.

"Shane?" I say hoarsely and for some reason my voice is trembling. My heart has started to race. "What did you just say?"

"Forget it," he says, looking away. "I'm tired. I've got to go."

With his head down he tries to walk past me but I grab him by the collar and slam him up against the wall, hard enough that the pictures along it shake.

"What the fuck did you just say?" I growl. "Del and…our baby? What baby?"

It doesn't even sound right coming from my mouth.

Shane closes his eyes, breathing in deep through his nose, rubbing his lips together like he's trying to maintain composure. "Fuck."

My grip on his shirt tightens. "Fuck what, exactly?"

He sighs and looks off down the hall, his eyes looking pained. "I wasn't supposed to say anything. She was supposed to tell you. I guess I thought she had…"

Fucking hell. "Tell me what? *What?*"

"I guess I've fucked up at this point so I might as well." He pauses, his head going back and banging against the wall. "Shit. Fuck."

I let go of him, waiting.

He absently smooths the collar of his shirt and says, "Del is pregnant."

What?

I can't…

Oh, fuck.

Oh, no.

No.

I'm suddenly finding it very hard to breathe. "She's what?"

"Pregnant."

"Are you sure?"

He gives me a wry smile. "Oh yeah. I had suspected it and got her to take a test. Then another one. I was there, I saw for myself. Then she went to the doctor and it was confirmed."

"Holy *shit*," I whisper, my hands going to my hair, making fists in them. I can't seem to focus on anything, the pattern in the carpet is moving in and out. I lean against the wall, dead-weight on my feet. "Fuck."

"Yeah. So she's been dealing with that. Only a few of us know. Me, Rachel, her mother. That's it."

"Del is pregnant," I repeat. How could that even be? "She said she was on the pill," I say meekly, as if that will just cancel the whole thing.

"It happens," he says.

"Fuck."

"I wish I wasn't the one to tell you."

I look him in the eye. "I'm not. I'm glad you did. I can fucking lose my mind with you…I couldn't do this with Del."

"If it makes you feel any better, she's freaking out too."

It doesn't make me feel better. In fact, it makes everything that much worse.

"Why the fuck didn't she tell me?"

Shane shrugs. "She was waiting for you to get back."

"Yeah well I fucking got back and let her know and she

didn't even answer. She could have called me. Texted me. Now I feel like I'm the last to know."

"You're not."

"You know, of all fucking people. My own brother knows before me. And why the fuck were you with her anyway getting her pregnancy tests?"

"I just was, okay?" he snipes. "Like you should have been."

"She still should have told me. I can't believe this. Is she, you know, going through with it?"

I know Shane knows. I know he knows everything about this, that he's been through it all for the last three weeks while I've been gone.

"You should talk to her about this, Fox. Not me."

"If she wanted that, she should have fucking reached out to me."

"She's been busy. She has the pub quiz night on tonight. Maybe she didn't even get your text."

But I barely hear him.

I can't be here anymore.

I need to see her.

I need to hear it from her own mouth.

I need to know why she's kept this from me for three fucking weeks.

I storm off down the hall, hearing Shane calling for me, saying I shouldn't drive, but I don't care. I get in the Jeep and roar off down the road, straight to the pub.

15

DELILAH

"Jesus, Delilah, I've never seen this place so packed. You got some dancing naked ladies happening later?" Old Joe asks me as I hand him his beer.

"You wish," I tell him.

"Only if it's you, honey," he says with an exaggerated wink.

I roll my eyes. "It's pub quiz night, Joe."

"You're doing that again?"

"Do you not even pay attention to the board outside? I spend a lot of time on that. You think it's easy to work with chalk?"

"All I pay attention to is what's on the inside, and that's you, sweetheart."

I sigh and nod toward his table. "Go sit down before someone takes your booth."

Terror strikes his wrinkled face and he takes the beer, shuffling off quickly to claim his territory.

A few weeks ago I decided to bring back pub quiz night, something I used to do a few years ago but then stopped because people lost interest. Because the slow season is now in full affect and I have a baby I have to think of, which means I need more money to support said baby, this could be a great way to bring in more customers and extra income.

And so far it seems to be working. The place is pretty packed and I got Rachel and Riley to help me out with creating the quizzes for everyone and giving me some extra help at the bar. I didn't ask them to but they insisted on helping out and won't take any money in exchange for their time.

It's been a welcome distraction, no matter what. After seeing Julie leave Fox's this afternoon, my heart has been in fucking knots. Even after he texted me later, telling me he was back in town, I've been too messed up to reply.

I'm angry. And hurt.

And yes, according to my mother, jumping to a million conclusions. Normally I'm a fairly straight-shooter when it comes to Fox (well, aside from never telling him how I really feel about him), and I'd like to think before the pregnancy I would have just called him up and asked point blank about her.

But now, I don't feel like myself anymore. I am just all over the damn place and these hormones aren't helping and it's like the world is this big crushing weight over my chest that I just can't seem to lift off.

So pub quiz night is turning out to be somewhat of a godsend and I'm keeping busy, though I think at this point Riley is starting to wonder why Rachel is acting extra concerned around me. I haven't told her yet that I'm pregnant, only because I know she'll tell Maverick and Maverick will probably tell Fox.

I also haven't told either of them about what I saw today. I guess because I don't know the facts, I guess because it might make it out to be a bigger deal than it is.

Even so, Rachel knows something is up.

"Are you feeling okay?" she asks me for the millionth time as I make someone a rum and coke.

"Just tired," I say quietly, forcing a smile.

"But what about up here?" she asks, leaning over the counter to press her thumb into my forehead.

"My brain is tired too," I tell her, noting that there are a few people sitting at the bar and listening to us.

She takes her hand away and lowers her voice. "You just seem sad, that's all."

Well my best friend and baby daddy that I'm in love with just had his ex-girlfriend over at his house and didn't even tell me he was back in town.

But that confession wouldn't go over very well the locals who are watching us. The last thing I want is for the whole town to have something new to gossip about and I know it's no longer the 1950's where couples are punished for having children (or even sex) out of wedlock but it would still be enough to get the tongues wagging. I would especially hate for anyone to think anything less of my mother. There's no reason why they should but it seems to always be that way. The mother gets the blame.

And for the umpteenth time, I'm hit with the realization that...

Holy hell. I'm going to be a mother.

A mother.

Me.

I'm not ready for this. I am so not ready.

"I'm fine," I manage tell her, sticking a wedge of lime on the rim of the rum and coke and hoping I can keep it together. "It's a busy night and--"

"Fox," Rachel gasps just after I hear the front door swing open with a slam.

I look up from the drink and see him come in.

Only he doesn't just walk in the bar, he storms in like he's coming here for a battle, his sword sharpened and ready to strike.

Any conflicting thoughts I have about seeing him here are shoved away once I see the wild anger in his eyes. Anger directed at me.

Shit.

Shouldn't I be angry at him?

"You're fucking pregnant with my baby and you didn't even tell me?" he roars, stopping right in front of the bar. "Does everyone know in here except for me?"

The room seems to hum with silence.

Every face is turned, staring at us in curiosity and disbelief.

"They do now," I whisper to myself.

Fox's face is red, his eyes flashing until they seem to realize what he's just said and everyone that he's said it in front of.

"Fox," Rachel barks at him. "What the fuck is your problem?"

But Fox is a stubborn shit. He points at me. "I need to talk to you."

I don't know how I manage to stand my ground. I feel completely humiliated and ashamed and angry and defiant and scared. Oh, god, I'm scared because this wasn't at all how this was supposed to happen, not even close.

I glance at Rachel. "Can you watch the bar?" I ask, trying to keep my voice steady.

"Of course," she says to me softly, then fixes a glare on Fox.

I duck under the bar-top and head toward the back room, not even looking at Fox and assuming he'll follow me. I open the door, though I was tempted to fucking kick it down, and then go inside.

Fox appears right behind me, practically slamming the door shut.

Whatever anger he stormed on in here with though has been transferred to me.

"Thanks a fucking lot!" I yell at him, throwing my arm out. "That was supposed to be a secret!"

"A secret?" he says in disbelief. "It seemed it was a secret only to me. Why the fuck did I have to find out from Shane?"

Shane? Fuck! Of all people!

"He wasn't supposed to say anything," I tell him. "And I'm going to kill him now. And you for fucking telling everyone like that."

"I didn't mean for it to come out that way," he says, his nostrils flaring, breathing hard. "I just can't believe you didn't tell me."

"I was waiting for you to come home so I could tell you in person. This isn't the kind of news to tell over text, phone or even Facetime! What, you wanted me to tell you that while you were out there fighting fires, do you know how dangerous and distracting that would be for you?"

He doesn't say anything for a moment, his eyes holding flames inside them. "I texted you today. You should have told me right away. When were you planning on doing it? Tomorrow? Next week? Never?"

Okay, so he's got me there. But not without reason.

"I was going to tell you as soon as you got back."

"So why didn't you, Del?"

"Because I saw you with *her*."

He flinches like he's been slapped. "Who?"

"Julie," I tell him. "I was going by your house to feed Conan and I saw her drive out of your place. She saw me, too."

He closes his eyes, throws his head back and runs his hands

over face. "Jesus." He looks back at me and suddenly I'm aware of how tired and strung-out he looks, though, fuck, I definitely can't blame him now. "I didn't know she was stopping by. No one knew I was home. I got dropped off last night and passed out before I could even text you. I slept for almost the whole day. I woke up to someone knocking at the door and it was Julie. She had a bottle of whisky and wanted to come in."

I'm not sure if he's trying to make me feel better or not but this is getting worse. "And you let her in."

"Of course I did. I was tired but she was there and she said that she had heard about Roy and the fires and I guess she was just sorry she dumped me, I don't know."

"And so you let her in," I repeat. "Your ex."

"Well, I wasn't going to turn her away."

I can't believe this. I shake my head, trying to breathe. "Fox. You *can* turn her away. She dumped you. Right?"

"I know but…"

I raise my eyebrows expectantly. "But? Oh my god, how is there a *but*?"

He shrugs, squeezing the bridge of his nose with his fingers. "Look, nothing happened."

And here's where it gets tricky. I do believe him because I know him and I usually know when he's lying about something and I'm not getting that from him now. But even if nothing happened, there's the fact that he doesn't really owe me anything because we aren't exactly exclusive.

He looks at me and continues. "We just talked. Or she just talked. I was still so exhausted, I wasn't even sure where I was. I just drank with her for a glass and then she went home and that was that." He takes a step toward me as if he's going to reach out and grab my hand then doesn't. "Del, you know I wouldn't do that to you."

I stare down at my shoes, pretending to study the scuffs

on the tops of my boots. "You would have been allowed. We're not exclusive. And you didn't know I was pregnant."

"It doesn't matter. I still wouldn't have. Del," his voice trails off and when I look up at him he's staring at me with awe. "I can't believe you're pregnant."

"Welcome to my world."

"Are you…are you going to keep it?"

I'm not sure how Fox is going to react to this. Now that he's here I should include him in on all the decision making but at the same time, it's my body and my choice.

"I'm keeping it." I don't have to tell him my reasons why.

He nods slowly, brows knitting together. "Okay. Okay."

Fuck. This is exactly what I thought. He would rather I didn't.

"I know it's scary, Fox," I say softly, reaching out and putting my hand on his bicep. "I know that this news is knocking you over right now and I get it. It's doing the same to me. But I haven't had to think much about whether I want to keep it or not. I just know I am. And…god, this is so weird to say because it's our baby, it's you and it's me but no matter what you choose to do, I'll be okay."

"What do you mean, what I choose to do?" he says sharply.

I inhale deeply. "If you don't want to be a part of the child's life, then I get it. I do. I'm making this choice for me, not for the both of us and I'm not going to be that girl that gets pregnant and holds a man hostage. That's not me. If you want to be involved, great. If not…I'll be fine."

He's speechless. His mouth is open a little, his eyes wide as they search mine. "Wow," he whispers after a few beats.

"What?"

"I can't believe you."

Oh god, what now?

"What? What did I do?"

"Do you honestly, seriously think that I wouldn't want to be involved? Do you actually think that I would have nothing to do with this child, with my own fucking child?"

"I'm just saying," I say defensively and I know that I was wrong in thinking it. "You've been away for three weeks, I've had to deal with all of this alone."

"Not alone. You've had Shane."

"Oh for crying out loud! Is this what you're pissed about? That I told Shane before you?"

"Fucking right I am!" he yells. "Do you know how humiliating it is for me to find out from someone else other than you, from my own brother who I barely even talk to?"

"Do you know how humiliating it is for me for you to storm on in here to my own bar and yell at me in front of everyone, on the busiest night possible, telling them all I'm pregnant with your child. You fucking yelled at me Fox, in public. You don't have the right to do that!"

It's suddenly hitting me now. All the stress and the strain of the last three weeks, of having to keep this a secret, of feeling alone, so terribly alone, are all coming up, forcing their way out of me. I turn my back to Fox and blink back the tears, my eyes and nose growing hot.

"I'm sorry," he says hoarsely. "I didn't mean for that. I just...I'm angry Del."

"Well I'm angry too," I say, my voice breathless, shaky. "I'm angry and lost and afraid and alone, so alone. You don't know what it's been like, to have to figure out my life all over again. This was never part of the plan."

"You never thought I was part of your plan?" he asks quietly.

Before I can say anything to that—what, I don't know—I feel his warm, strong hands on my arms. "Del, you're not alone in this. Whatever you've been thinking while I've been gone, forget it. It doesn't matter. Your thoughts and fears are yours to have but I'm here telling you that you're not going to be alone. I will be with you every step of the way."

Don't cry. Stay strong.

"You mean the world to me," he says, his voice beautifully sincere. "You are my world. You always have been. You'll never stop being my friend."

Oh fuck.

The pain is excruciating, the word *friend* is a quick knife into the heart and out, following the same path lined with scar tissue for the years of him saying it. But it hurts just as much as the first time, hurts because I should be overjoyed that he's sticking with me and not going anywhere even if it's as just a friend. That's the best I can hope for and I have it.

But god, I want his love. I want this baby, I want him to love the baby, and I want him to love me, too. Is that too much to ask for?

"Come here," he says quietly. He physically turns me around until I'm facing him and brings me into him, wrapping his arms around me.

Any chance of holding it together like I have been doing is gone.

I break down.

Into pieces.

His arms are the only things that are holding me together, preventing me from shattering into a million more fragments. Fragments of a girl I used to know.

So I cry.

He holds me.

Kisses the top of my head.

Makes me feel like he's going to turn back time.

Makes me feel like he's going to fast forward time.

Bring us back to a place where we felt safe.

Bring us forward to a place where we're happy.

He does this all for me and he doesn't even know it.

He doesn't know how he makes me feel.

But I can't tell him. I can only cry and sob into him and let the strength in his arms, the sound of his heart beating in his chest, soothe me like nothing else.

"It's going to be okay," he whispers, running his palm down the back of my head. "We're going to be okay. We have a great support system...friends, family, a whole town who loves you, knows you. This baby is going to be very loved, that much I can promise."

What about me?

But I'm a selfish cow for even letting that thought enter my head.

I push it away, bury it somewhere deep. It can be dealt with at some other time. Right now, all that matters is that I have Fox's support. I know he's angry and he's a mess and I'm a mess too but if we're both in it together, both on the same page, we might be able to make this work.

I wish this wasn't so damn complicated.

16

FOX

My world is on fire again.

It's a dream but it tells me that it's real, whispers my name.

Believe it, Fox.

It wants me to believe all of it.

I'm standing on the other side of a freshly dug fireline, the Pulaski axe beside me, across from a towering inferno.

But this time it's not a forest that is up in flames. It's the whole town of North Ridge.

All the buildings are burning, the high school, the grocery stores, the fire hall, the YMCA, the senior living apartment complexes, everything up in flames.

Even The Bear Trap Pub.

This is what I was trying to save.

Trying to save and couldn't.

The flames keep growing, coming for me, and yet without even glancing at the hose on the ground beside me, I know it will run dry. There's no stopping it, not this time.

And that's when I see it.

I had been searching the flames for the sign of the woman that I often glimpse, the one I want to save.

My mother.

I don't see her.

Instead I see a little girl.

She comes running out of the pub, the walls around her on fire, but she's miraculously unscathed. Light brown hair, bright hazel eyes that shine brighter than any flames.

It's my daughter.

"Come to me!" I try and yell at her but my voice is nothing more than a whisper. "Keep running!"

But my daughter doesn't hear me. I don't even think she can see me.

To her I don't exist.

But I do, I fucking do.

And I can save her.

I try and move across the fireline but there's an invisible wall, an unseen hand holding me back. I scream and pound my fists into it, throw my body into it, but it doesn't move. I try again and again, sweat pouring down my face, so real I can taste it, the heat burning my hair, the acrid smell permeating every inch of my soul.

I call for her. She has no name but I know her heart and I call for her.

Parts of the pub are starting to burn off. A window explodes here, a beam falls there. The front door swings on one hinge.

The sign above with the bear and his beer crackles in the fire, threatening to fall.

"Please run baby, run."

But the words die on my lips.

The building starts to implode.

The little girl stands there, unaware of how close she is to death, and that's when she sees me.

"Daddy!" she screams, arms out, just as the walls collapse and a giant hand of fire wraps around her, pulling her back into the building until there's nothing left but ash.

I think I wake up screaming.

I sit right up in bed and I'm soaked, my skin feeling it's on fire, sweating profusely. I cough and cough, as if I inhaled ashes right into my lungs, then try to get my bearings.

It's dark out but my phone says it's 7 a.m., which means morning is here and the darkness will be fading soon.

I'm alone.

Del should be lying here beside me. After last night at the bar, I wanted more than anything to bring her back here. She has that way of banishing the cobwebs, of giving me a heart-beat in the darkness.

But things are strained between us. I didn't want to push my luck, push her. And in some ways it's probably for the best that I left the bar when I did and came home. I have a lot to think about, a lot to process. My nightmares are constant proof of that.

I'm just starting to hate waking up in this big empty house.

Except for a squeak coming from the cage where I see Conan staring at me.

The fucking squirrel.

It's almost as if God was testing the two of us out when I picked up that baby from the ground. Thinking I could rescue it, save it, give it a better life.

I guess I had but it was all thanks to Del. With my work, there's no way I would have been able to take care of Conan. Del helped out, Del fed the little guy until he turns into a big, fat curious little thing with the fluffiest tail you can imagine. Del did it all.

Which means my dream isn't that far off.

I'm going to be a rotten father.

I'll never be home.

I'll always be out working.

Sure, half the year I will be here but there's still the other half where Del will have to raise the baby by herself, then the kid. I know it's no different than fathers who are in the military, who go off for long tours, if anything it's a lot easier doing what I do.

But still, even now as I'm trying to think about when Del could be due, that would be what, May or June? Fire season will be starting right then.

I'll miss everything.

And more than that, Del will have to do it all alone. I know she has friends and family, I know she'll get by just fine. But this is our baby and it's hard to be in it together when I'll be out of the picture.

Something in my gut twists, a pain that comes from someplace deep.

Fear. This is pure fear.

Fear that I'm going to be a deadbeat dad and fuck up this kid's life.

Fear that the easy comradery and friendship I have with her is at stake.

Fear that I'll mess up the one good thing in my life.

Because underneath all this fear, I know the truth. The truth that this baby may have been an accident, but it's not unwanted. It may change everything but there's a chance that if I can somehow 'grow the fuck up' as Shane so eloquently put it, get my life together, that this baby might be the answer to everything.

Or, for once, I'll be ruining more lives than just my own.

The melancholy is after me this morning, hot on my tail. I need to get up out of bed and get moving, even though this is the first time in a long time that I don't have any jobs to do. I should let myself rest or inquire at the ski lodge about returning for another year as a ski and snowboard instructor, something I do during the winter months to bring in extra income. But I know that if I rest too much, I'll think too much and my brain will keep going around in circles.

I say hello to Conan, who really wants to get out of his cage, and then head straight to the kitchen to make coffee and have a shot of Julie's whisky and a pill. The sun is starting up over the mountains and the shadows start to fade.

I notice a notebook on the counter that wasn't there before and open it.

There's a pencil sketch of a squirrel on the first page.

"Conan's Owner Manual by Delilah Gordon," I read the scribbled words out loud. And laugh.

This woman has somehow turned this notebook into a step-by-step instruction book on how to take care of him. It's got little drawings for each one, which reminds me what a good artist I used to think she was back in high school when we were in art class together.

There's also a little diary every other page, telling me how he was when she fed him and by the end, she goes on about how she can let him out of the cage with no problems and sometimes she'll walk around my place with him on her shoulder. Apparently he's also graduated from applesauce and now tries to eat as many avocados as possible, along with shelled peas, blueberries (but he tends to eat the inner berry and leave the squishy skin, as she says) and of course, nuts of any kind.

This little book was like a tonic to my soul. It's not the whisky, not the pill. It's Del and her sunshine heart. It's that while I was out there, she was here trying to prepare for the life inside of her while at the same time, making sure some silly squirrel was taken care of. Because she's looked after Conan with dedication and love and joy and I know this baby, our baby, is going to have the best mother in the world.

I think I know what I have to do.

I have to do the right thing.

There's only one person I need to talk to about that.

I throw on black jeans, a thick grey sweater and jacket and go out to the Jeep, scraping frost off the windshield, the cold biting my skin. It's early still and it's almost November and the world is covered with sparkling white. The clouds are a dull grey and soon they'll be bringing snow to our neck of the woods. Beyond that will be Christmas and the holidays and then a new year.

I can't predict how the year will go or what's in store but I know there are some things I can control. I may not be a great man but I am a man of honor and loyalty and my word and though this is beyond frightening, I can be brave for this too. I can at least try.

I get in the Jeep and head out to the ranch.

Because it's early I pull up to the house just as Shane and my father are standing on the porch, pulling on their shearling jackets.

"Hey," I say to them with a nod as I get out of the Jeep. "It's cold as balls out."

Both my father and Shane don't say anything. Shane looks a little wary of me and then everything from last night comes flooding back into my brain and I feel shame. Shame for the things I said to him, shame for the way I treated him, shame for stealing from my father.

Then I'm wondering if he told my father what I did.

Then I'm wondering if both of them know what happened at The Bear Trap.

If my father knows Del is pregnant with my baby.

"What are you doing here?" Shane asks with a hardened voice, pulling on his boots. Normally my father would reprimand him for being rude, especially since Shane is never rude, but he doesn't say anything, just stares at me like he wants to know too.

"I want to talk to Grandpa about something," I tell him. "Is he up?"

My father grunts. "Barely."

"Why?" Shane asks.

None of your damn business. The words are on my tongue but one look at my father's face and I know better than to press my luck with him.

"I need some advice," I admit.

"Advice? The damage is done, ain't it?" my father grumbles, stepping off the porch and walking away. "Not that you ever listen anyway."

Shane raises his brow at me like he thinks I'm complete garbage and then follows my father, walking toward the barn.

Shit. My father does know.

Suddenly I feel like I'm sixteen years old again and getting in trouble for who knows what. I'm starting to think that trouble might follow me everywhere, or maybe the trouble lives deep inside me.

I take in a deep breath and step inside the house.

My grandpa is walking out of the kitchen in red long-johns, his silver hair starting to get long and hang by his shoulders, a bandana over his head, sheepskin slippers on his feet. He looks like he could be Willie Nelson's grandfather and I mean Willie is pretty damn old.

He stops when he sees me, lifts his head up from the mug and says, "Well looky here, if it ain't Fox Nelson, hot shot, hot head, and an obstinate buffoon who can't keep it in his pants."

"So you know."

He snorts and shuffles over to his easy chair, settling down in it with a groan and placing his coffee on the side-table. "I'm sure everyone knows, thanks to you. What happened to announcing things privately anymore? I know you forget that you have family sometimes, but Lordy."

I frown. "I don't forget I have family."

He squints at me and then gestures to the couch. "Sit down."

I obey and lean forward with my elbows on my knees. "What do you mean I forget I have family?"

He takes a long slurp of his coffee, closing his eyes for a moment, until he opens them again and looks right at me, into me. They're sharp as tacks. "I don't pretend to know your job Fox, but I do know it's tough. I also know you've gone your whole life making things tougher. I get it. I do. I know. I've been in this house same as you have. You have a knack for making everything in your life more difficult than it should be."

I can't even argue with that. I'm hanging on to every word.

"You picked one of the toughest jobs. It's harder than Maverick's job. Harder than anyone's. You take the hard route because you want to punish yourself, maybe. Or maybe you think you deserve it. Or maybe because you feel you owe the world a lot, to make up for something. Who the hell really knows. And that's my point. Because we don't know, Fox. We're your family and we're your lifeline and you act like we don't exist half the time, most of the time. So wrapped up in whatever is going on behind that thick skull of yours, whatever is eating you alive from the inside. It ain't healthy, boy. It ain't good."

This is a lot to process. I stare down at my hands. Calloused, scarred by fire, hands that one day will hold a baby in them, my baby. How can these take care of something pure?

"You're doing it again," he says. "Try opening your mouth

and telling me something. That's why you're here, aren't ya?"

He's right.

I need to just say it.

"Grandpa, I know I don't usually ask for advice but this is the first time that my choices don't only affect me."

He cocks a grey brow. "So you say. You don't know that your choices affect all of us?"

"Okay, then this is the first time I've been conscious of it and I don't want to screw up. I want to do the right thing here. I want to be a good man for Del, for the baby."

His expression softens as he studies me. "You are a good man, Fox," he says in a low voice. "One of the best men I know. All you boys are. You were raised right. By your mother, by your father. By me, by Jeanine. You even helped raise each other. You were a big help with John and Shane after your mother died, don't you forget that."

I nod, but I'm brushing it off. "Tell me what I should do."

He chuckles. "I can't tell you what to do. What does your heart tell you to do?"

My heart. My heart is a constant whirlpool. I can't make sense of it, it's constantly changing, it's twisted with fear.

"My heart," I begin, clearing my throat. It feels almost silly to be talking about this, my heart, but Grandpa is serious. It's all so serious. "My heart wants to do the right thing. I think I should ask Delilah to marry me."

He looks at me with wide eyes. "Oh."

"You weren't expecting that?"

"I'm never sure what to expect with you."

"Do you think it's a good idea?"

"Do you?"

"I don't know," I say, running my hand through my hair, trying to get a handle on it all. "I just know that I want to be with her and the baby. I want us to be a family. I don't want to be cut out from their lives and I don't want her to go on and have her family, my family, with someone else. It should be me."

"Uh huh," he says, taking a long, thoughtful sip of his coffee. "If that's what your heart says to do Fox, then you should listen to your heart. But let me ask you this—is that what Delilah wants? And if it is, then you must ask yourself, would you be doing this if she wasn't having your baby?"

"Of course I wouldn't be," I say quickly. "I knocked her up, I'm going to do the right thing and commit."

"I see. And you wouldn't marry her otherwise?"

I shake my head, confused. "Why would I?"

"Well," he drawls out, "maybe because you have feelings for her."

"I love her, if that's what you mean."

"But are you in love with her?"

"What's the difference?"

My grandfather gives his head a shake as he sets the coffee back down. I have a feeling I've said something immensely stupid. "You know when you know, Fox. And you don't know." He exhales and starts coughing for a moment. "Fox, Fox, Fox. You and Del have had a very special relationship for a very long time. I can't tell you how she feels about you because I don't know, she's never told me. But I look at her and I see a girl who adores you, Fox. And if you do this… just know it has the ability to break her heart. You might do more harm than good."

"I don't see how this could do any harm at all," I tell him. "This is the right thing to do. I'm not going to be like those other guys who run for the hills. I love her, she's so important to me. And I'm going to be there for her, like a proper family. That baby will have a father and mother, together."

He looks like he's going to say something else but he doesn't. He just gives me a faint smile. "Then I think you know what to do."

"You don't have a ring or something I can borrow, just for now?" I ask him.

"So this is the real reason you came over?" he asks wryly, easing up to his feet.

"One of them."

"Hold on," he says. He shuffles away and up the stairs and as he does so, I catch a whiff of his coffee by his chair. I lean in closer to smell it. Whisky. Seems the apple doesn't fall very far from the tree for us.

When he comes back he's holding a little muslin pouch that he plops in my hand. "Here. I gave it to your grandmother."

"Grandpa, you shouldn't have. I just meant like any kind of ring. Just to propose with before I get Del a better one."

He elbows me with a smile and then sits back in his chair. "Open it."

I do.

It's a gold plastic ring with parts of the gold paint peeling off.

It says Cracker Jack on it.

"You have got to be shitting me," I say, turning it over in my hands. "I always thought finding rings in Cracker Jack boxes was a joke."

"It was a joke," he says. "I was just a poor rancher when I asked your grandmother to marry me and it was all I could afford. I'm just lucky I picked that box. To her, though, it didn't matter. When I got her a better ring, I think she liked this one more. The sentiment. Anyway, want you to have it."

"Are you sure?"

"Sure, maybe it will bring you good luck," he says. "If not, it's a funny story."

I'm fucking touched.

I just hope Del finds it as charming as my grandmother did.

17

DELILAH

I<small>F THERE'S SOMETHING CALLED BEING EMOTIONALLY</small> hungover, then I spent the morning being hungover as hell. My alarm went off several times and I hit snooze several times more. I was tired and more than that, my heart was tired. Everything ached with emotions drawn-out and ragged and filled to the brim.

When I finally did drag myself out of bed and to the washroom it was nearly eleven o'clock. When I asked my mother why she hadn't woken me up, she said that at this stage I should take as much sleep as I can because I won't be able to sleep well later.

She's probably right about that. The more I hear from my doctor and the books about what to expect during pregnancy, the more horrible it all sounds.

Last night...should have gone better.

I'm glad that Fox and I talked in the end and got everything sorted as well as we could.

I'm a bit regretful that he went home after. I feel like things are still left hanging, feels like we needed to be closer, to find our way with each other again.

Though it was probably for the best. I know the more I sleep with him, the more wrapped up and confused I become in my feelings for him. If I had just kept my head, kept my body in line, if my hormones could just be controlled for once, I wouldn't be in this mess.

But, dwelling on the past only holds you back from the future you deserve. I know that much. So I try and pull myself out of my funk and stay positive. I have to.

I've just had a long, luxurious shower, as if trying to wash my sins away, when I step out into my bedroom and hear voices from upstairs. My mother and a male's.

Fox.

What the hell is he doing here?

I quickly wrap my hair in a towel, throw on leggings and a sweater and cautiously head down the hall, trying to catch snippets of their conversation.

"I know this is scary," my mother says to him in a hushed voice. "But you'll get through it. You both will."

"I'm going to try," he says.

They both look up at me while I pause in the entrance to the kitchen. "Hey," I say, my eyes going right to his.

"Hey," he says back. He looks different somehow. Last night he was fueled by anger and confusion and all the things I can't get mad at him about because I've been feeling them too. Today, there's a glint in his eyes, a spark. He's gnawing on his lip like he's nervous. "I need to talk to you about something."

There are a million somethings we still need to talk about.

"Okay," I say, giving my mother a look. She shrugs slightly.

"I'll get out of your hair," she says.

"No, it's fine, stay," Fox says. "I was hoping we could go for a drive."

I nod. "Sure, let me just get ready."

I turn and hurry back to my bedroom, taking the towel off my head and pulling my wet hair back into a bun. I know I probably shouldn't go out into cold weather with wet hair, especially when pregnant, so I pull a furry toque down over it and go back to meet Fox who is waiting by the front door, my usual winter jacket in his hands.

He holds it out for me and I slip my arms in it while he pulls it on.

"Such service," I remark as we head down the steps to his Jeep where he opens the door for me as well.

He doesn't say anything as I climb in and he shuts the door. He wasn't acting like much of a gentleman last night but I don't bring it up. I'm curious as to why he's nervous, practically jumping out of his skin, wondering what he wants to talk to me about. I have a feeling it's something good since his mood is on the up instead of on the down.

That said, I'm not sure if he's entirely sober or not, a thought that crosses my mind when I notice his fingers tapping against the steering wheel in agitation, the way he almost ran a stop sign when he pulled off onto a road that takes you to Chairman's Peak.

"Are you okay?" I ask him after the silence has simmered in the car for long enough. "Where are you taking me? Hiking?"

"I'm fine," he says quickly, giving me a tight smile. "I just have a lot on my mind."

"You don't say," I muse. "That makes two of us."

"I know," he nods, frowning, seeming to take what I just said more serious than he should. "I know."

Finally, after a million switchbacks that snaked higher and higher up the mountain, he brings the car to the parking lot at the trailhead. We're the only people here and at this height on this side of the mountains, the frost is thick, white, and refusing to melt.

It's gorgeous.

Cold, but gorgeous.

"Here we are," he says.

I'm still absolutely dumbfounded as to what's going on, especially as he gets out of the Jeep and comes around my side, opening the door for me.

"So we are going hiking?" I look down at my Sorel boots. "I'm not sure how these will hold up."

"We aren't," he says. He waves an arm at the view, gesturing to the glittering frosted valley and the town of North Ridge below. "I just thought this was a beautiful place."

"For what?"

He takes both of my hands in his and squeezes them. Takes in a deep breath, the air clouding at his exhale. His smile is shaky.

What the hell is happening?

WHAT THE HELL IS HAPPENING?

"Delilah," he says. "I'm going to make this quick because I'm, well, I'm scared to death and I know you are too and the sooner we can move onto the next stage of our life, the better."

I can't seem to swallow properly. I'm hanging onto his every word, like I'll be freefalling when he's done speaking.

"I wish it was more romantic than this, but it will have to do," he says and just those words alone are hitting me inside my chest, rattling around my heart.

It will have to do.

He reaches into his pocket and pulls out a ring.

A dull, brassy plastic ring.

He drops to one knee in the frost.

And I am beyond stunned.

Beyond. Stunned.

This isn't what I think this is. This isn't happening.

Fox is not proposing to me...

"Delilah, I think we should get married. I know this would be better under other circumstances, but it will have to do. Will you be my wife?"

Again, those words.

It will have to do.

Why I'm focusing on them more than on everything, the words I've longed to hear from him my whole life, I don't know. But I am.

God, I want this to be real.

But I don't know if it is.

So I don't say yes.

Not yet.

There are a million champagne corks inside me ready to pop, streamers poised to come down, but I hold them back because I can't quite say yes to this as it is.

"Del?" Fox repeats and now there's wild fear in his eyes, maybe some anger too. "You did hear what I asked, didn't you?"

I manage to swallow, a heavy, sharp pain building inside of me. Those champagne bottles are fading into the distance. "I heard," I whisper. "But...I need to think, Fox."

"You need to think?" he asks incredulously, squeezing my hand, the ring poised to go on my ring finger. "Del, I want to marry you. I want us to be a family. I want this baby to have a family. It's the right thing to do and you know it."

"I know," I say, my voice hushed as I feel the tears threatening me. "I know you do. But Fox, we can't just get married because you think it's the right thing to do."

"Why not?"

God, he looks so afraid. That look in his eyes...

"Because. Because you need to love me. You need to love me Fox, you need to want to marry because you love me and can't imagine life without me." I'm starting to shake, everything is unraveling at lightning speed.

"I can't imagine life without you, Del," he says and now his voice is rough, trembling. "I can't. You are my life."

"But am I the love of your life?"

He presses his lips together, eyes searching mine like he's searching for the truth in me. Maybe he is.

But I know his truth. I know it because I know him.

It's the truth I've always known.

"I love you," he says. "I've always loved you."

He says it like a fact. Like it's something we both just need to accept.

"But are you *in love* with me?" I whisper and in that moment I feel the air around us still, the very cells inside me pause and wait, wait for the pain.

His eyes give it all away. The shame. So much shame.

"Delilah," he says, his voice higher, breaking. "Please. We have to do this for the sake of the baby."

"Are you in love with me?" I repeat, my voice rising too.

He gets to his feet, taking the ring back, squeezing it into his fist. He licks his lips, his brow scrunched with frustration. "Why does that have to matter? Why can't we just take things as they come?"

And there I have it.

The truth.

And now I have no choice but to share mine.

"Because I'm in love with you, Fox," I tell him. My words tremble and shake as they leave my lips, my blood pounding in my head. "I've loved you since the day I first met you, when I moved next door. I loved you and I continued to love you and somehow I'm even more in love with you now than I was at the start, even after all this."

I always imagined the day I told Fox I loved him would be like standing before him, opening my chest, letting a million doves fly free into the sky. But now, with the way he's looking at me, like he's been slapped, like my very words have driven fear into his heart, it feels like he's taking a gun and shooting down every last dove. Dead.

He's speechless, like he can't process it.

I close my eyes, trying to pretend he's not here.

"I'm sorry if you didn't know," I go on, a few tears spilling from the corners of my eyes. "I'm sorry I didn't tell you earlier, but there was never a good time. I didn't want to ruin our friendship. I know I mean a lot to you and you've meant all that and more to me. But I need…I need you to love me like I love you. I need it more than anything in this world. And I know it's selfish of me to want it. I know that I should accept your proposal because it's the right thing for the baby but I'm sorry." My eyes open and I can barely see him through the tears. "I can't marry you."

He shakes his head, his jaw tense. He looks away, his eyes absently scanning the mountains. "I don't know what to say."

"I know," I tell him. "I know, and it's okay."

"It's not okay," he says sharply, looking back at me with fiery eyes. "You're not even giving me a chance!"

"Fox, I can't marry you just because you asked."

"But in time, things change. Love grows. It happens. I'm just…I'm too fucked up right now to make sense of anything in life but this can change me. It will change me."

"No. This won't change you. A baby won't change you until you change yourself first. You won't love me until you love yourself first."

"That's not what's going on."

"Maybe it's not then," I say angrily, fed up, tired, everything coming to a head. "Maybe you just always saw me as a sister and maybe that turned into a girl you loved to fuck and maybe that's how it stays. Maybe you'll never love me in the way I need to be loved because you just don't feel that way about me. But sometimes I think, no, I know, that you don't even know what love is. You wouldn't know it if it hit you in the face. You wouldn't know it unless you were open to it and you're not. You never were. You're closed off. You're happy in your anger and your sorrow and you shun everything good."

"That's not true!" he roars at me, spit flying. "I want what's good! You're what's good, you and this baby. Del, you mean the fucking world to me and I'm trying to offer you my world and you won't even take it."

"I don't want the world. I want your heart!" I sob. "I gave you my heart!"

"And I never fucking asked for it!"

Whoa.

I am dead on my feet, my heart burning away inside, burning away all hope for us, for the future.

"I want you to take me home," I manage to say after a few heavy moments, a passage of time that stretches on, opening the wounds in front of him with each minute. "Please," I say, my voice breaking.

Fox is breathing hard, his nostrils flaring, a wild look in his eyes.

I'm so afraid that this is it.

That this is the end of us.

That for all his wildness and brashness and boldness, that it's become too much for me and not enough at the same time.

His heart. I just want his heart.

I know he has one.

Something red and big and beautiful buried beneath layers of darkened ash.

A heart that I won't uncover, no matter how hard I try.

"Okay," he says quietly, walking around to his side of the Jeep.

The drive back to my place isn't just awkward, it's painful.

I keep thinking over what I said.

What he said.

I keep thinking about how this is it.

That he proposed and I said no and I should say yes.

I keep thinking about how I finally told him how I felt and all my worst fears came to light.

I keep thinking that later, when the baby is born, she or he might wonder why they don't have a father and I'll have to explain that there had been a chance. That I ruined it. That I chose my heart over theirs.

I keep thinking that I just lost the love of my life.

I just lost my best friend.

I've lost almost everything that gave me joy.

He pulls up alongside my house and I look at him and I feel so much sorrow, so much love for him, that I have nothing to say. There are no words to express how I'm feeling and even tears don't seem to be enough.

He glances at me and I see that I'm not the only one who is hurting inside. He's hurting too. I just humiliated him. I just ruined something that he had faith in to fix everything.

"I'm sorry," he says to me roughly. "I just wanted to do the right thing."

I nod, my jaw clenching. "I know. I'm trying to do the right thing too."

"Well," he says. He clears his throat. "You know where I am if you need me. If both of you do. I'll be a part of your life as much as you'll let me."

"Thank you," I whisper and for a moment I think I might lean over and kiss him on the cheek but then I couldn't handle touching him for one more second. I'd dissolve in front of him.

I love you. My intentions like a prayer sent up high.

Then I get out of his truck and he drives off and that's how that ends.

WINTER

18

DELILAH

"Delilah! Your squirrel is trying to drink my tea!" my mom hollers from the living room.

I sigh, too tired to yell back. I look at myself in the bathroom mirror and realize I don't only feel tired but I look tired. I look like a truck backed onto my face, repeatedly. When people tell you expectant mothers are beautiful, they're lying. Either that or I just happen to be the exception.

I just passed my 28-week mark the other day which means I'm six months pregnant. It's been a hell of a six months and getting tougher every day. I haven't been sleeping well lately, my blood pressure is high, my stomach sticks out like a balloon, I'm beyond irritable (probably because I don't sleep anymore) and the baby is kicking the crap out of me from the inside.

But it's not all misery. I mean, there's a lot of that for some very obvious reasons that I'm dealing with day to day, but there's a big ball of sunshine growing inside me that I'm very much in love with.

I don't know how or when it happened but around the four-month mark, I'd realized that the baby I had inside me

233

was a little person. Not something that was happening to someone else but an actual human being inside me. I don't know why it took me so long to accept it but once I did, I started to enjoy it. It was like having a tiny best friend inside me that no one else could see, someone that I knew intimately without having to think about it.

Then when we found out the sex of the baby, that I was having a girl, the bond between us seemed to double. Now I talk to the baby constantly, I'm rubbing my stomach all the time, I'm absolutely, head over heels in love with her, someone I haven't even met yet but I know better than I know myself.

I don't have a name for her, I'm just waiting for the right one to come around. I just call her "little one."

But even though my little one keeps me going through all of this, I wish, desperately wish, I had Fox by my side.

After he proposed, after I had to turn him down, he withdrew from me. He didn't stop supporting us but he stopped being a friend and that was the worst pain I'd ever felt.

It was even worse than the admission that he didn't love me. I know I probably did the right thing in turning him down, but I second-guess myself all the time. If I had said yes, I would have a wedding in the future, security in our relationship. But not in his heart. And I know that the most unselfish thing to do would have been to say yes to Fox for the sake of our baby but my heart is a thirsty selfish beast and it wanted it all.

Now I have nothing. Now Fox took a job as an instructor in the ski hills of Whistler and he's been gone since the end of November. It's the end of February now and I still don't know when he'll be home.

He's missing so much.

I keep him updated, I send him emails and texts every

couple of days and he always responds and he always texts to ask about our little girl but...fuck.

Fuck, it breaks my heart. It breaks it over and over again.

He's not here. He's not with me.

He should be with me.

I should have said yes.

But god I was in so much pain even then.

I'm still in love with Fox though I wish I could stop and the fact that I had to turn down his marriage proposal, it kills me. It fucking kills me. It's like I had everything I could have ever wanted in my hands—this baby, Fox, a future, a family—and I turned it all away.

Now I'm alone.

Again.

Just me and the little one.

Of course I have my mother and my friends and the rest of the Nelsons. I should say, especially the rest of the Nelsons. With Fox out of the picture for now, his family has completely stepped up. Shane and Maverick are especially invested, constantly buying the little one the cutest gifts until my house is absolutely overflowing with them, trying to be the best uncle.

Even Hank has taken an interest in me. Hank is a hard-nosed man and a tough nut to crack but he's calling me now at least once a week outside of the weekly dinners just to see how I am. It's absolutely sweet.

I splash some water on my face and then dot on some supposed anti-dark circle under-eye cream that does shit all, then I join my mother in the kitchen.

True enough, she's shooing away Conan.

He's a full-fledged adult squirrel now and as cute as can be.

And fat, very fat. With a big pink tummy and a bushy tail.

He actually turned out to be a wonderful pet, even though

that was never Fox's intention. It just turned out that he was with us for so long that he eventually became too tame to be returned to the wild.

Then, when Fox said he was moving to Whistler for the winter for work, there was no point in me traveling to his place anymore to look after him, so Conan moved in with me.

And my mom.

She says she's not a fan but I think she secretly is.

Like right now, he's trying to lick up the honey that spilled over the edge of her tea and though my mom's hands shake, I think she spills it on purpose.

"Come on Conan," I say with a sigh, picking him up around his fat middle and putting him down on the couch. Several times a day we let Conan out, when we're home to supervise him of course. He's curious as fuck and gets into everything. Otherwise he hangs out in his giant cage that we've put in the living room so he can watch Wheel of Fortune with my mother, which isn't much of a bother since he doesn't smell at all and even when he's running around the house, squirrel poop is small, odorless and easy to clean up.

Not at all like a baby but I'm getting ready for that. I'm both excited that it's only a few months now that I'll get to meet my little one and scared to death that something is going to go wrong.

"Still not getting enough sleep?" my mother asks me.

I shake my head and pour myself a cup of tea. I would die for some coffee. Or a beer. But you know how that goes. The pre-natal tea I'm drinking gallons of will have to do.

"I don't know what it is. I just can't seem to turn off my brain but I'm exhausted and I just want to sleep more than anything. I get so tempted to get up and start vacuuming."

"You know with your high blood pressure that you're

supposed to rest and take it easy, have a bath or read a book instead," she says to me over her mug. "And sit down for goodness sake."

I'm about to, my hand on the back of the chair, when my lower abs squeeze together painfully, like a fist is pulling it inward.

"Oh," I cry out, spilling the tea as I hunch over, the water scalding my hand. "And ow, my hand."

"What is it?" my mother says getting to her feet.

I close my eyes, feeling the pressure and pinch of pain as my mother takes the mug away from me and rubs my back. Then the pressure relaxes. "Oh, it's gone," I tell her, straightening up. "I don't know what that was."

"Braxton Hicks maybe?" she says.

"I don't know, I thought I had those a few weeks ago but it didn't hurt. This one was—"

And I'm cut off as the pain comes back and now I'm doubling over. I cry out as it feels like a vice inside me has pulled my uterus and stomach and groin all together.

"You need to drink more water," my mother says, scrambling to get me a glass. "You're dehydrated."

"It's like bad cramps," I cry out, clutching my stomach. "Bad, bad cramps."

She tries to put the glass of water in front of my face but I can't do anything but try to breathe.

"Drink it, that's what it is," she says. "Your water isn't breaking, it's just Braxton Hicks, you're thirsty, tired, everything."

"This doesn't feel right," I manage to say and once the pain subsides again I drink most of the water down. "I should probably go to the hospital, just in case."

I give her a pleading look. I know that she's probably right and it's nothing but I'm just so paranoid, how can I not want to get this checked out.

"You're right. Let's go," she says, taking me by the arm.

"Can you put Conan back in the cage?"

Normally she hates this since Conan can easily scratch up your arms with his little claws, even though he doesn't mean to, but now she does it without saying anything and luckily he doesn't give her any trouble.

Five minutes later we're at the hospital in the waiting room and my doctor, Dr. Fielding, is there.

He takes us both into a private room and starts running the usual series of checks. The whole time, my contractions keep coming, sharp bouts of pain but they don't seem to be building in strength and eventually they get further apart.

"I'm afraid it's just Braxton Hicks," Dr. Fielding says, examining me as I lie on the table. "Of course that's a good thing. You're just dehydrated."

"That's what I told her," my mother says rather triumphantly. "She's also not sleeping well and she's very stressed."

"I'm fine," I speak up, not wanting them to worry. "Really."

My mother leans in closer to the doctor. "She's still training this girl to take over her bar."

The doctor looks at me in surprise. "You shouldn't be working at all at this point, especially with your high blood pressure. You should be resting. And nesting. Those are the rules."

"I'm almost done." And that's true. It took an awful long time to find someone suitable to run The Bear Trap while I'm on self-imposed maternity leave, but I managed to find Vanessa, who actually used to be on the swim team with me, though she was a few years older. Even so, I want to make sure everything is running perfectly before she completely takes over. The bar is everything I have at this point.

"And the father?" Dr. Fielding asks. He always uses the word father like Fox is he who must not be named. I mean, he knows who Fox is, everyone does, he's not Lord Voldemort.

"What about him?" I ask, feeling defensive. I know Fox is getting a bad rap for going off to Whistler and leaving me here instead of finding a job locally and maybe it's well-deserved. But I'm still the one who turned down his proposal and pushed him away. I want to yell that sometimes when people start talking about him like he's some deadbeat dad that wants nothing to do with me and the baby.

"Do you know now when or if he'll be back," he says. "There are still some classes he can do to catch up, that's assuming he wants to be involved."

"He'll be involved," my mother tells him, adamant.

"Good," the doctor says, shoving his glasses up on his nose and marking some things off on the chart. "Just want to make sure everyone involved with the baby is up to speed. Now, I'll want to see you back at the office in two weeks for your thirty-week pre-natal exam, okay?"

I nod absently, used to all these appointments by now.

"Oh and one more thing," he says, patting me on the hand as I slowly sit up. "Please make sure you take time for yourself. Stress has never done favors for anyone, especially not for pregnant women. Once you've got someone else running the pub, take time to relax. Start nesting if you haven't already. If you need help, don't be afraid to ask for it. I know you're strong and independent Delilah but you have a whole team of people in this town who would love to help you if you let them."

But as I go home later and crawl into bed, preparing for another night of tossing back and forth, the doctor's words crash through my head like rocks.

I have a whole team of people in this town who would be there for me.

But there's only one person in this town, in this province, in this country, in this world, that matters to me.

And I pushed him away.

I pushed him away because I wanted his love and now, now I don't have him at all.

I have texts and emails, empty words that don't even hint at the person leaving them. I know nothing about how Fox really is. I don't know if he's happy. I don't know if he cares.

But of course I know that. I know he cares. He just doesn't love me.

"Fuck," I sob, my hands making fists into my pillow.

Suddenly the hurt comes over me like a hammer.

It breaks me apart into pieces.

I had always said that I would take Fox anyway I could have him and now, now that there's actually a wonderful, beautiful reason for the two of us to be together, I decided it wasn't good enough.

And he left. Why did he have to leave me like this? Why did he have to go so far away when I needed him the most?

Why…

Why doesn't he love me?

"I miss you," I cry out softly, to no one, letting the words float in the air. "Please come back."

19

FOX

I DON'T KNOW WHERE I AM.

I'm cold.

So fucking cold.

So cold I can't feel a thing.

Not even sure I have a heart beating in my chest. If it's there, I can't feel it.

Maybe I never could.

"Get up."

A man's voice.

Gruff.

Angry.

Far away.

Maybe it's my voice.

Where am I?

I'm not dreaming.

My dreams make more sense.

My dreams have fire.

And death.

So much death.

I'm cold, frozen.

I'm numb and yet somehow in pain.

Maybe it's a pain in my heart.

"But you don't have a heart," I mumble.

"So you're alive," the voice says again, and then I do feel something.

A quick kick to my side.

My eyes open slowly. There is ice stuck to them. "Who is there?" I say but my words come out all jumbled, like alien speak.

"All right buddy, time to get up."

Hands grab me and I'm hauled to my feet.

There's a loud clank and I look down to see an empty bottle of bourbon roll away on the ice-covered pavement. "Hey there might have been something in that."

"You drank it all, pal," another voice says, and now I think there are two of them.

I try to push them away, but I can barely twist my body, so I let them drag me along the ground, it doesn't matter.

Nothing matters.

I wish I hadn't let go of that bourbon.

I watch the ground go past, snow, ice, cigarette butts.

There's music somewhere, in a dream maybe, loud thumps that rattle my chest.

Someone laughs, a girl, and says, "Look at that drunk."

I wish I was drunk.

Suddenly I'm thrown in the back of a car and my head hits the window and I sleep again. It's warm.

I'm moving.

Stopping.

My skin comes alive in pins and needles and it hurts. I start to feel pain again, the numbness wearing off.

Where the fuck am I?

I'm grabbed again, pulled away from a car and into a building, bright ugly lights that stare into my soul and then

I'm leaning against a wall, slipping down, down, down until I'm on the floor.

It's not cold here, not like outside.

I think I'll rest.

I think I'll rest forever.

* * *

"Fox Nelson."

I hear my name said from humorless lips but my head is too heavy to lift up from my hands. I don't care what Petey Paul has to say anyway. That's the cop's name or something like that. I don't fucking like Petey Paul since he hasn't let me leave this cell for twenty-four hours.

"Fox Nelson," Petey Paul says again. "Your brothers are here for you."

My head snaps up and I'm rewarded with what feels like a kick to my temples, the pounding is excruciating. I wince, blink in time to see Constable Paul walk away.

My brothers?

Jesus. That can't be right.

There's no way they would be here.

I'm only supposed to be held for twenty-four hours and then let go. I was arrested but I haven't been charged for anything.

It's a joke.

It has to be a joke.

I'm in Whistler, I'm nowhere near home.

And yet as I'm staring dumbly beyond the bars of the jail cell, Maverick and Shane appear.

I have a hard time believing they're real until Maverick speaks.

"Jesus fuck," Maverick says with a low whistle. "You look like shit, Fox."

"I feel like shit," I tell them, my voice ragged. My pulse is quickening and it was already racing all day, my stomach is twisting into knots and I fight down a wave of nausea.

I'm embarrassed.

Humiliated.

Ashamed.

They shouldn't be here. They shouldn't see me like this.

Their eldest brother in a fucking drunk tank.

"Why are you here?" I ask roughly.

Shane sighs quietly. "They called me. Said they called your work here at the resort and they gave them my number for some reason. Well, dad's."

"They said they wouldn't release you unless we came and got you," Mav adds. "What the fuck did you do, Fox?"

Honestly, I don't know.

I don't remember the last three days of my life.

I don't even know if I'll remember this moment later on, the drugs and alcohol still have their hold on me.

But if the cops called my work, then they know where I am.

"Do you know if I still have a job?" I ask feebly.

Shane shakes his head. "It's doubtful. They said that you missed a few shifts so you were in trouble for that before you were in trouble with the police, so…"

I groan, resting my forehead against my fist.

"There goes my fucking money. That would have all gone to Del."

"Hey, Fox," Maverick says in such a tone that I have to look at him. "Del just wants you home, brother. That's all."

She doesn't.

I lick my lips, they sting from being dry and cracked. "Did you forget what happened?" I ask in a steady voice. "I proposed to her. I asked her to marry me. I did the right thing and she said no. She doesn't want me home. She doesn't want me at all."

"She's in love with you Fox, how can you even come to that conclusion?" Shane says, then he runs his hand over his jaw, shaking his head. "No. No, I'm not doing this here, not through a jail cell." He jerks his chin at someone I can't see. "Can you let him out? We'll take him straight back home, promise."

Another cop appears, one whose name I can't remember. I just know I don't want to punch his face as bad as I do the other. "He needs help, are you sure that's something you can give him?"

"I'm fine," I snap and stagger to my feet, rubbing the heel of my palm along my temple. I don't think I've ever felt this hungover before. It's like all the pain I've ever felt has decided to gang up on me for one day.

"We've got him," Maverick assures them and the doors to the cell open with a loud clanging noise that feels like a jackhammer to my brain.

"Are you seriously taking me back to North Ridge?" I ask them as they practically escort me out of the police station. Outside it's cold and bright, snow everywhere. I can't imagine having to leave here and go back home so soon.

"We are," Mav says firmly.

"What if I don't want to go?"

Shane gives me a tight smile before saying, "That's why we're both here. We won't let you."

"This is ridiculous. I have a job here. I can't leave like this."

"You don't have a job, get real," Mav says, leading me over to his truck in the parking lot. "No one goes on a three-day bender like you did and skips out on work and ends up in motherfucking jail and still has a job. You're just a snowboard instructor here, Fox, some loud-mouthed Australian has probably already taken your place and is scoring all the hottest ass."

"I haven't scored any hot ass," I mutter as I get in the backseat of the truck.

"Good," Shane says. "Because if you had cheated on Del while you were here, I would personally beat your face in with my boot."

"Jesus, Shane," I tell him. "When did you get so protective? And violent?"

"Well you've been gone, someone has to take up your role as resident asshole," he says.

"He's kidding, of course," Maverick says, starting the truck and driving out onto the highway. "You will always be the resident asshole, Fox. But he's right about Del."

"I haven't done a thing," I cry out, showing my palms in a plea of innocence. "And again, for the record, we aren't together. I proposed to her. She said no."

"You told her you didn't love her," Shane says. "What the fuck did you expect her to do? Still say yes?"

I swallow. God, I need water.

"Can we swing by the hotel room first?" I ask. "I need to get my stuff."

"Already got it, it's in the back."

I crane my neck around and see my suitcase and duffel bag in the back of the truck.

Fuck.

"Oh, we found your drugs too," Shane says, lifting up a baggie of pills from his shirt pocket.

"Those are mine," I say, reaching forward trying to swipe them out of his hands. "I need them."

"You need a swift kick in the fucking ass, that's what you need," Maverick says, and in one quick motion he takes the bag from Shane's hand and undoes the window, tossing the

246

pills out onto the highway where they are quickly crushed under the tires of the oncoming traffic.

"Fuck you!" I sneer, feeling a strange restless panic work its way through my blood. "Do you know how expensive those were? You could have at least resold them."

"Not interested," Mav says, eyeing me in the rearview mirror. Mav knows me better than anyone, other than Del, and he's always been one to handle me with that easy going attitude of his. He rarely gets mad.

But this is different.

I've seriously fucked up here.

I've fucked up and I know that I have no idea how badly.

"Fox, we need to talk to you. Both Shane and I," Mav goes on. "You understand why, don't you?"

"Is this an intervention?" I ask warily, but suddenly I'm so tired. I smell my sleeve. I stink too. Who the fuck knows where I went or what I did when I was on my bender.

"If you want to call it that," he says. "Though you pretty much intervened with yourself."

"Where did they even find me?"

"Passed out on the ground behind a café," Shane speaks up. "It was snowing. You were out. And it was only luck that an officer happened to spot you there, otherwise, you were out of sight of people and that café was closed at night. You could have died, Fox."

I know I could have.

And I think I knew that in my dark drunken soul.

It was like I wanted everything to just be over, to submit to the cold, to the way I so royally fucked everything up. I ran away by coming to Whistler but it wasn't quite far enough. You can never run away from yourself.

I told myself I left because of Del. The fact is, I left because she made me realize the man that I'm not, even when I try to be.

But I don't want to give up.

Coming here was giving up.

Drinking and taking pills and trying to forget my existence, her existence, the baby's existence for the last three months. It hasn't worked. Because she's not the problem. I'm the problem. Even in my emails back and forth with her, getting as much info as I can without stepping on her toes, I've been too afraid to interject myself back in her life.

"I…" I start to say but I don't have the words. My mouth is dry like sawdust, my mind slugs along as if it's been poured with cement. I stare at the scenery going past, snow-covered trees, a beautiful, peaceful winter setting and I know that I don't feel at home anywhere. Not in the fires, not in the ice. Not in my head, not outside of it.

Only Del made me feel at home.

Only Del is my home.

Delilah and our baby.

Our little girl.

"I fucked up," I manage to say, the emotions starting to choke me. "Christ, I fucked up."

They don't say anything for a few moments, the only sound is the road under the tires.

"Fox," Maverick says delicately. "You know you have a problem. You have more than a few. But you have to recognize them now and you have to face them. You have to face all of them. And we've got nothing but time on the drive back to North Ridge."

"Okay," I say. "Let's begin, then. Let's have it."

They start with the obvious.

Over the years I've been relying on alcohol more and more, to the point where it's obviously become a problem and interfering with my life. I mean, if you ever end up on a bender and in the drunk tank, that's a clear sign right there that casual drinking no longer applies to you, even if you think it does.

Then there are the pills. The pills that at some point helped me, gave me clarity, took away the pain inside and out. But those pills only work so well for so long. It's not long before you need more, before they don't even have an effect on you anymore.

And yet they do. They continue to harm. Your tolerance bends and then it breaks and you break with it. The cycle continues.

"You can't do this on your own," Shane says. "I know you do everything on your own, but you can't do this. We have to help you, be your support. You need professional help, rehab, a treatment center..."

My denial doesn't run that deep. "I know. I know. I'll go."

I'll go because if I'm going to be back in North Ridge, if I'm going to try again for another shot with Del, then I need to be the best man I can be, even if that man seems as foreign as a stranger.

"And counselling," Maverick adds.

I look at him in surprise. I'm not sold on this one. "Counselling? What for?"

They exchange a look with each other.

Maverick nods at Shane, then looks back to me in the mirror. "Because you're fucked up man, and you know it, and all the rehab in the world won't make a lick of difference unless you get to the root of *you*."

"You blame me for our mother's death," Shane says so matter-of-factly it actually hurts to hear it. "And I refuse to take the blame for it. Which means you need to deal with this, Fox. You need help dealing with every ugly thing you've been feeling and hiding and burying or one day it will eat you alive. I promise you that."

"I don't..." I try to say but I feel all the strength drain out of me. The energy needed to confront this demon inside me, to give it a voice, it's too much.

But still I try. "I don't blame you." My words are a weak whisper. "I don't blame you, Shane."

He turns around in his seat to face me and I see so much hurt in his eyes that it hits me all at once. What a terrible brother I've been to him our whole lives. He was just a baby when our mother killed herself. Our sad, depressed, sweet mother. She was ill, she had her own demons and she never knew to watch out for them and they killed her.

Shane was just a baby. I can see him now, in his crib, innocent. He was the surprise for my parents, he was the apple of everyone's eye, even my mother's, even though she was in so much pain, she loved him.

I loved him. I still do. I was his older brother and I shunned him because I couldn't deal with myself, because I hated myself and it kept going and going and going.

A tear escapes my eyes, my head feeling hot as a tidal wave of all that's been buried tries to surge up through me. I try and hold it back, hold it back and chain it until it gets unleashed as anger. That's what I've always done.

But I let it out, just enough.

A sob rips through me and I clamp my hand on Shane's shoulder, squeezing it. "I love you, brother," I manage to say, my words thick. "I'm sorry I haven't been there. I'm sorry I failed you. I'm sorry I turned on you. I'm sorry that I haven't known how to love anyone. I'm so, so sorry."

Shane's eyes well up. "It's okay," he says, putting his hand on top of mine and squeezing it right back. "It's okay, Fox. I get it. We all get it. We all understand, we've all been through it. We just…we want you to get well. We want you to get better. And the only way that will happen is by talking through it and realizing you need to love yourself. You've been hating yourself your whole fucking life, man, and it's been painful to see."

I close my eyes, another tear spilling down, and nod.

I've been in pain for so long.

I've caused pain for so long.

To me, to everyone I care about.

I don't want to do that anymore.

I don't want to be lost.

I don't want to be angry.

I don't want to blame myself.

I want to be free, to have peace, a future.

I want love.

I want all the love I have and all the love I don't have.

I want Del's love.

And I want to love her. I want to love the baby.

I want to love them enough to make up for all the love I've never let myself feel.

"This isn't going to be easy," Maverick says gently after what feels like an eternity of the three of us sitting in the truck and getting emotional. Definitely a first for us.

"I know," I tell him.

"But sometimes we have to reach rock bottom. Sometimes you have to know what that feels like in order to lift yourself up from it." He pauses. "But a revelation isn't enough. You need action."

"Okay…" I say uncertainly because it sounds like he's going somewhere with this.

"I don't think we should take you back to North Ridge," he says. "I think you need to go to a treatment center first."

"But Del," I protest. "I need to see her. She needs to know how sorry I am for leaving, for—"

"Fox," Shane interrupts me. "Del has been doing fine so far without you. Not the best, but fine. The only way you can actually be sorry in this situation is to take control now and do this. Come back to her sober, refreshed. Start again."

"He's right," Mav says. "I know it sounds like a bunch of hokey bullshit but that saying that you can't learn to love anyone until you learn to love yourself, well that's fucking right. You need to work on yourself and get through your issues, at least start, before you can be everything you need to be to her. You need to do some serious fucking soul-searching brother, the kind that hurts."

They're probably right but I don't like it. My whole being protests against it. I want to see Del now. "I can't miss anymore of her pregnancy," I tell them, realizing that I'm practically pleading now. "I've missed so much."

"You'll catch the most important part," Shane says. "All Del will know is that you're still working in Whistler. She doesn't expect you back for a bit anyway so we'll keep on pretending."

"You mean you didn't tell Del you had to come here to get me?"

"Nah," Mav says. "None of her business. This is just between the Nelson brothers."

I breathe out a loud sigh of relief. At least there's that. She still thinks I'm working, which sucks in its own way but at least she doesn't know what happened. She might not let me near her and the baby.

"I text and email her every now and then to check on her and the baby," I tell them.

"Then email from there."

I don't even talk about what I've been doing in Whistler and she doesn't ask. I ask her the questions and she answers and that's the extent of our relationship now.

Shit, it hurts. It fucking hurts that this is what we've become, what we've been reduced to. And it's all my fault.

No, I tell myself quickly. *The blame stops now. It has to stop now.*

I take in a deep breath. "Okay," I say to them. "I'll do it."

Maverick gives me a broad grin that lights up his whole face. "Good choice, brother. Otherwise we would have made you and that wouldn't have been pretty. Though I'm pretty sure Shane here more than deserves getting a few punches in. You've had it coming for a long fucking time."

I smile. It feels like the first time in months. Years. It feels like forever. "He can try but Shane punches like a toddler."

"Oh fuck you," Shane says, but he's laughing. "Next time we stop for gas, you're dead."

"Shit," Maverick says. "Now I have to figure out which one of you to bet on. The odds are better on this than the scratch ticket I was going to pick up."

"Yeah right, I'd obviously win," I tell him, punching him lightly in the shoulder. "Remember that time..."

And as I go on about the fights we've been in, the three of us in general, scrapping like brothers do, I realize how fucking lucky I am to have these guys on my team. They've always had my back, always been great brothers.

Time for me to return the favor.

I'm doing this for them.

I'm doing this for Del.

I'm doing this for me.

SPRING

20

DELILAH

"Open mine first!" Riley shrieks, picking up her present from the pile and shoving it into my hands.

"Okay, no more mimosas for Riley," Rachel says.

"No," I implore them. "Please drink more mimosas. I have to live vicariously through you all. Besides, it's my baby shower and my rules and I want you all as drunk as possible."

"On it," Vanessa says, getting up and walking over to the mimosa station we've set up on the bar. "Good thing this place is closed tonight."

Riley, Rachel, and the new (temporary) manager of The Bear Trap, Vanessa, decided to throw me a baby shower here. It's as good of a place as any and it's been done up with white streamers and balloons and the most adorable cake with a stork on it that Vernalee baked.

I've been craving cake during this pregnancy like nothing else and honestly I just want to bury my face in it. It's over on the counter, taunting me, and I've already had three pieces.

It's not a large party—just Rachel, Riley, Vanessa, my mother, Vernalee and a couple of ladies I'm friendly with who frequent the bar, plus a few people I knew back in high school. That's the thing about staying in a small town and running a bar, you might not have a lot of close friends but you have a lot of acquaintances.

And it's nice, actually. It's not about the gifts, though the giant stack of them on the pool table will go a long way. It's about the sense of community. It's about having people around you that care about you, that have your back and give you cake.

It's funny, growing up, I always felt like an outsider. I think that's why I attached myself to Fox, because he felt like one too. I was shy and tended to throw myself into solo sports like track and field and swimming. Though my mother was my rock, I was still conscious of not having a father, thought it set me apart from everyone else and all the happy families you'd see.

I assumed that would change as I got older. I thought having run this bar for so damn long would have made me feel part of something and for the most part that was true. But it wasn't until I got pregnant that I really felt like people were there for me. That I wasn't alone, even though my heart was alone. I've learned to rely on people in ways I never let myself before, and honestly…it feels good.

"Open it," Riley says, slapping my knee.

"Hey, no hitting the pregnant lady," I joke. "You never know when this thing might pop." I rub my stomach appreciatively.

"When is your due date again?" one of my old friends, Susan, asks me.

"Supposed to be May 19th," I tell her. "But I mean how accurate is that really?"

"Another six weeks and your little girl will be out here in the world," Rachel says softly. I catch a bit of sadness in her eyes. I know she's happy for me but she and Shane are still trying and they aren't having the best luck. I think it's putting a lot of added stress on her.

I wish I could tell her to not worry, that things will get a lot more stressful when she finally gets pregnant, but I know how much it means to her. Sometimes I feel bad that I'm the one who got pregnant while on the pill and completely by accident, while she's actually trying. She has a husband, they're so in love and yet it happens to me.

I don't have anyone.

Fox is still in Whistler, working, and his emails between us have stopped. He still checks in via text every now and then to ask about the baby and how I'm doing but that's about it. It's already April, and I know that he'll be back soon, but he hasn't even said when and I've been too afraid to ask.

I've gone on the best way that I can.

It gets easier in a way, because I have so much love around me and so much to worry about and focus on.

But at night, at night the tears come.

He's the reason I can't sleep.

Everyone tells me it's the pregnancy. They tell me that it's my hormones and the discomfort and the anxiety of a baby coming. And while I don't doubt all of those have some part in it, I know in my soul that it's because of Fox.

He took a big part of my heart with him when he left.

And each day that passes I'm afraid I'll never get that part of my heart back.

It will be his forever.

Even if he doesn't want it.

Like a gift you're not sure what to do with. Do you throw it away, give it to someone else, or bury it deep in the back of the closet, to only notice it every now and then with a vague sense of sentiment.

"Get all the sleep you can," Vernalee pipes up, as if she

hears my thoughts. "This is your last chance before the baby is born."

"Well, I'm still not sleeping well," I tell her. "Though I'm definitely done nesting. I'm too tired to do anything. But hey, at least I can breathe easier now. The baby seems to have shifted lower, felt like she was all up in my ribs for a while there."

"Open. My. Present."

I roll my eyes even though I'm smiling at Riley's impatience. It takes a bit to unwrap it since she's done a good job, must be all those tourniquets she does for work, and my hands are swollen as hell, but eventually I pull out a tiny black onesie for the baby that says "My blonde aunt is the sexiest."

I burst out laughing. "Are you serious? Where did you get this?"

"Oh you can find anything online," she says. "Do you promise she'll wear it?"

"Of course."

"Hey," Rachel chides her. "What about her brunette aunt?"

Riley shrugs and has a sip of her mimosa. "Not my fault you didn't think of it."

When the baby shower is over, I'm exhausted. In fact, I left the party first so that the rest of them could continue drinking in the bar and living it up like I can't. I just want a nap, stat.

My mother drives me home and then, after she makes me a cup of tea and I lie down on the couch, she leaves to go back for the presents and some of Vernalee's enchiladas. I'm not much help in the kitchen anymore, though I try, and because of my mother's arthritis, some days she can't do it either, so Vernalee and the gang have been stepping in and making us meals most nights of the week.

Sleep finds me fast and I easily succumb, until a loud knocking sound, someone at the door, rouses me.

Ugh. My head is sticky inside, like my brain is full of mushed wet cotton balls. I'm over the forgetful pregnant lady phase (or the "preggo dumbs" as Riley calls it) thank god, but now I'm just plain out of it.

It's getting dark out too and I'm wondering where my mother is. Maybe she locked herself out, though we rarely lock our doors here to begin with. I slowly get to my feet and head to the front door.

I open it and a gasp freezes in my throat.

It's Fox.

It's Fox standing in front of me, in the flesh, completely real though this feels like a dream.

And he looks…

Incredible.

Not just in the way I thought he would, the way he always did when I hadn't seen him for a while. He looks incredible as in he looks like someone totally new.

The dark circles that were always etched under his eyes are gone.

His skin looks soft and vibrant.

There's a clarity in his eyes that make them even more green, a clarity that seems to look right into my soul, see what's in there, see me for all that I am.

"Fox," I say, breathless.

He blinks at me, then down at my stomach. "Holy shit."

When he left me I was barely showing at all, I just looked bloated. Now though, now I'm as big as a house, my stomach large and in charge.

"I know," I say, unable to keep the smirk off my lips. I rub my stomach. "It's like I'm having a baby or something."

He shakes his head in awe, runs his hand over his jaw. "I can't believe this."

"I can," I tell him. Fuck, suddenly I'm nervous. "I can't believe you're here."

"I wanted it to be a surprise," he says.

"It worked. I'm very surprised."

"Can I…can I come in?" And it turns out he's nervous too.

"Of course." I open the door wider.

He brushes past me into the house and I catch that scent of his, the hint of pine and soap clinging to his skin. It makes my stomach do flips, something unrelated to the baby, something I haven't felt in such a long time.

He still has this power to set my soul on fire.

"Del," he says again in that incredulous tone, looking me up and down as I close the door. "You look…you look…so fucking beautiful." His voice starts to quiver as he says that and I watch him, my eyes wide, as he tries to find the right words. "You just… you're the most beautiful sight I've ever seen."

He takes a step toward me, holding out his hands toward my stomach like a peace offering. "Can I touch her?"

I swallow hard, my emotions quick to rise up. "Yes. You're her father, Fox."

The word father seems to take extra gravity in his eyes, like it's dawning on him for the first time how real this.

How fucking *complicated* this is.

He puts his hands on my stomach, so softly, so gently, it's like he's handling a ball made of glass.

Just then, she kicks.

I giggle as Fox recoils in a mix of fear and absolute wonder. "Fuck. Did you feel that?" he cries out, mouth dropped open.

"Yes I felt that," I tell him, then I take his hands and I hold them against my stomach. "She does it a lot. In fact, I'm supposed to time the kicks but I'm not very good at remembering to do that."

"Why would you time them?" he asks, still staring down in fascination. I'm not sure I've ever seen him look so enthralled. There's this bizarre sense of power coming over me, mixed with tenderness. It's the same feeling I get during sex with him, that I'm able to bring these emotions and feelings out of him, that it's all on me.

In this case, I created this baby. Yes, he obviously had a lot to do with it, but it's different for the woman. I'm carrying it, creating it. I have a life inside me, a part of him mixed with a part of me.

"It's a way of making sure the baby is developing right but so far she's healthy in every way." I pause. "I do have high blood pressure which isn't good and my hands and feet are so swollen it's disgusting. So I guess there are some minor problems. But other than that, I mean, the baby is fine."

Fox looks at me through his lashes and I'm caught off-guard by the need in his eyes, this soft yearning that makes something ache deep inside me.

He quickly leans in and kisses me.

Sweetly.

Softly.

Just a brush of his lips against mine.

I think my heart might break free of my ribs.

I think my body might burst into flames.

The taste of him, the feel of him, this intimacy, the fact that he's still holding onto my pregnant belly...

It's too much.

I break it off and gasp. "What are you doing, Fox?"

Shame flits across his gaze. "I'm sorry. I just...I've missed you so much. You have no idea what this has been like."

I clear my throat. "I think I might," I whisper.

"I just want..." he starts to say and then takes his hands off of me, stepping back. "I just want us to find each other again."

God, I do too.

But I've been right here all this time.

"You barely contacted me, Fox," I remind him, trying to keep the emotion out of my voice, out of my body. It can't be good for the baby. "You've been too busy to even remember that I was here, that we were here. You *left us*."

He closes his eyes, pinches the bridge of his nose. "I was out of my mind."

"I don't care what your excuse is. You can't just waltz back here and expect things to go back to normal. Fuck, there is no normal for us. There never was. We were friends and there was no baby and then we were just fuck buddies and now we're this and I have no idea what this is."

"We could have been a family," he says stiffly.

"No, not the way you wanted," I tell him. "I know you thought you were doing the right thing by asking me to marry you but you have to understand why I had to say no. I didn't want our daughter to be brought up in a loveless marriage."

He glances at me sharply. "No. It wouldn't have been loveless."

"You know what I mean."

"And you don't know what I mean. Del, I've been away and I've made some terrible mistakes and I'll never forgive myself for leaving, for missing so much of you and the baby. But I've been doing everything I can to make it right."

I scoff, going around him toward the kitchen to get some water. All this is making me thirsty and the baby is kicking again. I know she can hear voices now, I know she's listening. Maybe she's picking up on Fox's. Maybe the last thing she wants to hear is me arguing with a stranger.

"By doing everything, you mean waiting until fucking April to come back home and see us," I tell him, pulling a glass from the shelf. "Jesus, Fox. You could have visited if you really cared that much."

"I know," he says, right behind me. "I know. I fucked up. You have no idea. Or maybe you do because you've been watching me fuck up my entire life."

"Don't start…"

"Del, I hit rock bottom out there. I ended up in jail."

Fucking hell. "What are you talking about? Jail? What happened?"

"I went on a bender. Drank, took too many pills, left myself to die out there in a snowbank."

Oh my god. I nearly drop the glass of water and have to put it down with shaking hands. I knew Fox was getting bad, I knew I saw signs of this but there was so much going on, I turned a blind eye. He was always so quick to shut you down and at the same time he was so bold in all he did. I wanted him to be okay, to have a handle on it.

I guess I was wrong.

"Fox," I whisper. "That's awful."

He shrugs. "I did it to myself. It was the bed I chose to lie in. And who knows how long I would have lain in it, accepted it as my life, my punishment. Then Shane and Maverick showed up to get me."

"What? They did? That's like a ten-hour drive!"

"They did. They saved me from myself Del. Just for a moment though, I had to do the rest myself. So I went into rehab, then a treatment center. Just got out a week ago."

"Oh my god," I explain. I can't believe it. "They didn't even say anything to me."

"My brothers can keep secrets. Sometimes," he says. "It was also their idea. They didn't want to tell you in case it didn't work, in case I didn't stay. But I did. And it will stay. I've started going to counselling and everything, working on myself, on my past. On my mother. On you. The baby. Found a good doctor over in Castlegar that I'll see once a week."

This is incredible news. I can hardly process it. Fox never asked for help once in his life, either from thinking he didn't need it or thinking he did but was too proud to admit it. This changes so much. So much.

And yet, between us, between my heart and his, it changes nothing at all.

"Look," he says, grabbing my hand and holding it tight. The warmth of his palm gives me temporary comfort. "I don't expect you to welcome me back with open arms. But I'm still the boy you knew Del, the one you had faith in, even if I didn't believe he existed. And this is just the first step to making myself a better man. This is just the first step toward a better life. Delilah, I've been thinking about you non-stop, I've been realizing so many things…how I really feel."

"Please, don't," I tell him, closing my eyes. "I can't…"

"Can't what?" he asks. "Can't believe what I have to say? You're everything I've been looking my whole life for and you've been right in front of me all this time. My heart, my everything, it belongs solely to you."

I shake my head slightly, my chest pinching. "But do you love me?"

He reaches out and smooths a strand of hair off my face, his fingers trailing over my cheekbones, down to my lips, my skin dancing under the touch of his. My eyes open to meet his and I see the honesty in them, the want, the need. His need to love me.

"I will. I promise you I will." He clears his throat and when he speaks his voice is choked with emotion. "I'm falling in love with you," he whispers. "A little bit more each day. It's spreading, like fire. Like wildfire. I can feel it ignite every part of me, from the deepest corners of my heart to the lost places in my soul. It will eventually consume me and I want to be consumed, Del. I want to love you, burn for you, until there's nothing else left. Just your heart and mine."

I blink away tears. I feel the intensity come off of him like heat. He burns for me and I burn for him. My fire rages and roars and his is just kindling, but it's happening all the same.

But things don't happen overnight.

It will take time for Fox to figure out if he loves me or not.

It will take time for Fox to love himself.

It will take time for me to believe him.

I think that's the biggest obstacle of all.

He kisses me again, this time on the forehead. "I'm going to go now."

"Where?" I ask.

He rests his hand on my stomach and bends down to kiss my belly and, god, I might just start crying again. I'm melting with love.

"To the ranch. Say hello. Tell my dad and grandpa that I'm back, telling them what happened. Ask for their support."

"Okay," I whisper, my throat closing up. "Anytime you want to come over…"

"Just text me," he says. "Or I'll text you. I've got a lot of catching up to do."

And then he turns and heads down the hallway.

We do have a lot of catching up to do.

I'm just not sure where we stand.

And where we're headed.

* * *

FOX DOESN'T STAY for long.

I get a call from him a week later telling me he has been called out to a fire. It's a bad one and they need all the hot shots they can get. It's broken out just outside the city of

Penticton. It's not normal to get fires this time of year but with an early spring and very little rain, the interior of BC is dry as hell.

The fire originated in a barn on the outskirts of town, probably from a cow kicking over a lamp into a bunch of hay or something like that, but it's raging out of control now and threatening a bunch of subdivisions, so of course Fox and the North Ridge Hot Shots are the first team to be sent out.

Of course, I don't want him to go.

Not even a little.

The stress I used to feel when he was gone fighting fires is even worse now that I'm so close to my due date. In a way, it was better when I thought he was in Whistler, when I thought he didn't care. Now he's here and I know he cares.

He cares a lot.

In the last week I've seen him a handful of times and he even came with me to my prenatal screening the other day. My doctor certainly didn't expect to see him, but luckily he was welcoming, albeit a bit condescending at times. Fox took it all in stride, eager to learn everything.

We're still in this state of limbo. We're not physical with each other. There's a distance that I'm not sure how to close. I know what I want and need from him and it's a waiting game, waiting to see if he's falling in love or just trying to. The act of loving someone should be effortless. It's not a push off into the unknown, it's a surrendering.

I surrendered to Fox a long time ago.

Time will tell if he'll ever surrender to me.

I try not to think about it.

It's pretty fucking hard when he's the father of your baby.

And still, I tell Fox not to go.

I tell him that I need him. Now that he's back, I want to keep him here. We're getting so close to the due date, I'm frightened that if he steps out now that I'll lose him forever.

I'm afraid that those flames will try and claim him after being lost to the ice and snow for so long.

I'm afraid that this is what happens on the tail of an epiphany. That life is that much of a sneaky bitch that the moment you realize you need to start it over, that it's going to be taken away from you.

I know I'm paranoid. I can blame the pregnancy for that.

But Fox can't stay, he won't stay.

I tell him that it's going to be hard in the future when he's gone all the time, when I have to worry all the time.

And he tells me that he knows.

But still, it's his job, it's his role, his identity.

The hero with a broken soul.

So he goes.

And I stay behind and wait.

I'm extra tired these days, as if that's even possible. Not only is my body preparing for this baby to be born, but on top of it, now I'm worrying about Fox. Anxiety has me upside down.

"You look a little green," Shane says to me, pulling back the sheet of foil paper to glance at the dish Vernalee cooked up. "So does this." Enchiladas with verde sauce for dinner. Again. I don't even like it, but the baby does. Can't get enough of that. Or cake. Sometimes both mashed together.

"I'm feeling a bit off to be honest," I tell him. "Thanks for bringing these, by the way."

My mother is having an off-day too, so the two of us are kind of hostage in the house today. Thankfully Shane and Rachel were able to drop off the food, plus Rachel brought more of that tea I'm addicted to. I can't seem to drink enough liquids and yet my body is retaining water like crazy.

"You're stressing too much," Rachel says, taking me by the arm and leading me over to the couch. "You need to rest. I'll make you some tea."

"How can I not stress," I say to them. "What if Fox doesn't come back?"

"He always does," Shane says. "He's the best at what he does and he's sharper now than ever."

"What if...what if he does come back but the stress of the job catches up with him again and causes him to relapse?"

Shane nods, rubbing his lips together anxiously. "I'd be lying if I said that wasn't something I thought about. But we have to let him do what he does. This is a part of his life."

"Though honestly, I think he should quit," Rachel says simply. Shane and I look at her in surprise. "Just being honest. This isn't the kind of job a new dad should have."

"But it's his livelihood," Shane says. "It's like me quitting the ranch."

"I know. I'm not saying it would be easy. I just think he should. Del and the baby need him around."

"Well," I say slowly. "I did do pretty well without him."

Shane gives me a sharp look. "You'll do better with him."

Ever since the two of them made amends, I've been noticing Shane's become more defensive of Fox and visa versa.

"He left me, Shane. He left us. Because I wouldn't marry him and he didn't love me. I know he's trying and everything and it's working but that sort of mark doesn't just heal overnight. It's going to take some time. To figure out how we work, to trust him."

"Why don't you trust him?" Rachel says quietly.

"Because I don't know if he can trust himself yet," I tell them. I sigh and then have trouble inhaling, my lungs feeling tighter. I shake it off. "I know I'm being silly..."

"You're not silly. You're just trying to protect yourself and the baby," Rachel says, patting my leg. "Your tea is getting cold, I'll go make you another."

"No, it's…" I trail off. Now it's even harder to breathe than the second before.

"What's wrong?" she says, and I look at her and I can't seem to focus. I look at Shane and it's the same thing. My vision is starting to blur.

"What is it?" Shane asks, leaning in closer, hand on my shoulder. "Del, are you okay?"

"My eyes," I tell them. "I can't…I can't focus. Everything is blurry."

"Just breathe, just relax," Rachel says, sounding calm. "You're under a lot of stress and you know your blood pressure is—"

"Fuck," I cry out as a stab of pain hits my stomach. It's like it's being carved right open. "My stomach."

"Okay, okay," Rachel says soothingly, but now her voice is shaking. "Is this Braxton Hicks? Is this the thing you had before?"

I shake my head. I can barely speak. I can barely breathe. I can barely see.

"Go…get my mother," I manage to say before I double over and roll onto my side on the couch.

Rachel gets up to run off just as I hear Shane say, "Oh shit."

"What?" I croak, trying to see what he's talking about.

"Del, you're bleeding."

"Oh my god," Rachel exclaims. "Fuck. That's not good, is it? That's not normal?"

"Miss Gordon!" Shane yells. "Jeanine. Wake up! Del is sick!"

"I'll go get her," Rachel says.

I can't respond to any of it, I can only close my eyes as I'm hit with a wave of nausea and pain, like the most powerful cramps I've ever had. I cry out, loud, my fingers curling around the couch cushions holding on as tight as I can.

"Are you in labor?" Shane asks me but I can't even breathe the words. My lungs are getting tighter and tighter. "Del, look at me."

I open my eyes and look at him, but his face is just a blur. Then I see the shape of Rachel's face, then my mother's right behind them.

"Delilah," my mother says. "Can you hear me? Where does it hurt?"

I only gasp as their forms seem to get further and further away. My lower back screams with a pain that I think I'm probably screaming too and then a black pressure closes in around my vision.

"Call 911," my mother barks at Shane. "Now!"

I feel her hand around mine. "You're going to be okay Del, just stay with me, okay? You're going into labor but you'll be fine. Just breathe."

But I can't breathe.

I can't breathe.

And this can't be labor.

This feels like death.

Death for me.

Death for the baby.

The last thing I feel is a sticky warmth gush between my legs, like life is being drained out of me.

Rachel cries out.

And then the blackness takes me under.

No more pain.

No more anything.

21

FOX

"So how is the missus?" Davis asks me as the truck bounces along the old logging road, heading to the station. The air is thick with acrid smoke, a sign that the fire is burning hot and quick and to everyone else this is just another day on the job, hence why they're catching up on the gossip they've missed over the winter.

It's not just another day on the job though. None of us expected to be called out in the middle of April to a fire for one thing and for me especially, this is the first time I've been out on the job knowing that I have a soon-to-be-born baby at home.

I'm not sure I like it. There's too much at stake now. Before it was just my life I had to think of and I didn't think much of it. Now I have to think about Del and the baby. Now I want to. I left them once, I don't want to do that again.

But duty calls.

"You okay, Foxy?" Davis asks, elbowing me in the side.

Normally I glare at that nickname but today I can't be bothered. "I'm fine," I tell him. "And she's not my missus."

"Oh. Shit man. I thought you were engaged."

"No," I say, staring down at my hands. "Not engaged. I proposed but she said no."

"Fuck," Simon, the other guy in the truck, says. "That's rough."

I nod. "She had her reasons."

"Like what? Isn't she pregnant with your child?" Simon asks.

Now I'm glaring. I don't appreciate the callous tone. "She is."

"Then what happened?" Davis asks.

I shrug and sigh, staring out the window at the fresh green leaves on the trees. Hard to believe anything is burning right now. "I asked her to marry me. She said no. She said she was in love with me. She asked if I was in love with her. And I told her the truth. I said no."

"She needs to get with the times," Simon says. "Half the marriages out there are loveless. My parents are a great example of that."

"Yeah and look how you turned out," Davis says dryly.

"Delilah has never been a girl to settle," I tell them. "She tried that once with someone, didn't work. She even tried that with me. Now she wants the world and I'm going to do whatever I can to give her that world."

"But you don't love her," Simon points out.

I give him a twisted smile. "The funny thing is, man, I think I always did. I just didn't know what it was. I think I know now."

"And what's love feel like to you?" Davis asks with complete sincerity, despite being dressed in our fire fighting gear, helmet in his hands.

When you're part of a team like this for so long, you grow close. I might be more closed-off than the others, I might not contribute much in way of my feelings, but there's an honesty and comradery that you don't get anywhere else.

They're as much my brothers as Shane and Maverick are, even if they don't know it. That's why losing Roy was so hard.

And that's why I don't shy away from telling them the truth, even over something as sentimental and vulnerable as love.

"Love is like everything I've ever lost has come back to me," I tell them.

They both stare at me for a moment, nodding. They get it. Both of them are married. They have babies too. They've been there.

For me, it's the first time.

But it's one hundred per cent real.

Now that I know what it feels like.

It feels like coming home.

It feels like creating a home.

Somewhere deep in Delilah's immeasurable heart, that's where I'll keep living.

* * *

THE FIRE TURNS out to be a fucking monster.

Our team responded to it pretty much right away and the local stations in Penticton and Kelowna were already fighting it, but even so, it's been growing and growing, and there hasn't been much we've been able to do to stop it.

Despite it being spring, with some trees and plants still budding, the fire is hot as hell, coaxed by a heat wave this week, a dry winter with very little snow, plus a solid month without any rain.

The fact that the fire started near town doesn't help either, the flames jumping from ponderosa pine to ponderosa pine instead of running along the ground. Normally, at least in the past, at least twenty-years ago when this subdivision wasn't here by the forests and fields, we would have let it run its course. When you bring homes into the question, that's when things get complicated. Instead of fire being a natural process of renewal of the land, it becomes something that must be snuffed out at all costs, and some of those costs are the lives of the hot shots like Roy.

So here we are trying to make the decisions based on the homes we can save. Everyone in the subdivision in question and the neighboring surrounds have been evacuated so their lives aren't at risk but their properties and possessions are.

And I understand. It would be horrible to lose your home. We had a fire at the ranch last year thanks to a lightning strike and it nearly burned both Vernalee and Shane alive. But it was their lives that were important. The house was just a thing. A thing we missed since it was used as the worker's cottage, but a thing nonetheless.

Maybe it's because I've found a home in Delilah that I've realized that a home isn't found in a building and so those buildings aren't always worth trying to risk your life for.

Maybe I've just become disillusioned with my job after this winter, after the counselling, the rehab, after losing Roy.

Maybe it's because I have Del and the baby waiting for me in North Ridge and I'm spending each minute more worried about them and how they're doing than saving some rich dude's home.

Whichever way you spin it, I'm fighting a monster and though I will do all I can to tame this beast, I'm starting to wonder if this might be a turning point for me.

Of course, that thought itself is scarier than anything else.

If I'm not a hot shot, a fire fighter, then what am I?

A father, the word shoots through my brain like an arrow. *A father, a lover. Maybe someday a husband. You're Fox Nelson, that's who you are. One hundred per cent.*

"Fox, we need help at the back burn," Mad Dog runs up to

me, breathless, face black with soot. Night is starting to fall but you wouldn't be able to tell with how thick the smoke is. "The fireline won't hold, the flames are a ladder, jumping from tree to tree and that first house at the end of the cul-de-sac has a line of fir along the back of the property."

I nod and pick up my Pulaski axe and drip-torch and follow Mad Dog, away from the fireline we've all been frantically digging, down the hill toward the houses, jogging all the way, breathing in smoke and fumes.

With a few of my crew as well as some members of the local fire station, we start digging a new line around the house, this one thick and wide, with plans to start burning down the firs on their property. If they burn first, controlled, they might stop the fire from reaching the house.

The only problem is, this fire is hot and getting hotter and completely unpredictable. With the wind picking up, the embers could be thrown in any direction. What happened with Roy is fresh on my mind.

"I don't think we have enough people," I gasp, as I pull down my mask to talk to Mad Dog who is right beside me, getting the drip-torch ready. "We need back up."

He nods grimly. "Go tell the chief over there by the garage."

I jog over around the house to the garage where a small outpost has been set up. I see the fire chief as well as some of his crew, plus some medics on hand. Beyond them is police tape and news crews filming the action.

I wait for the chief to stop talking before I say. "Mad Dog from NRHS says we need more men."

"All right," he says, giving a curt nod to the crew he was standing with who scamper off. "What's your name?"

"Nelson. Fox Nelson," I tell him.

"You look like you need a drink," he says, reaching into the cooler beside him and pulling out a bottle of water from the ice. "Hydrate yourself or else you're no good to anyone out there."

I nod and take the water, my heart racing all over the place, adrenaline fueling my cells.

"Take a moment," he goes on as I drink the water down. "Rest. Clear your head. Then get back out there."

And at that, he grabs an axe, slips on his mask, and goes around the corner to join everyone else.

I take my phone out of my pocket to glance at the time, not expecting to see a million missed calls and texts. I'm so used to fighting fires where there's no reception, the sight is jarring. And frightening.

I bring the phone close to my eyes and squint at it. I can't scroll with my big gloved hand but what I see on the lock screen strikes terror in my very soul.

Text from Shane: **You need to come back Del is in the hospital it's serious**

Text from Maverick: **I know ur out there in the fires but pls come back ASAP**

Text from Rachel: **Del went into early labor, there's a complication with the baby, she needs you, do what you can to leave**

I can't breathe at all now and it's got nothing to do with the smoke.

Panic floods me as I rip off my glove and start scrolling through the messages, aware that there's a fire raging at my back and not caring.

I can barely read them but I understand them.

That this isn't good.

I call Maverick and my phone gets put to voice mail.

I call Shane and it just rings. He doesn't even have voice mail.

I call Rachel and she picks up on the fourth ring.

"Fox!" she cries out. "Oh, thank god you got this."

"What's happening? Is she okay?"

"No, she's not okay," she says tearfully. "She was in labor, they're doing what they can. It's called preeclampsia, it has something to do with her blood pressure."

"The baby? How is the baby?"

The seconds between my asking that question and Rachel answering are scarier than that fire behind me burning me to the ground.

Rachel sobs. "I don't know, I don't know. Del lost a lot of blood, the baby is going to be premature and normally that's not too dangerous but with this thing, I don't know. I don't know, we're all freaking out and the doctors are working on her."

"Okay, I'm coming back now, okay? I'm leaving right now."

"Okay. Please hurry Fox. I don't know what's happening. You need to be here for them. Just get here as quick as you can."

I hang up.

And now I have to make the biggest decision of my life.

Choosing one love over another.

This fire, this job, my hot shots.

Over Del and the baby.

Maybe once it would have been a tough choice to make.

It's not a tough choice anymore.

I'm about to head over to the fireline to tell Mad Dog but I don't want to distract him, not now when so much is at stake, so I see Davis and pull him aside.

"Hey man," I'm practically yelling over the roar of the flames. "I have to go."

"Go?" he says. "Where?"

"North Ridge. Del is in the hospital. Something's really wrong."

"Oh shit. Sorry man. Yeah go, I got your back."

I glance at the fire and I swear the flames are waving at me goodbye. "We need more crew. I'm going to be needed here."

"I know," he says. "But you're needed more out there. We will be fine."

"I could get fired."

"You could. But you know what you're doing, don't you Foxy?"

I give him a shaky grin. "You're a good man Davis. I hope you remember I said that when I steal the truck and you don't have a ride home after this."

Before I can wait for his reaction, I turn and run toward the truck, away from the flames.

22

DELILAH

P<small>AIN</small>.

I know nothing but pain.

Pain is a mistress and my master and my world seems to be condensed to a black space with a chair that I'm chained to and there's no escape. There's only pain.

Pain and crying.

Somewhere beyond the black space there is crying.

A baby's cry.

My baby.

I gasp, trying to scream. "My baby, please don't hurt my baby!"

Then there is silence.

Hands on me.

"She's not responsive," someone says.

"Delilah? Delilah listen to me. You have to push."

I find words in my mouth and they spill out into the darkness. "No. It's too early."

"Delilah, you have to deliver your baby now, do you understand? You need to push, okay?"

"She needs more time."

"She has a better chance out here than in your womb. Push now, push."

I try.

I scream.

The pain takes over.

I'm yelling words that make no sense. They're rushing out of me on red rivers of pain.

Someone yells, "She's hemorrhaging! We need a transfusion!"

I wonder who they're talking about.

I hope she's okay, whoever she is.

Then it all goes back to black.

* * *

WHITE WALLS.

I was in a black, black world, cold and wet and fathomless. A place where things go to die, swallowed by the dark.

I lived in that world. I became that world.

And now I'm here.

I don't know where I am.

White walls.

I blink slowly, willing them into focus.

There are machines around me, also white, maybe cream. Lights. Beeping. The sound is comforting.

I close my eyes.

"She was awake a moment ago," someone says, a familiar voice. Excited. Worried.

My mother.

It's my mother's voice.

Why is she here in this place with the white walls?

"Delilah," she says. I feel familiar skin against mine. Warm. Soft. "Del, it's your mommy here. Can you hear me?"

I can hear her.

I try to tell her that.

But there's too much peace pulling me back down.

I surrender to it.

* * *

I HAVE a dream about a little girl.

Beautiful green eyes.

Blonde hair that shines like the sun.

The girl is my daughter.

We walk along the river bank and she holds my hand and squeezes it and she says to me, "I miss you, mommy. I miss you and daddy. I wish we had time together."

I say to her, "We have all the time in the world, little one. Just you and me."

"But where's daddy?"

My heart swells with sadness. "I don't know, little one. But I know he loves you very, very much."

"I wish we had more time together," she says again.

"But I'm right here, sweetheart." I crouch down at her level and smooth the hair from her face. "I haven't gone anywhere."

"But you're not here," she says and then she gestures to the river. It becomes a golden shimmering thread. "And I'm over there."

I frown. "Where?"

"Where I've always been," she says.

She lets go of my hand suddenly and runs for the river, her shoes kicking up tiny pebbles from the river bank that shine like glass.

"No!" I yell, but I'm unable to move or go after her.

She reaches the river and dives in.

The water absorbs her for a moment.

In that moment everything around me stills, even the flowing water.

She's gone.

She's gone.

She's…

She reappears on the other side, waving at me, translucent and shimmering like a mirage.

"This is where I've always been," she shouts across the water. "And one day you'll be here too."

Then everything on that side of the river starts to dissolve, fading into gold.

She's gone.

She's dead.

She never even had a chance to live.

I sit straight up and cough, still worried I'm in the dream, unable to scream what I need to scream.

Which is that my daughter is dead.

I gave birth to her and she died.

I almost died.

I should have died with her.

"Delilah."

I hear voices but I can't see them. I just see unfamiliar faces staring at me, their features blurred like masks, I can't make out who they are, who is talking.

I'm in a room somewhere, the white walls have returned.

I cry out, my throat garbling the words.

"My daughter."

"It's okay, you're okay," someone says and they take my hand and squeeze it.

"No, no my daughter. Oh please, she's gone. She's gone."

"She's confused, give her some space and time to make sense of it," says someone else in a strange accent.

The person holding my hand says, "You almost died, Del

sweetheart. You lost a lot of blood. You were white as a sheet, they had to give you a blood transfusion."

"My daughter," I croak. "What happened to my daughter?"

"She was delivered premature," the unfamiliar voice says. "You gave birth to her; do you remember that? She's in the intensive care unit now."

"My daughter," I gasp again, tears springing to my eyes. "My baby."

Oh god, my poor baby.

"Shhh," my mother says.

My mother.

My mother is here.

My eyes finally see her for who she is.

My mother, staring at me with watering eyes, holding onto my hand as tight as she's able to. "There's no need to worry," she says gently. "She's in good hands and she's strong. She's a fighter, just like you."

"Can I see her?" says a strong male voice from across the room. I look up to see Fox standing by the door. Fox is here. Fox. I'm in a hospital bed and Fox is here.

"She needs rest but yes, if you're quick," the voice says and in my woozy state my head lolls to the side to see a nurse with bleached blonde hair.

The nurse and my mother leave.

Fox approaches me quietly, moving like his feet aren't touching the ground. Like he's in a dream.

Is this a dream still?

"No," he says and I must have wondered it out loud. "This isn't a dream, Del. You're alive. You're awake. You're here with me."

I stare at him, taking him all in.

"You're here," I whisper.

He nods, grabbing my hand and holding it tight, his jaw muscle twitching. "I came as soon as I heard what happened."

"You were fighting a fire."

"I left the fire."

"They'll fire you."

He gives me a sad smile. "That was a pretty good pun, considering you just gained consciousness."

I lick my lips; my mouth is so dry. "Can I get some water?"

He reaches over and grabs a cup of ice off the stand beside me. "I think you can have ice chips," he says. He nods his head at all the IVs and tubes and drips going into me. "You're being taken care of otherwise."

"Have you seen her?" I whisper, because I'm afraid that everyone else was lying to me to make me feel better. "Have you seen our daughter?"

Another smile, soft and sweet. "I have. Through the glass. She's in one of those incubator things. Has your nose. I bet she has your smile too. She's going to be a heartbreaker, just like you."

I'd laugh if I wasn't so weak. "Heartbreaker. Right."

His features fall. Clears his throat. "Del, I didn't...I don't..."

I don't know what he's trying to say but right now, here, I can barely keep my head up. "Whatever you're saying, it's okay. You're here now. I can't believe you did that. You left in the middle of a fire."

He pulls up a chair right beside me and sits down, his elbows on the edge of the bed, still holding onto my hands. "There was never any doubt. I knew what I was doing. I was an idiot for leaving you in the first place. I knew it was a mistake to go."

"But it's your job," I say weakly.

"*Was* my job, probably."

"It was everything to you."

"No," he says, voice choking up, eyes going red. "You're

everything to me. There was no questioning what I would do. Del, I don't want to be brave for anyone else anymore. I only want to be brave for you."

Something inside me melts.

My heart, I think.

I still love this man.

I love him with a fierceness that burns even when the rest of me is lying here two shades away from death. I love him with an energy I've barely been able to contain.

"I'll never leave your side again," he says, kissing my hands over and over. "Not you, not the baby. I'm with the two of you forever, if only you'll have me in your life again." The last kiss he places on the back of my hand is a long one, a firm one, and his eyes stare at me with so much intensity I feel like I'm being healed from the inside out. "Take me back. Let me love you. Because I'm in love with you."

For the first time in my life, Fox is telling me he's in love with me.

And I believe him.

More than that, I need him with every labored breath and weakened cell in my body. I need him like I've always needed him, the way we seek out the pulse of another in the dark.

"I love you," I whisper back.

"I know," he says and grins at me.

I laugh. Trying to do a Han Solo impression always puts a smile on my face, even when it hurts.

"You really need to let her rest," the nurse says as she pops her head in the door.

"When can I see the baby?" I ask her, trying to sit up straighter.

"When you get some rest," she says.

"Okay," Fox says as he gets to his feet.

"Please don't go," I ask him.

"But you want to see her, don't you?" He shakes his head

as he stares down at me. "God, you're incredible. Do you know that? You almost died there and you were still able to give birth. You gave our daughter a fighting chance. I'll forever be in awe of you Del."

"Our daughter," I repeat. "We have to give her a name."

"Whatever you'd like," he says but I can tell he has something specific in mind.

"What about Emily?" His mother's name.

"Are you sure?" he asks.

I try to nod but end up yawning instead, my head feeling too heavy to keep up. "Yes. Emily. It's perfect."

"She's perfect," he says. "Just like you."

Then he leans over and kisses me on the forehead and I'm whisked off to a most blissful sleep.

23

DELILAH

"Good morning Delilah," the nurse Irene, my favorite nurse because of her lilting Swedish accent, says to me as she brings Emily bundled up in her arms. "Do you know what day it is?"

"Saturday," I say, my heart beginning to bloom at the sight of Emily.

"Oh, I'm going to miss you Delilah," she says as I sit up and she places Emily in my arms. "You have an answer for everything."

"I try," I say. "Hello little muffin," I coo to Emily, though she's sleeping. She's always sleeping. I suppose I should be thankful for that because I have a feeling it won't last.

"It's also the day you leave the hospital," she says.

I can't believe it's been ten days already.

After the complications with the preeclampsia, the doctors wanted me to stay on so they could monitor me, which worked out well since Emily was being monitored in the intensive care unit.

Those first few days were rough. There wasn't a moment where I wasn't thinking about her, fretting over her. Since I was still recovering from the hemorrhaging and some of the damage to my kidneys from the preeclampsia, which is basically my blood pressure going on a rampage, I wasn't able to be with her as often as I liked.

I remember the first time I touched her through the incubator, my hand so big against her body, and she grasped onto my pinky finger and I nearly lost it.

Okay, I did lose it.

I burst into tears and even Fox couldn't console me.

Probably because he was crying too.

It had just been so rough to not even remember delivering Emily, then being unconscious for the first few days after almost dying, that I was so scared to be without her. I wanted to bond with her immediately, I wanted to feed her, I wanted the reassurance that she was alive and was going to be okay. I wanted to take care of her.

But I could barely take care of myself.

Eventually I just had to trust the doctors that they were doing the best that they could to take care of her.

And Fox.

Fox was always here. If he wasn't with me, he was bugging the doctors in the ICU to see her. He was my lifeline, the bond between Emily and me, the one keeping us connected.

I'd like to think that he helped Emily develop so quickly. As I hold her in my arms, she's no longer the bright red little thing who was so weak she couldn't even feed. Now she's six and a half pounds, up from the five of her delivery and she's getting stronger every moment.

"Are you ready to go?" Fox asks, coming inside the room.

"I'll miss you too, you handsome thing," Irene says to him with a big smile. "My favorite lumberjack."

He looks down at the green plaid shirt he's wearing, his jeans and Timberland boots and shrugs. "She's got me there."

I give Emily to Irene and Fox helps me out of bed. I got dressed earlier, which was a tiring operation, but it was nice to be able to put on soft leggings and a giant tunic instead of the hospital gown. I wish that my prolonged stay in the hospital meant that I had lost my baby weight but I swear to god I've somehow gained while I've been here. The doctors say it's just water retention from the preeclampsia but whatever it is, it makes me feel like my legs, stomach, boobs and face have turned into jiggling bowls full of jelly.

But I'm counting my blessings. I nearly died, and I could have lost Emily too, and I didn't. I'm lucky to be alive.

Even luckier to have this man by my side.

The man who has never left my side.

The man who has given me his heart and I have no intentions of ever giving it back.

Emily goes in the car seat.

Fox carries it with one hand, his other hand strong and protective around the small of my back. He leads me out of the hospital to his Jeep.

I blink at the light. I've been outside a few times over this past week but today it feels like freedom. Like I'm getting a chance to start again. Like the world has opened just for me.

"It's so gorgeous out," I say softly, closing my eyes briefly as I let the warmth sink all over me. Spring is everywhere, all around us, in our veins.

Emily's birth.

Our rebirth.

Our love.

"You're gorgeous," Fox says to me, kissing me on the forehead. Then he bends over and kisses Emily. "And you're gorgeous too, sweetheart."

God.

My heart.

I might have to go back into the hospital if he keeps this

up, this big burly man and his tiny, dainty daughter. The love between them makes me want to melt into puddles and that's a problem because he's her father, and I'm going to be seeing a lot more of this scene.

But when we get ourselves all strapped into the Jeep, we don't head straight to my house like I thought.

"Where are we going?" I ask. My mother is supposed to be waiting there with cake. I want cake something fierce.

"You'll see," he says.

We head over the bridge over Queen's River toward Ravenswood Ranch.

"I thought we were going to my house?" I say.

"Change of plans."

"But the cake," I say feebly. "The welcome home cake."

"You'll get your cake you cake monster," he says to me with a grin. "Just have patience."

"Fox. I've been in the hospital for ten days with Emily. Our patience has run out."

He glances over his shoulder at Emily sleeping in the back. "She looks pretty patient to me."

"Fine. But if I don't get cake to calm these raging hormones and that shitty hospital food…"

"You'll what?"

"You don't want to know," I grumble. Probably just be a snippy brat, that's what.

"You'll get your cake, Del."

He pulls the Jeep up to the house and there I see what he means.

A huge *Welcome Home Emily & Delilah* banner hangs across the front of the house while white and pink balloons sway from the front porch, anchored in place by cowboy boots.

"Oh my god," I say, shocked to say the least, as I get out of the car.

Fox immediately comes around to help me, holding onto my hand tight while Rachel darts out of the front door of the house to snatch Emily from the back seat. I mean, she literally snatches the carrier and then gives me a quick, impish smile before running back into the house with Emily and closing the door behind her.

"What?" I cry out, pointing with my free hand. "Babysnatcher!"

Fox leads me to the house but then stops a few feet from the front porch.

Holds both my hands.

Faces me so we're inches apart.

Stares deep into my eyes.

And we've been in this situation before.

Only this time it's different.

This time I'm absolved of all fear.

Of all doubt.

Because I know this man loves me for all I am.

"I'm going to make this quick. Again," he says with a chuckle. He's still nervous though, which is absolutely endearing. "Because no one should have to hear my bumbling words twice." He takes in a deep breath, lets out a shaky one. Squeezes my hands.

I squeeze them back. "You know I'll hear all your words, Fox," I say softly.

He licks his lips, the pink of his tongue appearing for a second. "You've been in love with me for most of my life and though you never confessed it to me at the time, I felt it. I knew it on some level that you were the one for me, the one I was supposed to be with. But that's the problem with knowing things on some levels. Sometimes those levels are layers deep and you're able to bury everything until you were sure it never existed to begin with. That's what happened with us."

He goes on, voice soft as silk. "I pretended we were just friends because I never wanted to look deep inside myself for anything, let alone you. And then, I guess, things changed. Shifted. Little things moved in our lives so we could finally come together. Maybe it wasn't in the way we wanted or the way it should have been. It was messy. It was imperfect. Raw and real. And it was the way it worked for us. It was how we found each other. Then lost each other. Then found each other again."

I stare at him, soaking in each word, each piece of himself, because I've been waiting so long to hear it. In some ways it doesn't feel real but then I know it is because my heart is beating fast and my throat is dry and every single cell in my body is buzzing and alive.

So alive.

We're *so* alive.

"Del, I'm sorry that it took me so long to come around. To realize what you meant to me was more than I was willing to look at, let alone admit. But when I found a home in your heart, I realized that was all I've ever needed. Loving you is like every lost part of me has returned and made me whole and, fuck, I want to marry you. I want to spend the rest of my life with you. I want to be your husband and love you to death and love Emily and be a family and be all the things that I know in my heart that we are."

He drops to his knees.

Again.

Brings out a ring.

Again.

But this time it's in a velvet box.

He flips it open to reveal a sparkling diamond and emerald ring that catches the light like otherworldly jewels.

His voice is choking up as he speaks, "Emerald is the birthstone of Emily's original due date. It signals rebirth and the spring and things starting over. Not to mention it sort of matches my eyes." He gives me a sheepish smile at that one. I may have commented on his emerald eyes a million times throughout his life. "And the diamond is for now, when Emily was born. They're rare and unique, just like she is. They symbolize love, like the love I have for you."

With a trembling hand he takes the ring out of the box and holds it poised at my ring finger.

I'm crying and not even realizing it.

"Delilah Gordon will you marry me?"

I nod, the tears spilling, my lips quivering as I say, "Yes. Yes, I'll marry you Fox."

He grins, a dashing beautiful smile that radiates like the sun and he gets to his feet, pulling me to him, kissing me with so much love I fear my heart might burst.

"I love you," he whispers into the top of my head. "I've never known love like this Del, never thought I could. But I love you with all my heart. I am madly, chaotically in love with you. And I will do whatever I can to make you and Emily feel happy and loved, I promise you that."

He cups my face in his hands and peers down at me, tears in his eyes. "Do you want that cake now?"

I laugh.

Happy.

So happy.

And yes please, cake.

The front door to the house opens and then everyone comes streaming out, smiling, laughing, matching our joy. Rachel holding Emily, my mother with bottles of what look like kombucha, Shane, Riley and Mav with beers, Hank and Dick (just drinking whisky straight out of the bottle now). Then Vernalee with the cake.

My mother hands me and Fox the kombucha, something

for us to have since Fox quit drinking alcohol, and we raise our drinks in one giant group toast.

"To the newest Nelsons," Hank says. "Emily and Delilah. Welcome home. Welcome to the family. It's finally official."

"We've only been waiting twenty-seven years," Dick speaks up. "Now let's eat cake."

Amen.

24

FOX

Six weeks later

"Delilah, sweetheart, you need to give her gripe water."

"Mom, we've been over this. I'm going to a lactation consultant on Thursday. We'll figure it out."

"It's nothing to do with foremilk and hindmilk," Jeanine says. "It's just bad luck and Emily is a colicky baby. I'm telling you, you were colicky too and gripe water always worked. Plus, you could use more bone broth in your diet."

"Miss Gordon," I say as politely as possible. "I'm surprised that bone broth isn't coming out of your ears. Now what the hell is gripe water?"

Honestly, I have no clue what these two are arguing about, all I know is that our daughter has colic and has been crying for two weeks straight, I swear, from three p.m. to three a.m. Everyone is on edge.

"Gripe water is what I used to give Del," she explains, her voice loud in order to be heard over Emily who is screaming and crying in Del's arms as she attempts to swaddle her. "Back in the day, it had alcohol and sugar, so I'm not sure how effective it is now but it's worth a shot."

"I've read that it doesn't help," Del says, her voice raised and frantic, "and it can cause vomiting. I'm not giving it to her. It's got to be something in my body, what I'm eating but I've cut out dairy and gluten and sugar, what can it be?"

"I'm telling you, you need more bone broth."

I look at Del and see she's at the breaking point, her skin wane from lack of sleep, her eyes watering, lip trembling.

It hasn't been easy since we got back from the hospital, not even a little bit. We're both so grateful that the baby and Del are doing well that we've tried not to complain about it, but let's be honest—it's been hell.

Because I was out fighting the fires and Emily was born prematurely, our lives weren't really ready for her. Del had a nursery all set to go in the house she shared with her mother but ever since we left the hospital together, ever since I proposed and she, thank the lord above, said yes, we decided that it made more sense for both Del and the baby, and her mother to move into my house.

No, having your future mother-in-law live with you isn't ideal, but she still needs helps with some things and to be honest, we need help too.

Luckily, there's a lot of room and Jeanine has moved into Maverick's old bedroom, while we've turned his old office into the nursery.

Today we're almost done with the nursery too, only a few more finishing touches that I'll most likely be doing myself because Del just fed Emily which in turn spurned on the next twelve hours of colic-o-rama, the worst ride in town. There's absolutely nothing worse than the way she cries. Her little body cramps up in obvious discomfort and there's almost nothing either of us can do to soothe her. It's painful to watch.

And hear.

Still, Del needs a break. I need a break.

We need a moment to be alone.

"Jeanine," I tell her. "It would mean the world to us if you could put Emily in the stroller and take her outside. Just around the block a few times. It's sunny, it's a gorgeous spring day. The fresh air might help her."

"Fox," Del says. "She can't do that. You're asking too much of her."

Jeanine gives her daughter a sharp look. "I'm not crippled," she says. Then she seems to reconsider that. "Only sometimes. Not today. I could use the fresh air and exercise too, believe it or not." She grabs her stomach and jiggles it. "I'm not the only one who gained weight with this pregnancy."

I know Jeanine didn't mean anything by that since she's usually very supportive of Del but that was the absolute worst thing to say. Del's been extremely self-conscious about her weight gain, even though it hasn't been much and she's even more gorgeous to me now with soft silky curves replacing all that muscle. She glows inside and out, even when she's only getting three hours a sleep a night.

"Thanks a lot," Del cries out. "I'm trying my best. Everyone always says that with breastfeeding you drop, like, fifty pounds at once, like splat, it goes out with the milk." I wrinkle my nose at her analogy. "But it's not working at all with me."

"You look fine Del," I try to reassure her. "You look better than fine. You look like a warrior, a powerful human being who brought a life into this world."

She gives me the most unimpressed look. "Oh, cut the crap, Fox. I'm hideous."

Jeanine gets to her feet and takes the baby from Del's arms. "I'm going to take her out before you two start killing each other. Remember that you love each other and everything is going be okay." She smiles at Emily and takes her down the stairs to where the stroller is by the front door. I can hear her saying, "Grandma is here to save the day again."

We don't breathe, we don't look at each other until we hear the front door close and the crying starts to fade away as Jeanine and Emily head down the street.

"Thank you for that," Del says quietly, leaning back against the couch. "I was starting to lose my mind."

Her words are a trigger for me so I sit up straighter and take her hands in mine. "You are okay though, right? You just have the baby blues, it's nothing more serious? You know you have to tell me if you're having any bad thoughts, Del."

She gives me a weak smile, her head lolling to the side. "I'm just tired. Don't worry. I'm not thinking anything bad, I just want nothing more than to have a good night's sleep. I want to be able to eat the things I had to cut out for Emily. Like a pizza. A big pizza with extra helpings of gluten. And cheese. So much cheese."

"I promise you we have a whole future of extra glutton cheese pizzas ahead of us."

"And beer. And wine."

"And everything you want. And peace and quiet and long restful sleeps."

She laughs, the most beautiful, joyous sound in the world. This is the best part of being engaged to her, knowing I'll be spending the rest of my life trying to make this incredible woman laugh.

"You do know that we have to be parents beyond this colicky stage and I don't think we'll have peace and quiet or solid sleep until Emily is like eight years old, right?"

"I choose to be optimistic."

She looks me up and down and grins. "Wow. You really have changed."

"In some ways, yes," I tell her, leaning over her until my nose brushes against hers. "In some ways I'm exactly the same." I run my hands down the sides of her arms, wanting more but trying to be as respectful as possible.

Other than a few kisses and hugs, we haven't been all that physical with each other. I've wanted to, of course. I've never not wanted to. Even when it's four a.m. and I've fallen asleep in the recliner with Emily on my chest and a hairdryer in my hand (the sound stops her from crying), if I happen to see Del padding into the kitchen to get a glass of water, I want her. She's just the sexiest thing on earth in every way shape or form, and that will never go away.

But I'm used to functioning on little to no sleep and in some ways, taking care of a newborn is a lot like fighting a forest fire, albeit an unpredictable one that rarely responds to any of your techniques. I also wasn't the one who had to go through the physical transformation that Del did.

"Fox," she whispers.

I glance up at her with my brows raised, my hands resting at her hips, ready to back off.

"I don't think I'm ready for that," she says like she's embarrassed. "I'm not confident. I'm not ready for you to…touch me."

It hurts to hear that but I'm learning not to take things so personally. "I totally understand," I tell her, placing a soft kiss on her forehead. "Whenever you are ready, you know where I am. How about we take advantage of this quiet though and finish up with the nursery."

She agrees to that and I help her to her feet.

The nursery is between our bedroom and her mother's so it's the perfect location for either one of us to be there in a moment's notice. Del opted to paint it a soft yellow since she's not really a fan of pink and the other day we stuck fluffy clouds on the ceiling. All that's left is to pick which mobile we want and hang it up.

One of them has the sun and moon and stars.

The other one has squirrels.

Yeah.

The squirrels were Del's idea.

"I miss Conan," Del says with a sigh, picking up the squirrel mobile and gazing at it as she spins it around.

"But he's only living with Shane and Rachel for a few more months until we get settled, and then he'll be back here. So Emily won't be missing out. Plus, Conan can live into his twenties. We'll have that furry bastard for a long time."

She laughs again. "I know. But I still miss him. I miss having something that doesn't cry all the time."

Even though she had literally just told me not to touch her, I grab her by the waist and pull her to me. "Are you talking about me or Emily?"

She grins at me. "I don't know, you haven't been whining that much lately."

She's right. Ever since Emily was born, ever since Del came out of the complications alive, I feel like everything for me has shifted, out of the black and into the blue. It's hard to believe that I even had a life before Emily, like she hasn't always existed in our lives, like I haven't always been madly in love with Del.

And I guess I have. I know I have. It took time for my fathead to get around it but once I did it was like being shot with an arrow, only not Cupid's variety but something big and sharp with a firecracker at the end. I fell in love with her slowly throughout the years, at such a low level that I couldn't even detect it. Then, when I realized the truth, it hit me all at once. Loving Del started as a spark that needed just the right amount of time and heat for it to flame.

I know I lucked out. Emily is the best thing that ever happened to us and Del is the best thing that ever happened to me. Every day I count my blessings that this is the route my life decided to take though it hasn't been without it's struggles. You don't learn to love yourself overnight and being sober doesn't become easier either. But with weekly counselling sessions, I've managed to control my addictions and rediscover who I really am. I've learned to let go of the shame over my mother and that has been more freeing than anything.

"If I haven't been whining," I tell her, running my hand up to her face and cupping her cheek, "it's because you've been so incredible. Every day you impress me more and more. I'm starting to think you might not be human."

"Oh, I'm human," she says. "A very tired human who is just trying her best."

"And your best is a ray of sunshine, darling."

She closes her eyes and leans in, giving me a soft smile and a kiss on the lips. "Are you trying to butter me up for something?"

"Just being honest. I love you to the moon and back."

She pulls back and bites her lip and a flash of something carnal, something I haven't seen for a very long time, comes over her. "You're too good to me. Best father in town."

"Am I?" I ask curiously.

She nods and her hands slip down to my pants, undoing the button and pulling down the fly.

My brows raise.

I wasn't expecting this.

Not at all.

"I know I'm in a weird place now," she says, her voice becoming low and throaty. "And my body doesn't feel like my own anymore. But until it does, I can do something for you."

Jesus.

"Are you sure?" I ask. "You don't have to…"

But fuck, please, *please* do.

She drops down to her knees, pulling down my jeans and then my boxer briefs.

I can't think. I know we probably shouldn't do this in the nursery and I know that Jeanine and Emily could be back at any minute but…

She takes my cock in her hands, and I'm so warm, so fucking stiff, raring to go.

I'd barely been masturbating since Emily was born, there's just been no fucking time for it. I know I'm not going to last long.

"Del," I croak, my hands sinking into my hair. "You…"

She slides her tongue up and down my shaft expertly, taking her time around my balls, over the hardened ridge, the swollen tip before putting me in her mouth.

"God, your gorgeous mouth," I whisper and already I'm feeling everything inside me tighten, pressure winding around and around, building up the energy that's begging to unleash.

She murmurs something back and the vibrations make my eyes roll back in my head. Every hair on my body is alive, every inch of my skin hums from the sweet sucking of her mouth around my cock.

"Darling, don't stop," I manage to say, choking on my words. "Suck more. Harder."

She does, her mouth getting sloppy, more wet, her teeth razing my skin just the way I like it. I hold her head just right, thrusting up into her mouth.

"Suck, suck…more."

She groans again, getting into it and that's all I need to unleash myself.

"Fuck," I cry out hoarsely. "I'm coming, I'm…"

She gives me one last, long hard suck and I'm gone.

I grunt loudly like an animal, my hands tugging at her hair, my hips jerking as the orgasm tears through me and my cum shoots hard into the back of her throat. It doesn't end there, it just keeps coming and coming, my groans bouncing off the walls.

I'm seeing stars.

Galaxies.

Black spots that come into focus and fade.

"Fuck me," I say helplessly. "That was…"

I let go of her hair even though it makes me a little unstable and she gets to her feet, swallowing proudly. She smiles, a big infectious smile that makes this blow job that much better. "I think you needed that."

"I did. And I need you. I love you," I tell her, pulling her to me, wrapping my arms around her while my spent cock presses against her thigh. "You know it's for a lot more than spectacular blow jobs but I love you Del. I love you."

"I love you too," she says to me, curling up into my arms. "I love you, the baby, this life. This everything."

EPILOGUE

THREE YEARS LATER

"Mommy?" Emily asks as she toddles into the kitchen.

"Yes, sweetie?"

"Do you think I could have some anal beads?"

I look over at my mother, pausing mid-chop of the carrots I'm preparing for dinner. My mother's mouth drops open with a gasp.

That's definitely a phrase you don't expect your three-year-old to say.

"Where did you learn that word, sweetie?" I quickly ask Emily, crouching down beside her.

She's hugging her favorite stuffed unicorn to her chest, smiling wide, looking way too innocent to be using those words. "Riley. Riley and Maverick talked about anal beads and I like beads." She shows me her unicorn, Flutterbye, who has several beaded necklaces and jewelry wrapped around her. "Flutterbye could get some new beads."

Oh, I am going to *kill* those two.

"We don't use that word, okay Emily? The real word is adult beads and they're just for adults." God, it's hard to make up shit like this on the spot all the time. One of the most creative aspects about being a parent but I like to think I'm pretty good at it. Way better than Fox, who will bluntly tell the truth every time.

Of course, Emily looks absolutely crestfallen over these special beads that she can't have. "But don't worry," I go on, giving her a squeeze. "These beads are all boring and brown and grey."

"And they smell horrible," my mother adds.

I nearly laugh at that, giving her an incredulous look for a moment. My mother never indulges in potty humor, but ever since I had Emily, she's lightened up a lot.

"Yes, Emily, they smell horrible," I tell her, unable to keep from smiling. "Hey, how about you go upstairs into your playroom, let's play fashion show. While I get dinner ready, go and dress up all of your dolls, and when I'm done, I'll go up and be the judge of the fashion show, okay?"

"Okay," she says with a big nod and turns around, racing out of the kitchen and up the stairs to the playroom. It used to be Fox's bedroom but we've converted it into a playroom for every time she's over here at the ranch.

I look at my mom, shaking my head. "I'm going to kill those guys," I say and then march out of the kitchen and into the living room where Rachel, Riley and Maverick are all gathered on the couch.

"All right, which one of you was it?" I ask them, hands on my hips.

All three look up at me with innocent expressions.

"What are you talking about?" Rachel asks, looking extra innocent thanks to her huge pregnant stomach. She's due almost any day now and resembles a beach ball with arms and legs more than anything. I get to say that because I've been there. And naturally she looks extra beautiful. We've all been pretty excited about this.

"Not you," I tell her and fix my eyes on Riley and Maverick. "You two. Which one of you taught Emily about anal beads?"

Maverick nearly spits out his beer, clamping a hand over his mouth.

Riley bursts out laughing.

Still can't narrow it down.

"What?" Rachel cries out.

I point my fingers at them. "Emily just came up to me and asked if she could have some. Because she likes beads."

"What makes you think it was us?" Riley asks as she bats her big blue eyes which aren't working on me this time.

"Because she told me you were talking about it."

"Stop," Rachel says, laughing louder, gripping her belly. "I can't handle the laughter, I'll pee myself." She stops laughing abruptly, eyes wide. "Seriously. That was a close one."

"Well?" I coax them, tapping my foot.

Riley and Maverick look at each other as if sharing telepathic thoughts, then finally Riley says, "It was me. But I didn't think she was listening."

"She says you specifically told her the word."

She waves at me dismissively. "Oh, kids these days. They're getting older all the time."

"And when were you having this conversation around her?" Rachel asks. "As Emily's godmother, I'm equally as concerned."

Riley shrugs. "I don't know. Earlier at some point. Here."

I shake my head. "You too are crazy. Still. How long have you been together and you're talking about anal beads?"

"Who is talking about anal beads?" Shane says as he strolls toward us. "I'm guessing these guys." He jerks his head toward the kinky twosome before looking down at Rachel. "How are you feeling? Did anything happen?"

Rachel rolls her eyes. "No. How was the ride?" she asks him just as Fox walks inside the house, coming over to us.

"Fine, fine," Shane says quickly.

"Phff," Fox says, slipping his arm around my waist and kissing the side of my head in greeting. He gives Shane a discerning look. "The whole entire time all he could talk about was getting back here in case Rachel went into labor."

"I'm not going into labor," she tells him adamantly. "This damn baby does not want to come out."

"It's all about balance," I tell her. "Emily came early. Daphne will come late."

"I'm still not sold on the name," Rachel says.

"Well you better decide soon," Riley nudges her gently. "I think Riley should have been your first choice."

"I'm still sweet on Tabitha," Shane says.

I shake my head at him. "Tabitha? Where did you even get that name from?"

"Right," he says dryly. "Because Angelina is so much better."

"What, it is!"

"Yeah. So every time someone thinks of our daughter they'll think of Angelina with her tattoos and wearing a vial of blood around her neck and kissing her brother."

"Shane, what decade are you stuck in? Sometimes I think it's the 1950's, other times I think it's the nineties. Plus, they'll think of Angelina who adopts children and saves the world."

"I just don't buy it," Riley says with a shake of her head, plucking Mav's beer out of his hand and having a sip. "You don't go from wild child, because she was fucking wild, to Mother Theresa, just like that. You don't grow out of that stage and leave it all behind. She's still got the crazy free spirit in her; the wild child won't be buried forever."

While Riley starts a debate over Angelina Jolie with everyone else, Fox pulls me into him for a hug.

I smile against his chest, loving the smell of him when he

gets back from riding. Hay and sunshine and happiness.

A lot has changed since Emily was born. Some bad, mostly good.

Fox ended up quitting his job as an active teammate of the North Ridge Hot Shots, which was sad and tough for him but it was the right thing to do. I didn't want to be the wife that would tell him what to do, make him quit a job that brought him a lot of happiness and sense of identity.

But sometimes you have to be that person for more than just the two of you. With all the craziness around Emily being born prematurely and Fox not being there for it, we decided together that it was best he wasn't in a high-risk job. Being a hot shot is an extremely noble and dangerous job, but there's a reason why so many of them are young, and even though many do it with families with no problem, I wanted Fox as close to home as possible.

He also agreed to it because his passion for the job was waning. As extremely fit as Fox is, he couldn't keep up that level forever and the psychological damage of the job was becoming too much. He just wasn't operating at full capacity anymore and in his heart, he didn't really want to.

But all was not lost. He now does training which still sees him going around the province and even into the states during the summer, but he's not fighting the fires. He's only gone for a week at a time. Sometimes he'll still go out and help with the big fires, but most of the time he stands back and tells people how to do it.

I still run The Bear Trap though, so some things don't change. When I became pregnant and had to hire Vanessa to help run the bar, I really thought that maybe this was the way out. That maybe I'd realize the bar was better off in her hands, maybe I could sell it to her, maybe I could just focus on being a mother and eventually focus on being something else, having some other career and calling.

But that didn't happen. I missed the bar too much. I kept Vanessa on and together we figured out ways to bring more money to the bar without losing the charm.

One of those things involved cheap pub food, so we had a small kitchen installed in the back where one of us could easily heat up some prepared food. Another was to expand the booze menu and include cocktails, much to my grumbles and protests. Ain't nobody got time for that but apparently people do. Including the locals, like Old Joe when he discovered what a Manhattan tasted like.

Sadly, Old Joe died a few months ago. Lung cancer that he apparently had for a long time. Being a bartender, you hear a lot, but people still keep a lot of painful things to themselves, including when they have a terminal illness. I miss the guy, I have to say. He may have annoyed the hell out of me at times but he was sweet and loyal and the life of the bar. And as per Fox's suggestion, we named a signature cocktail after the old-timer. It's pretty much a Manhattan but extra strong.

As for everyone else, they're doing well. Hank and Vernalee still live here on the ranch, Dick is still alive and kicking though he suffers from narcolepsy now and is prone to falling asleep at the most awkward moments.

Riley and Maverick got engaged last year. I can't believe it took Maverick two years to actually get the nerve to propose to her. Riley was ready to ask him at one point. Luckily, she held off. Maverick's easy-going, but I think his pride would have been hurt, and it turns out that there was never any commitment-issues on his end, he was just psyching himself out trying to make it as epic and elaborate as possible.

According to Riley though, he proposed right after they had sex in their shower and he had hidden the ring in the soap. It sounded like a slippery disaster but at least the outcome was good. Both of them are still set on not having kids and I think that suits them just fine. Especially since they spend a lot of time looking after and playing with Emily.

Although, maybe now I oughta start supervising *them*.

Then there's Rachel and Shane. While Riley was waiting forever to become Maverick's fiancée, Rachel and Shane were waiting to become parents. They tried non-stop. They went to doctors and did tests. There wasn't even really a clear cause for their problems, it just wasn't happening for them.

Then, finally, one day, it happened.

The two of them have been absolutely overjoyed, as is everyone else. Especially Vernalee, who had been praying for a grandchild, and Emily, who is so excited about a cousin. Fox and I are still a bit unsure about having another kid and giving Emily a sibling, we're quite happy and satisfied with our unit of three, but with Shane and Rachel's girl, she'll have someone like a sister. Plus, I don't think those two will be satisfied with just one. Shane and Rachel will have their own little herd of cowboys and cowgirls running around here one day, I just know it.

"How was the ride otherwise?" I ask Fox, resting my chin on his hard chest and looking up at him.

"Good," he says. "We saw a wolf."

"Seriously?"

"Seriously. He kept his distance. He was alone. Gorgeous though. I have to say, it's nice being able to come across wildlife that's not running away from a burning forest."

"I bet."

That's another thing that's changed too. Ever since Shane and Fox had it out and actually started talking to each other and especially after Fox started seeing a therapist, the two of them have grown a lot closer. It didn't happen overnight though. It happened with them taking a horseback ride through the ranch and the mountains for a few hours before our weekly Sunday roasts. Somehow the combination of wilderness and brotherly bonding has really brought them both a lot of peace.

"Where is Emily?" he says, letting go of me.

It's funny, even though we've officially been together for three years, I still feel bereft when he's away from me. Even standing here, I crave his touch and his affection. His arms are still the safest place in the world for me, a place where I know everything is right.

"She's upstairs playing." I pause. "Riley taught her all about anal beads."

He pales. "She what?"

I grin, pressing my hand into his chest and patting him. "Turns out with all your biggest worries about having a girl, the biggest one should have been Mav and Riley corrupting her."

He shakes his head. "Our girl is staying as far away from those two as possible. Until she's at least thirty."

"I heard that," Riley pipes up.

"Well, I said it kind of loud," he shoots back.

"Delilah," my mother calls out, wiping her hands on her apron. "Get back in here and help."

I give Fox a pathetic pleading look.

"Fine," he says. "I'll help."

We head back into the kitchen and the three of us finish up the roast. Now that Rachel is severely pregnant, we all chip in with the cooking. It can get a little crowded in the kitchen. Especially when Conan is around.

"Hey," my mother says, shooing him away as he tried to take a carrot. "Del, Fox, what did I say about not letting him loose in this house when we're trying to cook?"

Conan makes a tittering noise of disgust and then does an impressive leap off the counter and onto Fox's arm where he scrambles up and sits on his shoulder.

"Well it ain't your house, Jeanie," Dick says coming around the corner. "And I love this little bugger, even if he doesn't love me."

He leans in to pet Conan but the squirrel literally runs up over Fox's head and onto the other shoulder. Conan doesn't like too many people and he's especially afraid of Dick for some reason. I think because he tries too hard.

Dick grumbles. "One day I'll win you over. You're just a rat in a good suit."

Or maybe it's because he's always calling him a rat.

Then Dick heads into the living room, taking a seat beside Rachel on the couch.

I share a warm smile with Fox and we go back to cooking.

Everything is just about ready when suddenly we hear Rachel cry out softly and then Dick say, "Jumping Joseph, Rachel I think your water just broke."

We all run out of the kitchen just in time to see Dick pass out right on top of Rachel's belly, completely asleep.

She looks at us with wide-eyes. "The baby is coming! Dick fell asleep on me!"

It's hard not to laugh at the sight. We quickly get Dick off of her so he can snooze away in his narcoleptic state, and then help Rachel to her feet.

Her water definitely broke.

Everywhere.

"Oh my god!" Shane exclaims, pretty much yelling, pressing his hands into the side of his head. "It's finally happening!" He jumps up and down. "It's finally happening!"

"Get their bags!" I yell and Vernalee comes running toward us with their overnight bags in her hands.

"Got it!" she says, starting to jump in the same way that Shane is, freaking out.

"Who is driving?" Hank asks, not freaking out.

"I will," Fox says. "I'm the only sober one."

I glance at my mother and she says, "I'll watch Emily. And the squirrel. Just go. And good luck!"

As quickly as we can we rush out to the Jeep, Shane and Rachel in the backseat, me and Fox in the front. I know the others won't be far behind.

"Are you okay?" I ask her as we roar off.

Rachel nods. "Yes. Yes. Definitely having contractions." She winces.

"You're having a baby, we're having a baby," Shane says excitedly.

"Shane, really, it's not a big deal," Fox says, smirking at him in the rearview mirror. "People have babies all the time."

"Shut the fuck up," Shane says but he can't stop grinning.

"This is so exciting," I tell them. "I can't remember Emily's birth so it's like I get to live vicariously through you."

"I know I'm going to wish I was passed out through the whole thing," Rachel says, starting to hunch over. "This fucking..." she groans loudly. "Fuck."

"Remember your breathing," Shane says, holding her hand.

"Taking your breathing and shove it up your ass," Rachel snaps.

Fox and I look at each other with raised brows. Whoa. That escalated quickly.

And it does.

It goes very quickly.

We get to the hospital and there's no waiting around with her. The baby is coming and fast so they get Rachel into the delivery room pretty much right away. Within four or five hours, the doctor is coming out to us all in the waiting room and telling us that there's a healthy baby girl that's been delivered.

"And the name?" Fox asks him.

"Raven," Shane says as he appears from around the

corner, looking proud as fuck to finally be a father. "Raven Tabitha Angelina Nelson."

"That's quite the mouthful," Maverick mutters under his breath.

Riley elbows him.

Hours later, we're all allowed in to see her.

Rachel is lying on the hospital bed, looking worn-out and pale but still glowing and gorgeous all the same. In her arms is a pink little newborn with a shock of dark hair, just like hers.

Raven suits her alright.

Fox leans across the bed and hands Shane a cigar. "Welcome to the club, brother. Glad to have you."

I hoist up Emily into my arms so she can get a better view of the baby.

"That's your baby cousin," I tell her. "Her name is Raven."

Emily smiles gleefully. "Do you think we'll be best friends?"

Everyone laughs. Some people are still crying. Definitely Vernalee.

"You'll be the best of friends."

"Do you think she'll like my Flutterbye and the ponies?"

"I think she'll like all those things, sweetheart."

"Do you think she'll like adult beads?"

Riley snorts. So loud.

Dick asks, "What on God's green earth are adult beads?"

"I have a feeling you don't want to know, Grandpa," Fox says.

Dick shakes his head. "Sometimes I wonder about all of you. How did we all even get here? What a crazy clan of loons I have."

Everyone looks at each other and smiles. A crazy clan of loons? I think that's about right.

Otherwise known as the Nelsons.

THE END

THANK YOU SO, SO much for reading the North Ridge Series! I absolutely loved writing about North Ridge and these amazing rugged brothers, their heroic jobs and the strong women who love them. It's been an honor to share these characters with you!

Hot Shot was the last book in the series about the Nelson Brothers but if you missed out on the others, no worries. You can pick them up here:

Wild Card (North Ridge #1)

Maverick (North Ridge #2)

Also, stay tuned for my next release, coming to Kindle Unlimited in March, 2018. It's one big-ass long and epic romance that I like to describe as Roman Holiday meets Shameless. Sexy, funny, emotional…this book is going to hit all of your sweet spots.

SO if you want to be the first to know the title, see the cover, read the blurb, or get more information about this "secret" book as it all gets released, please:

- Sign up for Bookbub alerts (they will email you within a few days of the book's release - just click FOLLOW)

- Or sign up for Amazon alerts (these are not as reliable, usually sent within a few weeks of release)

- Sign up for my newsletter (I don't spam people, I promise. I only send them around release days)

- Please join My Facebook Group (low-key, drama-free, tons of great readers and authors, lots and lots of giveaways)

- FOLLOW ME on Instagram (this is where you'll always find me! I post pretty pics daily): @authorhalle

- Twitter: @Metalblonde

ACKNOWLEDGEMENTS

This book could not have been possible without the love of Scott Mackenzie, the understanding of Bruce, and the patience of Roxane LeBlanc. Thank you guys so much for helping me make this book happen.

To my anti-heroes, you have my back. I couldn't ask for better readers, fans and friends.

To my IG and Twitter families, you all rock. Thank you for your support. Also shout-out to my favourite squirrels I follow on there :D

To Nina at Social Butterfly - you're my rock!

To anyone reading this, thank you so much for taking a chance on me and this book. I really appreciate it!

Remember to thank all the unsung heroes of this world! We need them now more than ever.

ALSO BY KARINA HALLE

Contemporary Romances

Love, in English

Love, in Spanish

Where Sea Meets Sky (from Atria Books)

Racing the Sun (from Atria Books)

The Pact

The Offer

The Play

Winter Wishes

The Lie

The Debt

Smut

Heat Wave

Before I Ever Met You

Rocked Up

After All

Bad at Love

Wild Card (North Ridge #1)

Maverick (North Ridge #2)

Hot Shot (North Ridge #3)

Romantic Suspense Novels by Karina Halle

Sins and Needles (The Artists Trilogy #1)

On Every Street (An Artists Trilogy Novella #0.5)

Shooting Scars (The Artists Trilogy #2)

Bold Tricks (The Artists Trilogy #3)

Dirty Angels (Dirty Angels #1)

Dirty Deeds (Dirty Angels #2)

Dirty Promises (Dirty Angels #3)

Black Hearts (Sins Duet #1)

Dirty Souls (Sins Duet #2)

Horror Romance

Darkhouse (EIT #1)

Red Fox (EIT #2)

The Benson (EIT #2.5)

Dead Sky Morning (EIT #3)

Lying Season (EIT #4)

On Demon Wings (EIT #5)

Old Blood (EIT #5.5)

The Dex-Files (EIT #5.7)

Into the Hollow (EIT #6)

And With Madness Comes the Light (EIT #6.5)

Come Alive (EIT #7)

Ashes to Ashes (EIT #8)

Dust to Dust (EIT #9)

The Devil's Duology

Donners of the Dead

Veiled

CPSIA information can be obtained
at www.ICGtesting.com
Printed in the USA
LVHW100724181222
735466LV00030B/792